Partnership from HELL

Partnership from HELL

by

Simon Whitmore

This is a work of fiction.

The events depicted in this story are entirely products of the author's imagination or are used in a fictitious manner and should not be construed as fact.

Where factual information is portrayed, it is intended to be as accurate as possible, and any mistakes thereafter are the author's own.

ISBN: 9798510525069
Imprint: Independently published

This book is dedicated to the memory of the victims, canonical or not, tragically immortalised for all the wrong reasons, and of whom many of us forget were real people.

May they rest in peace.

'Just for jolly.'

"London lies today under the spell of a great terror.
A nameless reprobate — half beast, half man — is
at large, who is daily gratifying his murderous
instincts on the most miserable and defenceless
classes of the community . . . The ghoul-like
creature who stalks through the streets of London,
stalking down his victim like a Pawnee Indian,
is simply drunk with blood, and he will have more."

The Star, 8th September, 1888.

PROLOGUE

Wending their way through vast human warrens, passing the many crumbling and cruddy grey common lodging houses, two figures made their way through the filth. The night air was thick with fog and quiet at such a late hour. On either side of them, all but lost in the murk, lay dull and damp brick archways, most of which led directly through to a dingy yard or narrow cut-out to one of the many seedy but always cordial bawdy-houses that cluttered the area.

On reaching the far end of Old Montague Street, the two figures revealed themselves as men as they stepped out of the turbid haze onto Baker's Row. The faintest murmur of crumpled gravel upon cobbled stones sounded underfoot and floated away, unheeded, into the night. About them, decrepit and run-down lodgings and workhouses basked in a perpetual skyline of slate-grey, all black chimneys jabbing up into a dark, madder sky.

Usually teeming with life the streets were now deathly quiet. A spectacular fire in the south quay docks earlier that evening had distracted all but the most indolent of insidious residents — people from the lowest part of society enjoying a welcome break to their dreary lives. Fog gave way to heavy smog which hovered gently above the foul cobbled streets, caking the two men in a leaden brew; the fog here known by the grovelling inhabitants of the city as a 'pea-souper' for its sickly tea green tinge and impenetrable gloom.

This was much further east than the two had so far ventured together. Now and then an intrepid gas-lamp offered them its dismal light; their sinister shadows mimicked them, following in mute acceptance, silently awaiting their passive participation in the events to come. Wraith–like the two men crossed the dirty cobblestones, gliding almost. Both of them looking, searching. Both hungry — hungry for such different things.

Heading southwards now, four soundless feet took a sharp left, kicking up swirls of grey mist that floated above the walkway, whirling, twirling, faultlessly executing its own corrupt macabre dance of the dead. Walking away from one of the unrelenting workhouses that lingered like a greedy old landlord who wouldn't go away, the two silhouetted figures approached a narrow and dim thoroughfare.

Through the deep fug, leaning against a shoddy brick wall that abutted to a wet and gangrenous wooden gate, they finally spotted what they had come for. Without so much as a sound they approached the shabby lone figure of a woman. Of course it was dangerous for anyone to be out so late in this part of town, particularly a woman on her own, but she would have known that only too well — she had to make a living one way or the other.

On spying her one of the men quickened his pace, taking the lead on the dingy pathway, the parting mist revealing his smaller frame as he advanced ahead of the other, taller man. His full face housed injurious beady eyes and large black moustache

— his facial hair striving in vain to cover the faint tic of excitement above his lip. He carried with him a small black bag. The taller man, his agitated gait longer, followed in his wake.

Even in the haze, the second man was clearly pale in appearance with a benign countenance, carrying nothing with him, only an air of submission and disquiet, his thinning face donning a sombre yet dogged look.

Pulling straight her heavy brown ulster and adjusting her new linsey frock the woman hastily began to smarten herself up. Happy that she looked her best — or as best a poor prostitute could in the small hours of a late August morning with a steady drizzle falling upon her shoddy drapes — she slid her prized piece of broken mirror into her pocket. Together, with her comb, they were her only belongings, her only treasures.

The woman stepped forward, the alcohol in her blood — courtesy of the Frying Pan Public House earlier — giving her surplus confidence.

"Sees anyfink ya fancy mister?" the whore asked as the two men materialised from the fog and came to within a few yards of where she stood. "I likes 'em big, ya knows," she rattled, extending a wide toothless grin.

Looking closely at her the two men could see that her once-pretty face looked younger than her years now portrayed. Her greying eyes and delicate cheekbones inside her darkened face incognisant of the ageing thatch of brown hair that hid under her black straw bonnet. The two men said nothing.

"Ere, step over ere an' give us a kick, one of ya's," she squawked. "I could really do meself wiv a good lump o' coke on an 'orrible night like this."

On finally reaching her both men stopped dead. A blanket of black cloud clung portentously about the dire cutting, courageous in its battle against a constant entourage of mizzle.

In the dark she didn't see the smaller man's upper lip twitch in exhilaration. *'Ere, that a uniform, one of 'em's wearing?* She thought she could see the dark navy colour in the taller man's attire but in the dim light she couldn't quite make it out.

The blackened path, overlooked and overcrowded by more frigid and bleak buildings, caused the light to falter further. The small gas-lamp stationed along the footpath — this one doing a less than pathetic job — was struggling to brighten the dank street through the ever thickening fog.

With his head level, his face still, the smaller man's petulant eyes glanced up into the night sky. He squinted as drizzle assaulted his brow. A faint orange haze, surrounding a thin sliver of light emanated from the low crescent moon, scarcely visible above London's grey rooftops. Unmoved at the beautiful celestial sight the smaller man turned his eyes to the other.

The taller man's troubled phizog returned his gaze, quiet contemplation in his face. After a while the taller man nodded in affirmation. The smaller man turned back to the woman against the brick wall, her outline blending almost perfectly with the speckled green constellation of moss behind.

"Good evening madam, I . . . I trust you are . . . well? And alone?" the smaller man asked in a bland but semi-alto voice.

Quickly sensing some action, and therefore a little money in her pocket for a drink or two later and even a doss down, she straightened herself up some more, pushed out her jaw in an attempt to hide her ageing, sagging chin.

More ennobled now, she put on her best posh voice. "O' course mister. Us girls 'ave us a job to do, we can't all work the same patch you know . . . an' you looks like a decent enough fellah to me, me jolly old buffer," she said, smirking, her face rabid with excitement.

Hesitating at the feigned compliment the smaller man continued with a curt nod in her direction.

"Jolly old buffer, eh?" he muttered inaudibly to himself. His shark-like eyes briefly scanned the shadows before continuing with the conversation.

"Thank you my dear. Well, I'm certainly no . . . er, bludger, as you might say," he lied, a friendly tone lifting in his voice. "Is there anywhere we can . . . Anywhere we can be alone?"

Yes. She had got him — maybe the both of them. A little work, some fumbling in the dark, a bit of pushing and pulling, and it would be drinks all round back at the Commercial Tavern later! Besides, she'd need something to swill out her mouth with afterwards.

"Well, I'm certainly no blowsey, neiver. The only place round 'ere is that cosy little doorway ova 'ere," she said, pointing behind her. "That's, o' course, if ya don't take offence at it?"

The smaller man had already taken offence as soon as she had opened her mouth and uttered her first words. *Women*. With a cursory glance up and down the street again he fixed his gaze upon the doorway.

Evidently reading the signal in his eyes the woman readied herself to move. "Orwight me darlin' but one at a time, eh?" she winked, her lip curling up as her face contorted.

Pushing herself away from the grease of the mossy wall, she nearly stumbled as she stood fully and turned. Pulling back her shoulders, she shoved her breasts together, squeezing her cleavage high in the air and let go. With a curled out finger she began ushering the smaller man into the dark recess of the doorway.

Again, the smaller man looked to the taller man. The taller man thought for a moment before nodding again. The woman was clearly poor, her old spring-sided boots and muddy-brown skirt and blotchy complexion instantly gave her away — the fact that she was this far east even more so. That was good though, it was precisely what they wanted. Needed. Quite impervious to moral persuasion, London — or more precisely, the East End — had a knack at looking the other way and ignoring others' misfortunes.

Prostitutes, drunks, the vile and wretched were rarely missed this far out. Society had a way of ostracising the weak and vulnerable without a second's thought. Most had dropped so far by the wayside that death could be considered a welcome respite. The woman in front of them tonight did, however, show some spirit still, a charismatic lust for life — the zeal in her voice at earning some quick and easy money had been apparent to anyone who bothered to listen.

Watching her as she headed towards her destiny the taller man began having second thoughts. *Maybe we should move on? Find someone else. Just walk away.*

He did this often — too often. *No.* He was hungry. Hungry for now, not for later. He had been without for too many days. He reasoned again. *There isn't anybody about, it's getting late, she'll have to do.*

"Isten, bocsássa meg nekem," he whispered as he let the whore and his confederate step away. *God, please forgive me.*

Approaching the high-arched doorway, and following the prostitute, the smaller man negotiated the gutter at the side of the road. He lifted his bag in his right hand and released the dull bronze catch with his left, flicking it open. His left hand darted into the bag and, while in full motion, he deftly pulled something out.

Something sharp.

The woman was deep in the darkness now, invisible almost, as he too stepped in.

Immediately, she was on him. "Come on then big boy, let dear old Polly do sumfing wiv those trousies o' yours," she said, twirling towards the smaller man and pulling frigidly at the thick black leather of his belt.

Instead of obliging her as his intentions had promised, his hand shot up, grabbing her under the chin. Like a tightened vice, she was stuck. In natural reaction her own hands came up to her neck and tried to free herself from her assailant. Desperately pulling, clawing at his cast-iron fingers, she attempted to cry out. With one single swift impassioned blow the smaller man punched her hard in the stomach.

The woman doubled up, wincing, the wind knocked out of her. Raising her head slowly, she tried to look about for help through watery eyes. A second blow came as he dug his fist hard into her mouth. She mewled, her throat constricting, a scarlet trail drivelling from her lips. Pain engulfed her condemned body. Her eyes blinked as her aggressor spoke softly, calmly into her ear.

"Fear not my dear, this shouldn't last too long."

ONE

Using all but the last of his depleting strength, the young man ducked out from his camouflage of watery caskets. And ran. His head down, the slabs beneath his feet were cold, wet and slippery. It mattered little, his determination carried him forwards. Leaping awkwardly he launched himself high into the dawning air and landed on the large vessel as softly as he could — his height and slender build aiding his saltation.

A chance had arisen — had shown itself only moments before — and the vessel he now stood on would soon be leaving its berth in Belgium; it should be heading for the south-east coast of England.

Biztonsági – Safety.

At least that is what he hoped. It was now or never.

In a rare state of clarity he stole aboard and, poking around, ducked down behind some crates, searching for a better hideout. He pulled a canvas up and over him, now totally out of sight. The short but tumbling journey made him terribly sick — it was the first time he had ever been on a ship — and he was no sailor. Safe in his concealment, he groaned, dribbling, dropped his head into his hands and rubbed at his scalp through thick black hair, unable to halt his queasiness.

How long had it been? For two, three or even more winters he had meandered through the huge heathlands of Europe, a semi-daze clouding his brain throughout. Groggily, he totted up the years through the haze of his numbed brain. *Could it really be 1882?*

Cold, dirty and ravaged, his mind was a constant state of turmoil, and had been for a long time. The nausea he felt deep down in the pit of his stomach was not only caused by that of the choppy seas but by that of the reality of his situation, of home sickness.

He missed home; he missed his beloved mama and papa. A tear welled in his eye. He wiped his sleeve across quickly, trying to banish his thoughts. After all this time on his own, scraping an existence, he still had no idea why he and his family had been singled out. By now he knew it didn't really matter why, only that they had been, and that now he was stuck on a strange ship in the middle of the English Channel, and nothing was ever going to change that. That was why he was here now — all alone, cold, hungry, on the verge of vomiting, and feeling like shit.

The last few years had been the bleakest period of his pathetic short life. After finally escaping Europe and the violence that seemed to forever grip it, he was certain — hopeful at the very least — that England was going to offer him the solace he had begged for since he had gone on the run, his life and spirit ripped from him.

He dropped his chin to his chest, clasped his hands to his face and groaned again — and waited for the trip to end.

He didn't know how long had passed; luckily he had managed to get some much needed rest. He rubbed at his face.

As the ship approached the western edge of the harbour he inched forward to spy overboard and take his first look out onto an alien world. Still feeling bad — but better than when he had first boarded the vessel — he was totally unprepared for the sight of the massive flat-faced mountain of sheer alabaster that loomed above. For as far as he could see huge cliffs towered over all below as if to crush him, his spirit, and everything else it deemed unfit. He gulped. *Maybe I shouldn't have come.* He saw himself then, walking away from the docks back in Belgium, not getting on the ship, slowly but surely disappearing into the distance, headed for another life. France maybe.

But no, he was here, now, facing an almighty shield of blanched gypsum. In relation he knew he was just a tiny and insignificant speck of dirt on the world. He closed his eyes and shook his head.

Noises brought him back and he scanned his new surroundings. Bunches of people, mostly men but some women, were all racing about the docks, shouting, laughing, cajoling. Far below, the imposing waves continued to crash against the indestructible wall of solid white in an unrelenting attack of water against rock — a monumental display equal to that of a small splash against the homely banks of his *Magyan Danube*. He shivered and ducked back down again, biding his time.

As the sun slid below the horizon, the initial flurry of activity on the harbour began to die down. The day's work obviously finished, tired bodies with hardened leather faces were heading towards the local taverns for a well-earned and timely ale. The rest of the work could evidently wait until tomorrow.

He looked up and down, making sure that nobody was around before rummaging forward. As quickly and quietly as he could he jumped off the vessel and sneaked away from the mooring, tripping on numb legs as he went but instantly feeling much better for being back on solid, dry land.

Careful not to be noticed by any of the authorities on the new shore he crept away. Admittedly, the place was quiet but staying hidden had become easy for him — he had spent years dodging and avoiding anyone and everyone, whether they appeared to be a threat or not. Blending in and aversion had become a personal art form. One of life's little games of endurance.

Away from the boat now and safe from any prying eyes and dubious questions that may follow, he turned to look back. Perched high on top of the immense brilliant wall of white was another almighty sight. A castle, now ruined, sat there resolutely as if in a constant state of age-old awareness, silently governing and observing the seas. High above the waves it asserted its singular dominance. He could make out the old castle walls; stretching along the ridge like a huge two-fingered claw of stone, they eerily reached out. Complete with sickly brown and grey jutting carbuncles of toppled buildings, it 'gripped' the top edge of the chalky precipice, clutching the key to the kingdom firmly within.

From where the young stowaway stood, he saw the humble boats bobbing insignificantly in the harbour way below, their tiny masts resembling a hundred archers strung and poised, aiming true, in a futile attempt at taking the great ramparts.

Sadness washed over him as he wished his parents were with him. *Hiányoztok - I miss you.* His mama would have loved the ancient castle. Not only could his mama clean, cook and embroider, but as soon as he had been able to read and write his mother had taken it upon herself, indulged in her own interests, and taught him a thing or two about history.

Initially he had only learned about his homeland and its neighbouring countries, focusing heavily on the Austrians and the Romanians. But then his mama had turned her lessons and his attention further afield. He had learned that the people of this place, this place called England, were originally derived from the Germanic tribes of the Angles. *With any luck, perhaps they won't be so different?*

He knew of Henry V, once King of England in 1415, and how he had famously taken the French by surprise at Agincourt. The English king had immediately been visited by a cautious King Sigismund of Hungary in an shameless attempt at shifting his allegiance away from France and appease Henry's might, to align himself with the winning side. With Henry accomplishing what many thought impossible, defeating the French with his small band of brothers, Sigismund had then inducted Henry into the *Sárkány Lovagrend* — the Order of the Dragon — King Sigismund's own personal order of Knights. Staying on Henry's good side, it was a clever political manoeuvre by the Hungarian - his own ancestors' king.

As he thought back to his teachings as a youth the young man felt an ancient kinship with the place; Englishman and Hungarian — not quite a dragon but standing side by side in history. Throughout the years and the history books he had also learned that William the bastard, landing further along the coast

13

from where he now stood, had conquered the English, becoming famous for his bloody battles and subsequent rule.

It appeared that death had reigned, not only in Europe, but in England too.

Taking a final look at the oppressive sight he left the patriotic castle to its singular duty and started off, heading towards the town; the sheer ivory cliffs stretched out as far as he could see, looming over the sea, hovering high above like a giant white spectre, a phantom of the ocean.

It discomfited him.

A bad omen?

TWO

The young new migrant was a little leery at first, concerned that his foreign accent might make people wary or even suspicious of him. This however soon wore off as he found out that, along with the native Britons, there were also a great many immigrants to this new island: Germans and Jews and Poles, French Huguenots from the Protestant Reformed Church, Africans and Chinese, all fluxed and fused in a mingle-mangle of creeds and races.

Now there was even a young Hungarian. Alone, he was safe, away from Europe, away from the brutality. This was going to be a new start for him. Yes, he still missed home — he would always — but time was helping, the anguish inside him slowly subsiding.

To keep him from dwelling on the events of his past and sliding off into a dark mood, he decided to make himself useful, to stay busy and make his parents proud. He would get his head down - work. That is what they would want. It would mean fewer questions. He could do something, become someone worthy - maybe. If he could just get things together for long enough he would follow the intellect of his countrymen and enter into the history books — maybe not.

Whether it was the good people of England affording him pity he didn't quite know but he soon began to earn his keep in this strange land, proving himself a suitable and strong asset as he set about running errands for people in exchange for food or a bed for the night.

Sometimes he would get both.

His command of the new language wasn't exactly good and so he decided that simple labour would do for now. No talking, just point and work. And work.

There were times when he would even get paid on top of food and board. This he enjoyed. Immensely. As his various employers dropped money into his hand he felt like a king. He would look at the few coins, tiny in his hand, and roll them around in-between his fingers, chinking them in his palm. He liked the sound.

Work was good, he was in demand. 'Get young Magyar to do it,' became a familiar saying. The locals never knew his name; just Magyar or Hungo, but he didn't mind, he only wanted to forget. The constant trickle of work kept his tormented mind occupied, it kept him strong. He had money in his pocket.

His sorrow diminished further.

Crossing Europe had been difficult. During his inflicted travels he had spurred himself onwards, forever thinking, forever asking himself what would his parents do? Of course he knew his once radiant mother would have studied the place, traversed the land quite merrily, taking in all she could. He decided in that moment that he too would learn more about this new country;

even learn how to speak better English. It was to be his home now for the foreseeable future, so why not?

With his new interest he turned to reading. He read adverts pasted on to walls, signs on billboards and in shop windows, even borrowed books if he managed to draw up the courage to ask for them in his unusual dialect. Struggling but eager he steadily learned the letters, the syllables, the meanings and pronunciation of the peculiar words that made up the English language. He reflected on his history lessons. *The English language.* He soon found out the French William of Normandy had well and truly lived up to his illegitimate name and, as soon as he had been victorious at Hastings, he had set about changing the country he had defeated, including bastardising the language of the Angles even further. Twisting his own Uralic tongue into strange vowels and different nouns his English began to slowly improve.

Constantly mindful of his past — it was his reason for being here — he decided it would perhaps be safer if he kept on moving. Complacency was another of his enemies. He had survived the trek across Austria and Germany by sheer determination and need, but also by not stopping in any one place for too long.

The small town of Dover was not as dour as its name suggested but he soon resolved that the strategic port simply wasn't going to be enough for him. Stuffing his crude money into his breeches he got up one morning, looked at the town one more time and headed west.

He stopped briefly in Folkestone, only for a few days, then turned inland towards Ashford. While there he worked as a general labourer and then as a market trader's mate.

But work wasn't as plentiful as it was back in Dover so he packed his things again. This time he walked north-east to Canterbury with its magnificent Gothic cathedral, staying on for a few months. He found each town would have its own identity, subtle differences, oddball characters, and workloads. Eventually he headed off again, north, towards the coast, arriving in the tiny placid sea-side town of Whitstable.

In wandering the length and breadth of Europe, crossing the Channel on a boat that made him seasick, working his way through several southern English towns, he decided it was time to stop – at least for a while. Surely he had moved on enough? *Az utazás itt ér véget - The journey ends here.*

He rubbed at his facial hair, the stubble of his chin prickly on his fingertips. He had finally grown into a young man — that's if a lonely, strange and bewildered boy who had lost the singular love of his parents can ever be said to be grown.

Having chosen the English as his new neighbours he continued with his work and his studies. Time passed quickly and he realised he had now been in the south-east for around a year. Still, it was a strange country to him with much changing all the time. Industrialisation and development was busily working around the clock. Times were moving forward. It made the people busy too — and that wasn't a bad thing, it meant less time to interrogate him on his past, to rake up painful memories.

Although the young Hungarian felt comfortable in his new surroundings he often felt a strange sense of foreboding creep up on him and close around him, stifle and suffocate him. It depressed him, he was lonely, and he still missed his parents. There were times he would wake in the night, feverish and sweaty. As safe as his new place was he wanted nothing more than to go home, to see his papa's kind and broad face and hear his mama's soft voice singing to him as he lay.

He knew it wasn't to be.

His mind may soar now and then but at least he had settled in well enough since arriving in what was known locally as the Pearl of Kent; the fishy town famous for its oysters. There was no going back, pearls or not. Whitstable, along with its friendly inhabitants, had immediately accepted him, again because he was prepared to work — and work hard.

Being a young man, he found, was to his advantage; his father had taught him well on the farm and in the workshop. He too had his father's strength but, thankfully, none of his bulk. *Köszönöm papa - Thank you papa.*

One day, he had climbed out of bed way too early and, deciding he was not able to get back to sleep, had dressed and was eating his breakfast, nibbling on some bread, when he sat down and began thinking of home:

The year 1850 had seen an end to the violence and civil bloodshed that his little country had endured. A decade had gone by since the revolution had finally been smothered, chiefly by the Russian Army. It was then in 1860 that he had unceremoniously entered into a hostile and brutal world, covered from head to toe in mucous and blood and shit. He had no actual recollection of being born of course, had been told by his parents, but he was only seconds old when he had floated high in the cool air, supported by the huge rough hands of his father.

Like a pink plucked chicken being taken to the boiling pot his papa lifted him up and exhibited him lovingly to his beautiful mother. Tears of happiness and fatigue pearled his mother's cheeks. Dear, dear mama. Exhausted, she lay upon the small stained bed looking up at his descending form and instantly said to his tiny but perfect uncomprehending ears, 'My beautiful Jakob.'

She took him then, lifting him tentatively from her proud husband, the new father, and gently cradled his raw body. Brushing her soft warm hand across his cheek, over to his wild new hairline, she regarded him lovingly and proudly said aloud: 'Uros.' - My Little Lord.

Jakob remembered his father being much taller than his mother — and much wider. Over six feet high, a thick black beard covered his full face. His papa's size and strength had always marvelled him. Sometimes as a small child he would hide and watch his father for hours at his work if he could get away with it. Spotting him sitting quietly in the thick of the straw that lay around the small barn his father would pretend that he hadn't really seen his son watching. Then, walking round as though to pass Jakob by — an actor at play almost — his papa would suddenly pounce like a massive hairy wolf onto him. Jakob would jump in fright, startled to the core, as this mighty man-mountain moved towards him. He would be swept high into the air before his father would fake a fumble and catch him again, laughing deeply to himself. Putting him down gently on the ground again, after a quick tickle, his papa would lift him onto his shoulders and show him the animals, teach him their habits, their names.

For all his size and bulk his papa was really a big puppy dog — hard to believe when Jakob would watch him manhandling a big old ewe like she was just a tiny ball of cotton wool.

Jakob? Was that really his name? He felt the life that he had conjured in his mind, his past, belonged not to him but to some other happy and carefree soul. It couldn't be him – could it?

But Jakob it was, named by the woman who had been his mother. Slim and tall she was always attentive, responsive and caring, a beautiful black-haired woman with sharp features. Her defined cheek-bones gently housed her narrow nose. Slender and strong from her daily housework she would always offer a helping hand.

He remembered how happy she was, how she would hum simple folk ballads, all the while dutiful in her chores. High spirited and fun (although she could be stern if she needed to be), his mama was the cohesive force, the glue, that bound his family, not only to one another but also to home and country — Hungary.

He always knew he would stand accused of having a biased opinion whenever he remembered his mother. Soon he would stand accused of many other terrible things.

THREE

The sun hugged the horizon far out to sea, a huge shiny capsicum eye peeking over the edge of the world, the early morning sky shifting to a light blue. Jakob looked out beyond the harbour at the rolling waves. He buried any memories of his parents before going to work but thought of them fondly as he stepped out the door.

Isten áldja meg mindkét - God bless you both.

He wiped his sleeve across his tired eyes; he now wished he had at least tried to get back to sleep. A soft breeze blew in from the sea. In the fresh air he felt better, a little more awake. Salt and ozone, mixed with the odour of kelp, helped to clear his nose. The early morning birdsong and the sound of rolling waves wallowing against the harbour wall soothed him while he strolled. As he approached the boats a dozen or more seagulls rode the early thermal winds, all darting about him; they swooped and screeched at the idea of an easy and tasty morning meal.

Fresh fish had arrived in the harbour from several small fishing boats; the day's catch. Still early, the place was already alive, thriving with workmen. He remembered the feverish crew back in Dover on the day he arrived. He was one of them now.

The water within the harbour walls was almost still, rippling lightly, and the boats swayed gently, pulling at their tied ropes, while people buzzed along the length of the wharf like busy bees around honey. A hive of activity, all workers and no queen.

Jakob wasn't particularly fond of the constant smell but he was at least happy for the work. He looked down at the latest catch that the boats had now offloaded, where several large cartons of fish and oysters lay. Opting this time to carry the fish, he finished tying his apron and bent his tall frame down and lugged some of the slippery catch into his arms. With his hands full, he turned, walking towards the street front, and the fish market.

The load was heavy, and he straightened his back, tightening his muscles. He fixed his eyes on the drop-off point up ahead, concentrating hard, not wanting to slip or fall. He had only done that once and it was a lesson well learned, as he had been the laughing stock for most of the day. From the corner of his eye, walking slowly and gently, he saw her.

He nearly tumbled.

Saját maga királynő - *My very own queen.*

Emerging from the morning light, encased in a golden glow of low sunlight, she appeared; ghost-like, a hazy apparition of beauty. Her green flowing skirt bounced softly as she walked, her shoulders tightly wrapped in a scarlet shawl, matching her flowing hair. Suddenly Jakob didn't mind being a simple drone, a mindless worker bee. He could watch her

Forgetting the ungainly salty and smelly cargo in his arms, he slowed, almost to a halt, and eyed her longingly. She was the loveliest woman he had ever seen in his life, her young pale soft skin pearlescent in the morning sun. She was about twenty-five years old — he had enquired about her later in the day to a colleague at the fish yard, Tom Parker, whose family knew her from her work as a nanny. Tom Parker had eyed him curiously before laughing and teasing him. His face had reddened as he spewed verbal diarrhoea about why he wanted to know. There were lots of ums and ahs in his unconvincing replies.

He looked down at the cargo in his arms and then at her again. Her *vörös* — ginger — hair, giving off the look of deep burning embers in a dying fire juxtaposed her milky white, almost porcelain skin. She was at least a head shorter than him but she emanated a presence and confidence that aroused him.

Gyönyörü — Beautiful.

To him she was perfect, like a minuscule and exactly formed sea-horse. To everyone else she was simply the pretty young redhead who worked at the big old house a little further along from the town centre, in Seasalter.

He gulped deeply again at the fresh sea air. *What would she ever see in me?* Here he was, an ungainly foreigner with strange moods who sometimes suffered deep bouts of depression.

Strengthening his resolve he buried any negative thoughts and, as he did so, he walked up to the front and plunked down the fish onto the slate surface. He turned and, again, watched her in awe as she moved closer. Closer. Gracefully, she approached, a large cat slowly stalking its unsuspecting prey.

His stomach cramped.

Ever so gently and poised she drew nearer, closer, to him. He couldn't help his eyes wandering. He looked her up and down and noticed her dew-dropped brown boots were muddy and stained. They stood out against her spotless dress. He looked up her shapely body again, coming to rest on her pretty face. He soon forgot all about any dirty boots.

Ő gyönyörű. She's beautiful.

Seeing this new stranger eyeing her, this tall scaly man in front of her, she gave him a wry glance. She fixed her eyes on his.

Going for broke, it was Jakob who spoke first.

"*Szia* . . . I mean, um, hello," he said, forgetting himself.

"Mornin' to you, sir," she responded, all bright and cheery.

Her voice held an odd accent. Since arriving Jakob had stayed only in the south and was not familiar with any other tones or accents, if there actually were any.

"It's a good morning," he reported, sounding rather dull and stupid.

"Yes, 'tis a fine morning and should be a lovely day," she answered with confidence, her eyes on him. "Good for the soul to be sure."

Like a puppy dog Jakob nodded excitedly. Pushing his luck he reached out his hand towards her and said, "Erm, pleased to meet you, young lady."

Looking down at his fishy and scale ridden hands she smiled, tilted her head, then looked up at his face.

Spotting his outstretched arm he realised his daft mistake. He frowned. He drew his arm back not knowing what to do with the embarrassing limb. Without thinking he ran his large dirty hands through his hair.

"Sorry, I'm a little . . . I'm a bit fishy," he said nervously, wiping his oily hands down his apron.

Her smile gripped him momentarily before it faded as she spoke. "Tis not a problem but I'd rather keep my hands clean just the same. The children will wonder whatever it is I've been up to," she said. "It's nice to meet you, too. My name is Emma."

Her deep, powerful eyes drew him in. Unable to move, he was instantly seduced. He was transfixed, could feel himself floating towards her. Standing there, gazing into her deep blue eyes for what seemed an eon, he felt a sudden hard slap on his back.

"Are you going to stand around all day while us real workers pick up your shift?" It was his colleague, Tom Parker. He would have a word with him later.

Startled, Jakob nearly slipped over before regaining his composure. He glared at Tom and then turned to Emma who had let slip a discreet but obvious laugh.

Amused, Tom winked at Jakob, nudged him in the side and trundled off again to fetch some more of the day's catch, the market wouldn't wait.

"I'm sorry about that," he said as his face flushed. "That's Tom . . . he's a bit of a joker. I'm Jakob."

Seeing his awkwardness, she giggled.

After that first meeting in the harbour, they met often and it wasn't long before they became close. They would get together as much as they could; an eager Jakob struggling to wait till he finished his shift; he found himself buying more bars of soap to scrub away the odour of his daily labours.

For hours they would talk, deep into the night, leaving Jakob tired for his early morning shift. He cared little, he was with her.

One afternoon she readily told him that she wasn't from around the area and, of course, in his reply, neither was he — in that, they were the perfect match. The locals would notice them together around the harbour, around the town. As in all small communities tongues soon began to wag. Apparently it was no longer peculiar to see such a young woman without a chaperone; it was just, as someone had put it: "She's a bit different."

Jakob knew she was different, savoured that she was different in so many ways; it was why he was so drawn to her, so attracted to her. Jakob also knew that she worked and lived in a large house owned by a rather odd but wealthy reclusive couple who worked in London, and Emma had the 'honoured' task of looking after their two children aged one and three, a boy and girl respectively. It was because of this, due to her work commitments she had said, that she couldn't always see Jakob — or not nearly as much as he wanted to anyway.

When they were together it was like he was living in a dream. He floated on the air, found himself humming strange tunes. He had boundless energy, would listen intently to her every word.

Since leaving Hungary he had yearned for the comfort and compassion of a kindred spirit. Someone close, not to replace his mother, but someone to replace the void he felt deep in his heart and soul.

In short, he was falling in love.

Red-headed and fiery she lived up to her looks. Emma was exactly what he needed. They got on so well.

After a few months of being together, Jakob realised he still didn't really know much, in fact, anything, about her. Yes, they talked, but about what? Jakob shook his head and his cheeks flushed as he knew it was just soppy stuff. He hadn't even been to the house where she worked. It seemed everyone knew the big old house on the outskirts of the town except himself — apparently a place so large it could house several families at once and they would never cross paths in the many complex rooms and corridors.

Emma had been left to fend for the two children on her own. Her employers obviously trusted her but Jakob didn't exactly like the idea of her being alone in the house. The owners, away all the time on business, were rarely seen — if ever.

FOUR

It was a perfect day. The sun shone out from a cool sky. Red-brown leaves filled the rounding autumn trees that lined the shallow banks, almost orderly in fashion. The town, readying itself for the coming season, bathed in an ocean of baroque orange. Sitting on the edge of the luxurious Danube, to the north of Pest, the once prehistoric settlement had matured through battle and devastation next to the medieval castle ruins. Brisk white clouds patched the blue sky, threatening to open up. She was with him now, Édesanyám — his dear mama — making their dinner, rich and abundantly spiced with bright orange and red paprika, it was his favourite; gulyás — goulash. Sitting down together to eat, she rubbed at his nose as he let the hot broth flow through his sinuses, across his tongue and down his throat — he loved it . . .

Jumping awake, his clouded sleepy head instantly realised he was late. *Szar - Shit.* Jakob berated himself at his laziness and at his stupidity.

He was meeting Emma today in the town centre. They would often go for long walks along the coast or simply stroll through the town hand in hand, just pleased to be together. On occasion they would catch the train to Canterbury after meeting at the station. That was where he was now supposed to be.

Come on.

With the speed of a young leopard and the grace of an orang-utan, he rapidly made himself presentable, pulling his best white shirt over his head. He slammed the door shut behind him and made off down the road. Low sunlight twinkled off the dewy grass, half blinding him as he went, and he stumbled. Careful of his next steps he put his head down and walked steadier, faster.

It was still early in the morning, not as early as his work shift, and most of the regular townsfolk were only just rising themselves. He gave a cursory nod and the odd greeting as he went by. Thankfully he had remembered to bring a little money and a bag of food that he had hastily thrown together before leaving his room.

Seeing Emma in the distance through half-open eyes he smiled at her, letting out a yawn at the same time — a sort of yawn-smile. She was wearing a deep bonnet, more red than pink with a ribbon at its sides and a fine lace trim around the front. He could see her face framed within. She smiled back at him.

When he reached her he greeted her, apologising for his lateness (and his bleary eyes), and together they walked down to the little station and boarded the train. Not so long ago, the *Invicta* steam locomotive — built immediately after Robert Stephenson's *Rocket* — had run along the same railway line, the *Crab and Winkle*. From Whitstable town centre, along a short straight track, it soon descended into Canterbury.

Peering out of the coach at the countryside of green pastures, Jakob thought of home. *Kocsi*, the first horse drawn wagon (or coach), had been made in the humble Hungarian village of *Kocs* only a few hours journey west of Pest. The word Coach, now anglicised, had been adapted by the English. His mind reeled. *Why my parents? They were so gentle.*

It was a barbaric world, he knew, but why? *Why had they been chosen? What had they ever done?* His mama had loved life, had loved to bestow her knowledge on him. She had taught with such vigour and tenacity that it had been infectious. History was a subject that he now, as a young man, enjoyed himself. He suddenly realised that since meeting Emma he hadn't actually thought too much about his parents. *Was that a good thing?* He didn't know and he began to feel a little guilty. In his heart he knew that they were always with him. Everything he had become was because of them — his caring, gentle mother, his hard working father.

Sensing his mood, Emma drew nearer to him, touching his hand. She leaned in closer still and kissed him gently on the cheek. Perking up at the show of affection from the girl whom he now adored, he smiled at her. The touch of her hand was cold. They kissed again, their lips locked together for a long moment — a moment of delight. It was the first time that she had kissed him properly, really properly, and her lips were cold too, almost blue, he realised.

"Are you all right, Jakob?" she asked. "You're not saying much."

He looked at her, tried smiling. It was during the first couple of months of meeting her that he had told her about his parents. But then he had clogged up and gone silent, and had never mentioned it again. She had not pursued it at the time — she knew he would tell her when, and if, he was ready. Turning to her pale and beautiful face he croaked and cleared what felt like a dead amphibian from the back of his throat.

"They . . . my parents, they were the kindest people. I miss them. Family was an important thing to them. To us."

Emma squeezed his hand.

He closed his eyes:

His best friend Miklós was visiting with his father. Leaving mama in the house he and Miklós sneaked past their papas, leaving the men discussing animals or work or whatever Hungarian farmers spoke about. Together he and Miklós headed off, armed only with a few tools. Tramping across fields of green for what seemed like miles (but was really only just past the river bed) they ended up near the old Roman ruins, spending hours playing and running and trying to capture wild rabbits. It was a lucky day and so they returned, muddy clothed, heads held high like triumphant soldiers traipsing back into town after an impossible battle with their doleful catch. Dinner that night consisted of fresh rabbit. Mama cooked it perfectly and it tasted excellent.

After a long pause he opened his eyes, his stare fixed upon the opposite seat of the coach. Without looking up he continued.

"The years before I was born had been a violent time in my country. Not that you would know, or probably care even, but the people of Hungary had been prosperous for a long time under the rule of the Austrian Kings. Civil unrest was growing, the new citizens demanding change. Small riots and fighting were breaking out all around the country, the majority of it little more than a simple skirmish here and there. Nobody thought it would ever come to anything.

"The Habsburgs were great rulers, proud; their roots stemmed from the Romans themselves. They had controlled Austria for over six centuries, ruling Hungary since Charles VI. I don't really know, I was too young, but Hungary wanted its own voice, its independence; this is what my mama told me. The armies, including our own soldiers, were fighting and dying in the foreign wars; for Austria, in Croatia, the Banat and in Transylvania.

"Revolution broke out. The uprising started in Pest around 1848, gathered momentum quickly and a new Hungarian army was formed. There were bloody battles close to us, to the west at *Komárom*. The Austrians were not happy at the resistance and began looking for support in greater numbers. So they called the Russians into combat, sharing cold steel alongside one another. Despite some courageous victories, the rebellion soon met with heavy losses and by the following year it was defeated. The bloodshed had turned our once-green pastures a deep crimson.

"I was born some years later, a portent of things to come my mama always said. Even in defeat the people of Hungary had managed to bring about radical change. Although the future looked bright there were still many dangers and isolated brutality continued around the country — misguided fanatics, men with a grudge to hold. There was talk of a dual monarchy. Like I said, I was young, I did not really understand. I was just happy to go to school and help papa at the forge and tend to the animals."

An image of his father at the anvil, a heavy hammer in his hand, made him proud. Struggling for further words, Jakob said, "We lived close to Pest, a little to the north, so we were safe. Or so we thought."

FIVE

Shattered at his story Jakob left his head down, his chin resting on his chest. His mouth was dry, his eyes still closed. He had survived the perilous journey across Europe and so he knew he was strong. *Come on now Jakob, pull yourself together.*

He looked at the girl next to him and allowed her beauty to caress him, to embolden him. Emma had just sat there and listened to him all the way. She was lovely and he soon began feeling better. Outside, a loud whistle blew and fizzed away into the Kent air. They had arrived in Canterbury.

Emma drew him close and put her arms about him and he stayed there for a few moments, smelling her natural sweet fragrance. With his face buried safely in the bouquet of her chest he hugged her hard before they headed out into the brightness and the mid morning air.

The ancient town was breathtaking. At least there was still some beauty to behold in the world. To try and brighten his mood Jakob took it all in, absorbing its grandeur, marvelling at its magnificence. He had been through Canterbury before on his travels, but had been busy working, staying anonymous, and had never really stopped to appreciated its exquisiteness. At the time sight-seeing was the last thing on his mind.

The town had stood since before the time of the Romans who rebuilt the new streets in simple grid formation. It was steeped in history, particularly with the infamous death of Thomas Becket. Years ago Black Death had diminished the local population by over two-thirds but it had still survived. Here, Death, for a long time, had hung around, loitering, taking indiscriminately, but the town and its inhabitants lived on.

Emma and Jakob strolled on, alongside the Great Stour, the river water gleaming, skimming the sunshine into their eyes as it beat down causing them both to avert their gaze. Children played on the banks, chasing, screaming and giggling. Well-dressed gentlemen and women strolled by, nodded their 'hellos' and briskly walked on.

Walking as young lovers often do, oblivious, unaware of their surroundings, swinging their arms, they careened into a man, knocking his black bowler hat from his head and nearly into the water. Grunting profusely, obviously he wasn't amused; he stooped to pick it up. Brushing dust from the retrieved hat he placed it back neatly on his head, glared at them both and charged away. Together, Jakob and Emma offered their apologies to the man and staggered away, tittering.

Eventually they reached their destination.

"Here we are," Jakob said.

Leading her by the hand they ducked inside. The old Germanic ruins of Canterbury Castle were said to have been built in the first quarter of the twelfth century. They stared with delight at the humble surroundings. Emma had brought with them a small blanket and so she set about arranging it on a stretch of clear flat ground. There was a still silence in the place

— no bird song, no buzz of insects, nothing. It was as if they had entered and stopped in the middle of a painted landscape.

Enjoying the peace they sat and talked.

Jakob started off by telling Emma about his mother, about how as a child he had struggled in earnest with his school work, trying in vain to follow the dynamo and electric motor principles of Edlik Ányos István, the Hungarian inventor and engineer. She knew nothing of the names and places, just sat, listened, and smiled.

Going on about more history he mentioned King Stephen I and the Ottoman wars. He told her of Attila the Hun with his legendary sword and whose empire stretched all the way from Germany to the Ural River and from the Danube to the Baltic Sea. The Mongols, too, had invaded Hungary in the year 1241. In fact, the grandson of Genghis Khan himself had attacked the Hungarian people in *Mohi*, near *Erdély* in Transylvania. The Mongols had ended up in Jakob's own beautiful borough of *Vác,* slaughtering almost everyone.

Jakob realised he was ranting on, talking about a morbid subject. As Emma continued to listen to his every word he decided to change the subject. He looked over at Emma, her red hair burgeoning forth from her bonnet like a flower germinating in the gleaming sun but her countenance showed the opposite. She looked to be upset, nervous even. He reached out to her hand, apologised and asked about her home, her parents, instead.

She said nothing, dropped her gaze, looking at the ground. Jakob stroked the back of her hand, her skin soft and cool. "Emma?"

She ignored him.

"Are you feeling all right?"

She nodded. Barely.

"It's only me — Jakob."

Again she nodded, letting her hand be caressed.

Eventually she started to speak, slowly and gradually. But whatever she said, she seemed to do her best to avoid any detail. Distracted, her words were vague, she acted as though embarrassed, and she would trail off into reticence. She did manage to tell him that she had once lived in the Welsh valley's some time ago, but exactly where and who with she did not elaborate on.

Her descriptions of the rolling Welsh countryside, again, reminded Jakob of his own but he could not understand why she was being like this, tight-lipped and secretive. *Surely we have been together long enough by now?* She had always seemed to him to be confident with a strong resolve and a clear head.

Perhaps she was hungry — he knew he was.

He clutched the small bag of food that he had brought along, opened it up and placed it in the middle of the blanket. It contained some broken bread, a little home-made cheese his landlady had prepared, some small apples and a whole tomato. Taking some of the bread and a knife, he sliced at the tomato, shovelled the juicy bitter-sweet fruit into his mouth and started to tuck in.

Halfway through his mouthful he realised how rude he was being. He stopped chewing and looked at her.

"Thorry," he said, his mouth full of fresh fruit flesh. "Ladies first." He pushed the food towards her, inviting her to take some.

"I'm not hungry," she said, giving the food a rather squeamish look.

"It's good," he insisted. "And fresh."

Abruptly she turned her face to his. "I said no, didn't I? I had something earlier on anyway, before I left the house."

He knew he had upset her — he put that down to her being scared of his silly stories — but he was totally unprepared for her major outburst. He shut up for a few minutes.

There was an uncomfortable silence.

After a while, he decided to try again. "But—"

"But what?" she snapped back at him.

"It's just, well, it is just I never see you eat," he said, a little concern in his voice.

"So? Do you have to scrutinise everything I do? I'm simply not hungry. I told you."

"Fine."

"Fine." She folded her arms.

Reaching an impasse he let her be, thought about what she had said. No he didn't have to scrutinise her, yet he could not recall a single time he had ever seen her eat — she did have an exquisite figure. But then so had his mama and she had loved food, loved cooking, had been a great cook. It was in her blood. *I wish mama could see this place.*

He left Emma be and gazed at the sheer beauty of the surroundings. The peace and quiet was replete. Soon forgetting the food and Emma's outburst they lay back on the blanket, enjoying the day. Emma kept on fussing, moving into the shade, complaining about the heat. He looked at her. *No wonder you are so pale.*

After lunch — well, after his lunch at least — they packed up and strolled arm in arm around the castle grounds for a while taking in the serenity of the place. Silently they walked, Emma still upset. Jakob imagined ghosts of weary soldiers lurking in the shadows, waiting for them to step around the next corner and into their eternal spectral battles. Hungary had been raised on bloodshed. It was no different to anywhere else he reminded himself. There had been wars and revolutions, kings and queens betrayed and beheaded throughout history — why should it be any different here? Of course he just wanted to believe, truly believe, that he was now in a place of kindness and compassion — and peace.

Toward the end of the day they had put their little disagreement behind them and were now back in the town, the great cathedral towering over them as it did the whole town. It was getting late in the day so they decided to head back to the train — they did not want to miss it. It was not that far back to Whitstable, Jakob had walked it before, only this time he was in the company of a beautiful young lady, a woman that cared for him, would never hurt him. It would not impress her if she had to walk.

At that precise moment in time he knew his life was on the up. He had endured the worst he was sure. He had a job, a place to stay. He had found Emma and was not going to give up on her. Yes, it was starting to feel like things might get a lot better.

He didn't know how wrong he was going to be.

The man in the black bowler hat watched them from a good distance. He had been following the lovers for several days now, unnoticed, until that afternoon when he had almost given himself away by getting far too close — and he had nearly lost his hat in the river. *Amateurish*. He chastised himself. *Maybe I shouldn't drink so early.*

He had to face it, he was growing weary, tired in his lonesome quest. He needed to recruit some help. Also, he badly needed another drink. It had been a long time since he had lost his innocence though and he had found he could kill quite easily now, without conscience. He slept well, too.

He knew that what he was doing, what he *had* to do, that only the Lord himself could judge him. Sitting down alone on the bench opposite the mighty cathedral he sighed heavily, his eyes never leaving the two he closely followed, he contemplated his next move.

He would bide his time, wait a little longer. Victory would soon be his, he sensed it. Yes, the drink could wait; he needed to stay alert, strong. He was going to need a steadfast durability for the bitter showdown, an act of love, for his gracious sister. A showdown that could end only in death, and not that of his own.

SIX

Arm in arm Jakob and Emma walked up the path towards the big old house, the gravel beneath their feet popping and crunching loudly as they went. They had enjoyed the day's delights in Canterbury and the ample stroll from Whitstable. The air outside was fresh now as the sun lowered.

Inside, the house was dark, still, all the curtains drawn. Elegant furniture wowed Jakob as he inspected each of the rooms in turn. There was no heating on and it was cold — much colder inside than out — he could see his own breath in the stale air. *Oh, my Lord. What about the children?* He knew England suffered from bizarre weather patterns and realised that on any day in any season it could be cold. The children would freeze to death in a house as large as this without any heating on. *But where were they? Away with their parents?*

Emma leapt out in front of him as he came out of a finely decorated lounge and back onto the varnished wooden floor of the huge passageway. Grabbing at him she skipped and giggled and led him by the hand, ushering him towards a large oak door at the end. Placing her index finger up to her lips she mimicked that he be quiet.

"Shhh."

Going along with the game Jakob obeyed her, watching her reach into her petticoat. She pulled out a large cast iron key. Quietly and effortlessly she slipped the key into the ready-made hole and, with a loud clunk, the lock gave way.

As she opened the door she looked back into Jakob's face. Excited, her eyes shone and she ducked into the gloom of the blackened doorway.

Jakob followed her into the dark loneliness of what appeared to be a set of stairs that led to a basement below the great house. She let go of his hand and marched down the steps into the pitch black. Slowly allowing his eyes to adjust Jakob followed her gingerly. After several steps he reached solid ground. He padded his feet around just to be certain.

Kkkkssshhhh.

The sound of the igniting match gave off a small pool of light. Jakob recalled his school teachings. It was a loud scrape, a Lucifer match, not the noiseless type invented in 1836 by chemistry student János Irinyi in Hungary. Aided by the tiny quivering flame Jakob could now see something, movement.

Stretching out her shadowed arm to the lamp Emma lit the gas and threw the depleted match to the ground. There was a hushed pop and light slowly flickered into life, grew and intensified.

It revealed a morose scene.

Piros - Red.

Red on the floor, the walls. *Had the tiny piece of wood, tipped with a combustible phosphorus chemical, somehow summoned Lucifer himself?*

No.

It was blood, Jakob recognised it, could smell its coppery odour in the damp cellar air. He looked around, trying to make sense of what his eyes beheld. *No, it can't be.* Bit by bit, his eyes focused fully on the appalling sight: the mire on the walls, the steps, and, at the end, the . . . the cage?

Realisation hit him hard and he suddenly retched. Sharp acid, defying gravity, left his bowels, hit the back of his throat and burned. Prostrate and still, he saw the bodies in the cage. Laying there, smeared in dregs of clay and dirt like a family of demonic sloths, the four shapes slowly began to emerge — a man, a woman, two small children.

A faint shuffling came from within the cage.

"Ungh." A voice penetrated the silence.

Ó, Istenem — Oh, God — they are still alive!

Jakob looked at her for answers. "Emma . . . what the hell is going on?"

Through the darkness he saw her face, her lopsided grin.

"I have to tell you, Jakob . . ."

"Have to tell me what? Please, what is this?" he asked.

"You need to understand, Jakob. About me I mean. It will probably be easier if I just say it outright. You see, I'm a vampire, one of the undead," she confided.

Jakob, still bent over, just stayed where he was, silent, numb. The smears of blood all around and the bodies confirmed Emma's bizarre statement.

"I was lucky enough to meet you Jakob, and now I've *chosen* you. I've chosen to give this to you. To give you our gift, the gift of eternal life. Because . . . because I love you," she announced proudly.

44

Jakob could not fathom what he was hearing. *A vampire? But Erzsébet Báthory was just a legend, surely nothing more?*

Seeing his shock, Emma pointed to the cage. "It's not so bad Jakob, they *are* alive you know." she said. "Although I think the little one may be struggling a little, if not dead already."

She continued with her horror story, telling him how she had to keep them alive, piercing them, cutting and slashing at them so she could feast on their blood. After all, she was only a petite girl and most likely was going to struggle wrestling a grown man into revealing his jugular vein so that she may happily chomp away at his neck.

And she *had* to choose a rich family — it made it so much easier — to live off for as long as she could. She had no money troubles that way and could easily keep up the pretence of merrily trotting into town, a pretty picture of youthful exuberance, where she would fetch the groceries, even smiling at the store owner and tipping his wife on her way out.

"I give them just enough to keep them alive; it's not as if they'll be using up any energy."

Oh dear Jesus! The woman he had fallen for was for real, a reincarnation of the beautiful and deadly *Lamia*, the child eating demon from Greek mythology. But she was so sweet, so pretty. *No. A fehér liliomnak is lehet fekete az árnyéka - Even a white lily can cast a black shadow.*

Needing to get out of the place as quickly as he could Jakob turned and bolted up the steps, slipping on slick pools of old plasma. At the top the door was locked. Emma must have quietly back-tracked up the stairs and locked the door while he was busy retching. He turned and peered back down the stairs.

There she stood, radiant in the quivering lamp-light, a sweetly innocent young girl.

Even in the half-light, her blue eyes jolted him back to her — *into* her. Something deep within his soul stirred and he had to go to her. Had to be with her, near her, touching her, feeling her. Gliding downwards again towards her beautiful and treacherous frame — it was more an ironic ascension into heaven than a plunge into the depths of Hades — as he was about to find out.

On reaching her she tip-toed and kissed at his needy mouth. Passion flooded them both and soon they were pulling at each other's clothes, frantic to be together, as one. She kept her eyes fixed on his at all times, the spell unbroken. In the cold, bleak mucous and blood covered basement, clothes pulled to one side in the desperate need to unite, they made love.

Reaching climax quickly Jakob curled up his frantic body, his head in a daze as she pushed herself off him, not quite contented.

From the corner of a misty eye he saw a flash, something gleaming in Emma's hand. A knife. Sitting there spent Jakob could only watch in horror as she took the sharp blade in her delicate hand and began cutting, slicing deep into the flesh of her forearm. Thick blood oozed from the fresh wound.

The less-than-perfect heart shape on her arm, she said, was to be a symbol of their unity and everlasting love. She stretched out her left forearm towards him, showing — offering — him her juices. "Kiss it Jakob, taste me," she rasped.

With diffidence he took her white arm and began mouthing at her self-inflicted wound, now feeling more aroused than ever. The metal taste of the dark crimson liquid that flowed from her seemed to gently stab at his frenzied tongue. Filling his mouth he let the blood flow to the back of his throat, about to burst.

He swallowed.

Pain engulfed his body, his throat on fire. Gasping, he fell forward and clutched at his throat and stomach. *Dear God, the pain.* What in the name of heaven and hell was happening to him? Looking up through bleary eyes he saw Emma, his lovely Emma. She was no longer the vision of beauty that his mind remembered but now a wicked, evil, malevolent beast.

She looked on fervently as his stricken body writhed around on the cold floor.

"Help me . . . please," he said as he clawed at the ground.

In fascination Emma stood by and watched.

"Segitsey," he pleaded. *Help.* Clutching at the cage for purchase Jakob attempted to stand.

"What was that, my love?" she asked, not fully understanding his Hungarian outburst.

"Help," he strained in English.

"Oh. Oh but I have helped you," she said, stepping back to give him some room to manoeuvre.

Leaning heavily against the side of the railings he tried to steady himself, his knees still half bent. Again he clutched at his guts, grimacing. He nearly fell back. He braced the railings harder.

"Just let it happen. Jakob, 'tis too late now, you've drank my blood, the blood of a vampire. 'Tis a poison if ever there was one to any living being, man or woman. I'm sorry my love, but 'twill soon be over and then we can be together. Forever."

The pain intensified and Jakob felt himself drifting away. This time he fell, felt himself descending, tumbling into a foul darkness that consumed his body, his mind, his soul, taking his final breath with him.

SEVEN

Jakob and his father trudged back to the house, pleased to be finished for the day. Both tired they were looking forward to dinner.

The screaming started as soon as they entered the small farmhouse. Together, father and son jolted into action. Papa told mama to stay put in the house, safe. They picked up some tools as they sought the direction of the screams, papa grabbing the axe from the wood pile. Jakob picked up some shears.

As they approached, cautiously, the screaming increased. Loud thudding against the ground gave way to horses. Bursting out of the dark copse they came — renegade soldiers on horseback. Barbaric and blood-crazed the soldiers galloped towards them. It was then they saw the screaming woman, her dress soiled from falling, her hair a thorn bush atop her head. She ran at them shouting wildly, terrified, seeking safety. The szablya — sabre — in the mounted soldier's hand swung down, chopping angrily into her flailing arm.

The woman fell, badly injured. Ignoring her the soldier carried on, kicking at his horse. Needing help, the woman stretched her good arm forward pleading for assistance. Assistance that they could not offer her. The second horse cut her down fully, the front hoof knocking her forward and face down, the rear hoof crushing her chest as it pushed away from the clumsy human obstacle.

Realising the intent of the wild soldiers, papa looked back at the house. His voice broke as he shouted out in panic.

"Mama."

The message was clear — mama was alone in the house. They spun around and ran back, retracing their footsteps. The first horseman was already at the house. Rigorously jumping from his horse, they could only watch as he kicked down the door, yelling out in a strange babble, and entered.

Russians!

On reaching the front of the house he and his father stopped. The soldier appeared. Following in silent submission, bent over like an old crone, was his mother.

Mama!

"Let her be," his papa growled.

Understanding their foreign tongue the Russian soldier grunted. "You bastard insurgent."

What's he talking about? The wars are over.

The soldier pulled his mama up by her flowing dark hair, leered at her, and repeated. "She bastard insurgent."

Mama stumbled on the mud beneath her but the soldier, grim in his determination, held on fast. Squealing gently she kept her resolve. She was strong, inviolable. Her even stronger husband was being forced to watch helplessly as his beloved wife was assaulted.

Tightening his vast grip on the wooden shaft of the axe papa spoke. "I said let her be, Kutyafasza." — Dog's dick.

By now the rest of the soldiers had reached the house, their beasts panting loudly. Steam from the horses filled the air.

Rearing his head back the lead Russian laughed, then spoke. "What? What you do? I soldier . . . I fight. Kill Hungarian pigs."

"The wars are over . . . finished years ago. You ignorant rat," seethed papa as he took a step forward.

"Stay where you are, pig!" the Russian shouted.

With a knife up to his mama's face the soldier screamed at Jakob and his papa. "Stay back . . . or I cut her."

Looking to his father again Jakob watched a lonesome tear fall down his papa's face. He had never seen him cry before. Such immense strength, so much power in those arms of his, but with mama in the hands of the heathen Russian he was breached. Breached but not beaten — at least not yet.

Jakob was terrified. The woman back in the field had not stood a chance against only one of them. With more armed soldiers maybe they didn't either.

"But we're just farmers," Jakob blurted out.

"Shut up, boy," a voice said from behind. A new soldier entered the scene.

"She looks . . . good woman, yes?" the new soldier said, and laughed at his comrade.

Walking towards his mother the new soldier grinned at the soldier who still gripped her hair. As he faced Jakob's mama, the soldier grabbed her chin and poked his tongue into her face, his acrid breath making her pull away. He forced his lips onto hers . . . then let out a muffled scream, staggering backwards.

Papa exploded into action. The woman they both loved, being violated by two uncouth Russian rats was too much for him to bear. His fatigue forgotten, papa pulled the screaming man down and punched him. Hard. Falling face down in the dirt the man stayed down.

The other soldier who still had hold of his mama dragged her closer to him. Mama raised her head in compliance and spat out a chunk of flesh, ripped from the new soldier who had tried to assault her with his kiss. The torn upper lip left her mouth and dropped to the dirt next to him, reunited.

As his papa reached them both, the other men closed ranks, surrounding him. What now? Mama had taught Jakob not to hurt people yet here she was mutilating them. Papa too, he had gone berserk, there was blood everywhere, the soldiers in retreat.

The punching and kicking continued. There was a flash of steel and his father yelled out in surprise. Standing back the Russians looked on at the beaten Hungarian man, now kneeling on the floor.

Papa.

The long blade entered his papa's back, disappeared beneath his clothing, then reappeared at his front.

No, No!

"Jakob," muttered his father. He directed his dying, blood-spattered words at his son. "Run!"

In sheer panic Jakob let out a cry, turned on rooted heels, and ran.

Jakob woke, his past real again.

Where am I?

How long had passed? His eyes slowly focused and he knew exactly where he was — sitting on the floor of . . . Hell. Dazed but cognisant, terrible images ran through his head.

Sitting up he expected to see the Devil, his horns bearing down on him, conjuring some everlasting torture.

Instead he saw bodies. The family of four, Emma's employers and their two children, confined in their wiry tomb, ensured of their destiny. Getting up from the floor Jakob drew closer to the cage.

Carefully he reached out and shook the man. The dead man flopped to one side; dry blood caked his gaunt face and body. An image of his father violently came to him again. He shook it off and tried the woman. The same. Finally, he looked at the little girl. She was blue; the chill of the cellar had coerced any sign of life from her frail, tiny body well before the vampire had drained her.

The chill. Suddenly he could not feel it. It had been cold down here when he entered but now Jakob felt nothing.

A familiar voice came to him from out of the darkness.

"Jakob, my lovely Jakob, you look wonderful."

It was Emma.

Reality dawned. She stood there, triumphant, covered in blood. It ran down her chin and neck, dripped from her fingertips.

"What have you done? These people are . . . They are all dead. You killed them."

"Jakob, I have to eat," she said. "They're no good to me, to *us* now."

"But . . . but, what are you?"

"I told you. I'm a vampire."

"A vampire?"

"That's right, a vampire, a creature of the night. But now you are too, my love," she stated, matter-of-factly. "I'm lonely

Jakob. I need someone who can understand me. I mean, really understand me. One of my own."

She sidled up to him and took his hand in hers. Incredulous at her revelations he drew back and tore his hand out from her feeble grasp.

"Leave me the hell alone, you . . . you witch, you succubus. You seduced me and then made me drink from your blood, you twisted sick bitch," he cried. "What have you done to me? Why did I pass out?"

Cowering gently, she said, "I'm sorry Jakob, you didn't pass out. You . . . you died."

"Don't be stupid, I am here, right now, talking with you," he said.

"No. Yes, you are talking to me, but you *are* dead," she said again. "Well, undead really. Look at your skin if you don't believe me. It's lily white like mine. Tell me, can you feel your pulse?"

Repulsed, he stepped further away from her, he looked at the pale skin of his arms, reached up at his neck to try and find a heartbeat. There was nothing. Nothing.

"There is no such thing as vampires; they are made up stories to get children into their beds. My father enjoyed telling me all about them," he growled.

"Jakob, please—"

"No, this is a trick. I cannot be here, alive, and not have a pulse."

"But you're not alive, you're undead," she told him again.

Confused, Jakob pulled back and sat down, his head in his hands. After a moment he lifted his head and looked at his ashen arm, felt again at his throat, realised that he no longer felt any chill.

"But— You killed me. Why? I loved you."

"Yes and I still love you Jakob, that is why I had to do it. But no, I didn't kill, not really. Instead I gave you a gift. We can be together now, properly, as one," she said, her faint, sweet smile creeping through. She was still so beautiful.

"No, I do not believe you. Yes. This is some kind of trick," he shouted.

"Oh Jakob, my dear sweet Jakob, please listen to me. You're a vampire now. I'm a vampire. *We* . . . are vampires."

"If you are a vampire then where are your fangs?" he fumbled for reason as he stood once more, repelled by the surrounding sight. The young girl's tiny shoe poked out from the railings, the delicate foot a still sign of the foul deed that had occurred. He shut his eyes.

"Oh, that. Yes there are stories and legends, but basically they're all lies. 'Tis just a silly myth that we have fangs or that we can turn into things like a bat or a wolf. That's the reason I had to keep them like that," Emma said, pointing towards the family in the cage. "We all must eat to survive."

"But you have taken everything from me; my dignity, my self-respect and now . . . my life. I cannot live like this. Why? You know about my parents, how they died horribly. Now you have done the same to me, only you have done much worse, you have left me undead. I would never hurt you. *Utálom a kibaszott neked,*" he screamed. *I fucking hate you.*

Jakob turned to run up the steps again, this time to find an exit. Nearing the top, a candle flittered and hovered, ghost-like, above him. Emma watched as Jakob sprang up the steps. Only to stop.

Someone was barring his way.

"Going somewhere, you filthy blood-sucking vermin?" a stern voice said from the top of the stairs.

Jakob froze.

"Who are you?" Emma called out from below. "What do you want?"

"Never mind you loathsome beast, you can call me . . . Death. It seems you already know my sister," he gestured at the fallen dead woman in the cage. "You killed her and her family — although I never really liked my brother-in-law much — and now I'm here to return the favour. Only I'm sending you back to Hell where you belong, you demonic hedge-whore."

"Leave her alone. Please. There's already been enough killing," Jakob interjected. "Let us leave. Please, sir."

"You stay exactly where you are young man. I've a job to do. The wench dies . . . and then so do you. You're next."

Alerted by the man's death threats Jakob ran at him, hitting him square in the stomach with his lowered right shoulder. Jakob had to get out of there. The man cried out and slammed back into the forced door frame, splinters raking at them both.

Kicking the man — Mr Death? — to the floor, Jakob shoved him back with the flat of his boot. Losing his balance the man tumbled down the slippery stairs, dropping his candle. The small candle and its flame descended innocently into the cellar. The diminutive ember landed clumsily on a pile of discarded rags that lay in a heap at the bottom. Flames erupted.

Picking himself up the man headed straight for Emma and together they started grappling. Getting hold of her firmly the man slapped her hard and threw her down. With a dull thud she hit the ground and cried out. Cried out for Jakob.

Jakob panicked, didn't know what he should do. He had, only moments before, found out that he was a vampire and now a total stranger had appeared and told him that he was going to send him straight to Hell. His head whirled. *What have I done to deserve this?* With moulded hair and glass eyes Jakob stood at the top, looking down like a deranged papier-mâché shop mannequin.

Catching alight quicker now the flames started to grow higher. Jakob dithered. S*ave Emma or leave the two-faced bitch here?* He loved her, but now she had turned on him, turned him into a monster? She had killed an innocent young family, had enjoyed it even. *Is this her comeuppance? An eye for an eye?*

A figure jumped through the rising flames, arms wide like a giant cross, and headed towards Jakob. *Too late.* The man, a starry silhouette with the raging flames behind him, faced Jakob from a few steps below. He was clearly injured, clutching at his thigh.

"Leave her. Go. You cannot save her now, her dead flesh will burn as good as any flesh that ever lived," the man said. "My sister and her family can be at peace now. The vampire has met her end. At last."

"But, I—"

"Go now, while you still can. But know this: I will find you again. And I will destroy you," he said, doggedly.

"I did not do anything. I am sorry," Jakob screamed at him.

"Sorry?" the man huffed, his face set like stone. "You let her take you into the realm of the damned." He shook his head. "There is only one outcome for those who are damned."

Jakob turned away, thinking he could hear screams through the cacophony of fire that roared below. He paused.

"Go, now, and get out of my way," the injured man said as he crawled up the final step, his leg bleeding badly.

Jakob did as he was told, backing off as the injured man hobbled past, glaring at him as his face turned orange against the billowing flames. The fire was too intense; it was too late for Emma. *Viszlát.* His mind screamed as he ran frantic into the night. *Goodbye.*

EIGHT

In terror Jakob fled the house. *What had just happened? Who the hell was that man? Oh my God, Emma?*

In bare feet he ran through the night. Coarse grass strafed his toes, brambles tore at his clothes. He tripped. Falling awkwardly he crashed heavily into the ground. Getting up he realised he was not hurt. The pause in his mad dash now gave way to another pause — for thought.

Why run? Emma? He fell to his knees, rolling onto his back. Clawing the damp soil with distraught fingernails he screamed. Anguished and stricken nothing came from him, no sound. He sat up and leaned forward trying to breathe. Nothing. *What's going on?* He couldn't — no, he *wasn't* breathing.

Jakob clutched at his chest, thinking he was having a heart attack. Surely, he should be hyperventilating? He did not have time. *Emma. I must go back.* Trying to regain composure he weighed up his options. There had been many times in Germany where he had been in a similar position, unknowing of what he should do next. *Go back? No, no she is gone.*

The man in the bowler hat, he would not be there now. But he could at least try. No, Jakob had to face it, the man would be gone and Emma . . . incinerated. *No.* He wondered where his tears were. The unknown man had avenged his family because of Emma's deeds, her hideous actions as grand gaoler of Hell.

Was what she said in the basement true? Was he really now a vampire? If so, would he ever breathe again? *I should go back.* Picking himself up, he hesitated. Standing there for some time he weighed up the odds.

Instead of going back he turned and headed west.

The small graveyard looked peaceful. Moonlight smoothed the grey headstones, displaying practised etchings that spelled out forgotten names of the strangers who posthumously resided beneath. Several men lay interred, together in rebellious rest, killed in the last battle on English soil. In 1838, the woods nearby at Bosenden had seen an armed uprising of agricultural labourers led by John Thom, they had swiftly been despatched by soldiers from Canterbury.

Jakob looked longingly at the graves, wishing he could lie down, be with them in the afterlife. Only he was *already* in the afterlife, but a completely different one altogether. One inhabited by demons. Scrambling on hands and knees he searched around the side of the church and spotted what he needed. A small piece of slate, a loose shard from the rooftops, lay beside the old church. He picked it up and turned it over in his hands, examining it closely.

Sitting, his back against a wall, he raised his head. He thought of Emma. He had loved her; only a few hours earlier they had been walking arm in arm along Saint Dunstan's Street in the wake of the Stour. When they had returned she had finally shown her true colours in that unspeakable cellar, seduced him, reached into him with her heart, and ripped out his unwitting soul.

He hated her.

I did not know you. How could he have been so gullible? *Aki délelőtt bolond, délután is az - A fool in the morning is a fool in the afternoon.* Only now the fool had just one thing in mind: he would save the dreadful man in the bowler hat a job. Jakob would join Emma and his parents.

He lifted the slate, gripping it firmly before dragging the naturally sharp edge across his jugular. His flesh and muscle gave way, opening up immediately. There was no pain, little blood.

He waited.

Nothing happened.

He sat there, threw the slate at a stone wall. It clinked as it hit, and rolled away into longer grass as if trying to hide from the evil-being that had just used it as a crude execution tool. In wanting to die he had forgotten the fundamentals of being a vampire — he couldn't die; he was already dead.

Again he tried to scream, to shout. He looked about, confused. Placing his fingers to his neck he felt for the gash that was there, that had not killed him. He pulled away, a thick ooze webbing his fingertips. An old Latin phrase that his mama had often used came to mind. *Memento Mori - Remember, you must die.* It was ludicrous. He tried to laugh but only managed a twisted grimace as he started back to his feet.

As he leaned forward he ran his hands through damp grass, ridding himself of his own filth. To his side a discarded chrysanthemum lay rotting, the petals turning a putrid brown. Back in his home town the same flower was used in remembrance of dead relatives each November. Picking himself up he shook his head and started walking away from the small graveyard, into the night. He kicked at the decomposing gold flower.

The black of night turned as he went. Behind him the sky was a deep shade of ever-lightening blue, morning was coming. He panicked. *The sunlight?* He started running again. What looked like a small bell tower up ahead appeared in the greying dawn. Spotting a forlorn looking narrow church in the distance, he headed for it. It would be empty this time of the morning and he had to get out of the coming sunlight.

An old arched wooden door barred his way. The inscription above showed the numbers: 1717 — the same year Maria Theresia von Habsburg had been born — not that he cared much about the former Queen of Hungary at the present moment. There were more pressing matters on his mind. He tried the handle.

The door swung open with a dull creak. Inside, he started up the thin wooden stairs. At the top, a shallow ledge circulated a large dusty bell. In the shade he screwed himself up into a ball. For now, he was safe.

The days passed like the tardy movements of a great glacier. In his blunted mind Jakob replayed the scene in the basement over and over again. *Was there to be no peace?* His escape across Europe had been a brief respite compared to this. The depths of despair and self-loathing that he experienced now reached new lows. He had to face it — he was a vampire.

His wounded neck had healed in the first few days. But a strong desire for blood kept on at him, clawing at his throat, growling in his stomach. He left any thought of straying outside or eating for as long as he could. Soon, he became weak as his cravings grew worse. In the end he had to succumb, give in to the lust.

He must drink blood.

Darkness had fallen some hours ago. There had been no activity in the church since he had arrived. Starting down the stairs he stepped out into the little cemetery. The village was quiet, everyone asleep. *Time to feed.* He headed through the humble headstones towards the open fields. The hedgerow was thick, rich in foliage, giving him perfect cover.

Crouching down, he waited. Patience had long since become his companion. Before long a few rabbits scurried into view, inspecting the ground. On a late night forage, the largest one to the front of the group, sat up and eyed the landscape, its nose twitching furiously.

Ravenous, Jakob discharged himself from the hedge like a bullet, the small herbivore caught in his weakening grip. It kicked and bit at his fingers but Jakob held on, firm. The rabbit recoiled and writhed in his hands. Pulling it close to him he wrapped his arms around the animal, restraining it. *Now what?*

Slowly the rabbit's natural escape mechanism began to cave in. The fatigued little mammal in his grasp was tiring, breathing heavily. Jakob looked down at its long ears. In its face he saw fear. *I cannot kill you.* The pretty ball of fluff was simply too beautiful. He could not bring himself to do it. But he had too. The need for blood — *his* need — was strong.

Lifting the rabbit, he held it up, staring at its closed eyes, its submissive face. *I . . . I cannot.* He dropped down to the ground, onto his knees, and gently placed the rabbit on the grass in front of him. Letting it go the terrified rabbit did not move. He nudged it with his toe. *Go on then.*

Rooted to the spot he waited until the rabbit moved away tentatively, its fear subsiding, before breaking out into a full run, relishing the open fields again — and freedom. Dejected and hungry Jakob turned back to the haven of the bell tower.

For several days Jakob just lay about, he didn't move. In the end he had no choice but to go. Activity in the church below was increasing. A man (most likely the churchwarden) had been flitting in and out of the place regularly now for the past few days. Jakob did not know how long it would be before the churchwarden or someone else decided to inspect the bell, only to find a frightened and starving vampire sheltered there. Under cover of darkness again he left the relative safety of his latest home.

The nights all drifted into one, became one long bad dream. He dossed down anywhere he could; old barns, outhouses. It was not long before desperation finally led to his first kill.

He found the wounded rat in a barn, the victim of a cat or overzealous terrier. He looked down at the ravaged hirsute body, its smitten, anguished form. A mercy killing. Already defeated, motionless, he picked up the rodent, its tiny life etching away. *Must be quick.* He wrapped his large hands around the body and wrung it out like a thick black towel.

Limp now, he raised it to his lips, sucking at the wound. Disgusted in himself, he squeezed, draining the dead rat as fast as he could. He left the rat's body in the huge wooden crypt of the barn. Not long after, Jakob did it again, only this time it was a family of shrews he had found under an old discarded gate. He hated himself for killing such a beautiful set of miniature animals just so he could eat — it amounted only to the equivalent of a few teaspoons. The bloodlust he felt, overwhelming him with a determination to kill, meant he had to do it — to survive, and so rodents and small mammals became his regular fodder.

When all the blood had gone from any one of his misfortunate victims he would sit, throw his head back, and suck at the muscles, the sinews, extracting all that he felt he needed, anything to save having to kill another.

I am a wild animal. He shook his head violently. No, he had not quite gone that far yet. Killing humans was not his style. His parents had been murdered in the most terrible way — he was not going to start killing his fellow man. *Fellow man? But I am a fiend.* The thought was abhorrent, laughable.

In truth there was only one man or group of men that he wanted to kill — the evil cowards who had killed his parents. Anyway, wanting to kill and *actually* killing were two different things. He would probably break down and cry or run off again. He was good at running.

Killing had clearly not bothered Emma in the slightest. Like the early bird that catches the worm, she took to it easily. *The early vampire that guzzles the blood!* She had been a vampire for many years she had told him proudly. Had no doubt killed many. He loved her. No, he hated her. *Fine, be a vampire, just leave me the hell out of it.* The thought of being 'out' of Hell, now that would have been a wonderful place indeed. But no, she had to turn him, make him one of them.

Living as he was, nocturnally feeding on small rodents, like a tall flightless human owl, he existed through the months. He did not notice the passing of seasons. He felt no cold and only ventured out in the small hours. Repulsed at his own being he roamed from town to village, back from village to town, scouring the south and south-east. At least when he had been crossing Europe it was out of a basic need — to stay alive. This time his so-called life had absolutely no meaning. In a retarded tempo he aimlessly circled the south of England, steadily turning months into years.

It must have been on his third time round that Jakob finally stopped in the hamlet of Pluckley. He had often used the thick natural canopy of the nearby woods as daylight cover. An old windmill close by — but not too near the village — was ideal for shelter. A shoddy ramshackle of a building it looked likely to tumble to the ground at any given moment — even without the wind blowing the enormous makeshift sails around. Because of that it had few visitors. The miller came and went, dutiful of his work but always mindful of the opening hours of the Black Horse pub back in the main village.

The windmill was a spectacular place to be when there was a lightning storm. It was small relief to the chores of hiding out and sucking on the discarded bodies of animals. The long stretches of tedium crushed him. From his vantage point in the cap of the windmill Jakob could see way out across the fields. It was a good thing he could too. It was no mean feat negotiating the great spur-wheel and milling stones, climbing past the dust floor, to squeeze into the very top of the man-made grinder, without the payback of a good view.

At the top now, the lightning storm had begun only a few minutes before. He looked out from his hidden vantage point. A bright flash lit up both the sky and the surrounding countryside. He waited momentarily before an almighty crash reverberated through the timbers. The storm and the rain had settled in for the night. Like waterlogged pebbles huge droplets bombarded the windmill.

The noise. He watched the storm gather momentum but the hammering inside the cap of the windmill was becoming unbearable. Another sheet of light across the night sky and a crack later he decided to head back down. In his hastened descent Jakob cut his forearm on the great tentering gear as he slid past.

Once down he poked his head out to make sure nobody was around. Driving down hard, the rain seemed to be increasing. *They would have to be mad if anyone was out in this.* He stepped out into the rain and looked up. Stretching his arms out wide he tried to feel the rain against his body, his face. His body should have been pummelled down, drummed into the soil. Instead he felt nothing. It may have been a clear and balmy day for all his insentient body knew.

He looked down at his arms. Black-red oozed from the cut on his forearm. *Damn.* Diluted in the heavy downpour it ran freely round to the underside of his arm and, messily obeying the laws of gravity, fell away into the mud.

Something appeared ahead of him. For a split second it was there, in the lightning flash, then it was gone. *What the —?* Forgetting the storm he lowered his arms and peered out into the blackness. Ahead of him, and all around, the fields were swathed in bitumen black.

Deadly still he peered and waited for another lightning bolt to light up the scene, to see if there was anyone or anything out there with him. The rain continued, relentlessly thrashing the ground. The noise of the rain, coupled with little or no visibility, left him disoriented. Minutes passed as he stood there, an invisible mute scarecrow. He watched and waited, waited and watched, pleading the lightning to return. *Come on.*

A wail and a screech drowned out the drumbeat of the rain as something came at him. All arms and hair, the 'something' jumped on his back, sinking teeth deep into the fresh wound on his arm. He yelped, more in surprise than of pain, and then more surprised that he had actually managed to utter a noise.

With his free arm, he reached up and tried to grab whatever was clinging to him. It wriggled maniacally, biting down harder on his wound. He released any grip that he may have had on it and dropped to the ground. Like the little church mouse that he had dined on earlier he resigned himself to its onslaught — he wanted to die anyway. *Maybe it is a rabid fox? Whatever it is, with any luck, it will bite my head off.*

As if reading his thoughts the creature on top of him gave up on its assault. Perhaps it only relished the sport of taking a life from someone who still had a desire to live? As it climbed off him Jakob managed to roll over and sit up. By now the storm was abating, the rain had stopped and the clouds were thinning, allowing a sliver of moonlight through.

In front of him stood what looked to be female. Her silhouette was that of a tall woman with hair so untamed she made Medusa look like she had spent days brushing and carefully grooming herself. Like some other mythical creature she shifted to and fro.

"Phlugh." She spat out the contents of her mouth. "Who are you?" she asked.

Jakob watched the dark figure carefully before he opened his mouth, forcing himself to speak. Like a baby, he gurgled. And then smiled morosely.

"Your blood tastes disgusting," she said, then wiped her mouth with the back of her hand. "I see you are one of us. It's a good job I am too, or I'd be in serious trouble now after swallowing it. Phlugh."

He looked up at her and motioned to his open mouth and shook his head.

In the faint light she saw his difficulty. "Ah," she said, "you must be newly turned. Haven't mastered the art of talking again yet, have you?"

Again he shook his head. Getting up, he waved his hand at her to follow.

She looked at him sadly, remembering what it was like to be turned. "I bet you *did* talk after you were first turned," she said. "I remember I did. It's quite common. The body goes into some kind of panic mode, desperately clinging to life. It doesn't realise it's already become a slab of lifeless meat. I suppose there must still be air in the lungs or something."

She trailed behind him as they walked towards the windmill. Stopping outside the mill, she walked by, turned to look at him. At three quarters full, the gibbous moon shone down giving them enough light to regard each other. Jakob noticed her plain and simple looks. She lacked any distinct or individual characteristics. Except, of course, for the crow's nest of hair on her head, sitting restively in search of an innocent passer-by to turn to stone.

Jakob tried, again, to speak. Nothing came from him. He clutched at his throat.

"I can see you need some help," she said.

NINE

Jakob's new visitor kept on talking, and trying to decipher whatever it was that Jakob was attempting to say. In quite some time she was the first person whom he had come into contact with let alone communicated with. Scared and confused, he had not noticed the time. At the first sign of dawn, Jakob became agitated and dashed into the mill, beckoning his unexpected visitor to follow.

She laughed gently, her hair shifting up and down as she did so.

"Nnghh," he attempted, as he waved at her furiously.

"Whatever has come over you?" she asked.

He jabbed his finger towards the east. She turned to look and saw the lightening sky.

"Oh," she said. "You poor lamb, that's not going to hurt you."

He backed into the shade of the windmill, doubtful of what she was saying.

"Oh dear. Listen, I think there is something you should know."

Jakob listened carefully from the shadows. She told him how she had been made a vampire around fifty years before, by a good looking but effeminate corset-maker from Portsmouth. He had seduced her during an amorous fitting of her corset.

"It certainly wasn't the tight-lacing that stopped me breathing — although that didn't help," she said.

The sun was starting its daily trawl, slowly inching over the horizon, taking its first glimpse of the new day. It lit up the woman as she adjusted her, now bedraggled, corset. Jakob flinched, expecting her to turn into a fireball.

Nothing happened.

He could see her properly now. She was not pretty but she was not ugly either — an ordinary woman you might see anywhere and dismiss immediately, unless she was sucking on your blood. Again the myths that told of a vampire being harmed or killed by exposing themselves to the sunlight just was not true. He wondered why he had been so scared of it and for so long. After all, hadn't he wanted to die — properly die? Why had he not just walked out into the sunlight sooner?

In many ways it made it easier to fit in, being out in the day, in the sunlight. Over the next few days the friendly and crazy-haired woman explained to him the simplicity of breathing. Jakob was dead and therefore did not need to breathe but this caused other problems.

"You see, people can only talk when they exhale air across their voice-box thingumabob, which makes it vibrate, and the sound comes out." She looked happy with herself.

Of course, why hadn't he thought of it before? He was angry with himself. He tried it. It took all his energy and will. Concentrating hard he expanded his chest, his lungs, enough to fill them with a little air and then he forced it out.

"E . . . Ello." he muttered with pride.

"Ello," she mimicked in reply, surprised at how well he had done on his first go.

He tried again, this time extending his hand. "Jakob." It was a bit muffled and slow, but really quite clear.

"Well done Jakob," she answered. "I'm Lucinda."

Although he had managed to utter a simple word, his name, the art of talking — in prolonged sentences — was much harder than he recalled, taking him some time to fully master it all over again. The process, however, had the odd effect of making his speech more English sounding. *How bizarre.* In the next few weeks with the help of Lucinda he lost nearly all traces of his old tongue — and his old Eastern European accent.

As soon as he could converse fully he told her about Emma, warning Lucinda of the bowler-hatted madman who had vowed to hunt and kill him, and all vampires. Lucinda said that her corset-maker had met his end in some strange way. Supposedly, he had fallen from the roof of the church in Portchester Castle grounds and decapitated himself against a granite headstone — his body dutifully obeying the laws of gravity whilst his chin, conveniently caught against the upper edge of the solid memorial stone, had not.

It was not long before Lucinda showed Jakob how to kill a goat, or a sheep. He hated it, glad that Lucinda did the lion's share of the killing. Once the animal was dead, he would justify: It's a waste if I do not eat. The strange thing was that he felt hardly any feelings, he was almost numb. It seemed he was incapable of doing so. So why the pangs of remorse? His parents had instilled in him, so deep, the simple truth of living a good and honest life and maybe a fragment, a minuscule piece of his humanity, had remained to make him this timid monster.

Together the two of them walked for days, months, in the sun and were fine. It became a gypsy's life for them, only easier than before. Travelling, perceived as a couple, they were much less conspicuous.

It was a bright winter's day when Lucinda returned from the town. She had gone out to steal some clothing. Her existing attire was worn and old, shabby, not to mention well out of fashion.

Jakob watched her approach and went out to meet her, noticing she had a wild look in her eyes, her dress freshly ripped down the side.

"We've got to go," she said.

Jakob was taken aback; he was only now coming to terms with his existence in the countryside, foraging out at night for badgers and rodents to feed on.

"Someone was watching me in the town."

"What do you mean?" Jakob asked.

"What do you mean, what do I mean?" she said. "It's not a trick question. A tall, horrid, ugly man was following me."

"What do you expect if you go out with the intention of stealing?"

"No, no, it's not that. I saw him earlier on and then again later on in the day. There was definitely no–one around when I took these." She held up the clothes she had 'taken' in her hand.

"What did he look like?"

"Tall, slim, with a gaunt face. A bit like an oversized two-legged starving ferret," she answered. "He chased me, grabbed at me, tore my dress." She pointed to the obvious ripped material. "I was lucky to get away."

"But why? Who is he?"

"A vampire hunter. We're not safe here anymore."

Jakob tugged at his bottom lip, deep in thought for a moment. "Did he have a bowler hat? Or a moustache?"

She shook her head rapidly.

At least that was something but it still meant that someone was aware of who — and possibly what — they were.

He nodded. "Yes, you are right we'll have to move on. Now. And be more careful in future."

"I agree," she said, looking away. "But I think we might fare better if we split up," she said.

Split up? The thought had never occurred to Jakob. He had been alone for far too long and ever since he had met Lucinda — even though she had once jumped on his back and munched on his arm — he had come to enjoy her company.

"No, no, I have a better idea. We should go to London. If they can find us here in the middle of nowhere they will soon find us again. What we need is a place where there are plenty of people; we could hide out in London forever. Nobody will ever find us. Safety in numbers."

She thought for a moment. "No. No, I'm going to go back to Reigate," she said. "They got a good look at my face. They know me now, I'll only be putting you at greater risk."

Jakob knew Reigate well. It was near there in a place called Outwood that he had stayed in another windmill, reputedly the oldest one in the country.

"Please come with me, I am sick of roaming this damned place on my own. And I would rather not do it alone. Anyway, what's in Reigate?" Jakob asked.

"Nothing, it's where I come from, originally," she answered. "And I know it like the back of my hand. I'll be safe there."

Jakob was surprised he could not convince Lucinda. Although they were not lovers they had been together for such a long time now and he assumed they would be together, in damnation, forever. They were after all both undead. He remembered how he had felt the day he had mastered talking again after her instruction and how she had shown him to kill efficiently. Being immortal, one could be alone for a long, long time.

"Please?" he asked again.

"No, I think it's best for us both," she said.

Jakob cast his mind back to the basement, the strange man and the fire. The thought of the same thing happening to Lucinda was unjust and, he convinced himself, it would be his fault if it did.

"Yes, you are right," he agreed, finally.

TEN

Much more time had passed than Jakob had realised. In the beginning he had been wallowing in the deepest and darkest recesses of the countryside, trapped in the foulest abyss. Then he had met the wild but friendly and helpful Lucinda. Unfortunately things had to change and she had decided, for whatever reason, that she was not going to London with him although he had pleaded with her for some time.

It was the year 1887 when Jakob finally emerged, alone once more, after what seemed an age of self-imposed exile. He was a young reptile that had finally grown, shed its skin, become the deadly serpent that he knew he should be — almost.

It was on sure feet then that he ambled into the south of London, stopping at the river. Reaching the Thames in the late evening he stood and allowed his lifeless eyes to take in the panorama. From his position, the south-end of Southwark Bridge, he observed great blocks of grey, besmirched white architecture, big and small, that made up the fascinating city. Off to his left in the distance a large dome protruded famously above the rest of the horizontal brickwork. The huge, head-like dome stretched to the heavens as if awaiting its violent removal from its shoulders — as had happened to the real Saint Paul.

Starting off again Jakob marched across the bridge into the City proper. He was not tired. He did not need sleep, had not slept for years, as long as there was some blood in his system. Blood was the only thing that kept him going, kept him strong. He found he had no appetite for anything else. But then he was a vampire, a dead man . . . walking. He scanned the area as he went.

London, he knew, was a metropolis for the greatest empire the world had seen. The grand capital of England was undoubtedly the most powerful city in the world and highly regarded by its royalty, the prestigious and the wealthy.

In the massive city he would have to act normally — not that he knew what normal actually meant anymore. Not surviving on blood would be a good place to start. He took to fitting in as best he could again. He found out that life, or death, would constantly repeat itself and it could soon get really boring, especially if you lived forever.

In fitting in again, Jakob took jobs here, jobs there, but he was always watching his back. In order to find his way around, each night he would cross the city far and wide, trying to commit the labyrinthine layout to memory. It may help him one day if ever he needed a quick getaway, he reasoned. Somewhere out there was a stranger, a Mister Death, complete with bowler hat, who was hunting him, who had vowed to find him and end his sorry existence.

It was an odd city, even the better areas of the massive layout housed small pockets of dingy, slum areas intertwined by crude alleys and cut-through back-streets. The task he set himself was enormous, almost impossible, but he felt compelled to do it. His home town had been so small; he had no experience of doing anything on such a large scale. And he missed Emma . . . and Lucinda.

Blood, too, was harder to come by than he had at first imagined. So during his moonlit jaunts he took to stealing chickens in the night from the backyard pens of the bigger, wealthier houses to the west. He killed rats by the London docks as they scurried on by. If he could still survive on the blood of animals, then that is what he would continue to do.

Having arrived during the latter part of the year it was not long before he decided that he would, in the new year, make a fresh start and lose himself in the depths of the East End. It was by all accounts a haven for immigrants and ingrates alike. A place where all the thankless wretches of London existed. He could disappear in there completely, easily fit in. After all, he was from east Europe, why not then the East End? It felt almost natural.

Mindenki a maga sorsának a kovácsa — Everyone is the smith of their own destiny.

The Tower of London, like a huge gargoyle on the City's eastern edge, sat vigilant in its unremitting guard, keeping the stinking residents of the East End at bay. Over the years it had quietly done its stalwart duty and if the Tower could talk it would bellow, from its ornamental armaments, woeful tales, not only of the treacherous prisoners it had once held and the swift executions it had once seen but also that of the struggle for daily survival of the pitiful creatures that lived beyond its eastern border.

The great city was indeed splendid in all its pompous expense and grandeur — it had recently celebrated Queen Victoria's Golden Jubilee — but once one had continued east, having passed the old City walls at Aldgate, the splendour abruptly ceased and the moral decline was blatant.

The River Thames, the lifeblood of London itself, had long ago become a dumping place for the rich man's waste. Affluent effluent. Further west it seemed, ignorance was bliss. What did they care? The river flowed away from them, fluxing eastwards, taking all their stink and shit along with it.

The British Empire may well have established *Pax Britannica* — peace on the high-seas — with its almighty naval force and appointed itself in the role of global policing but here, on dry land, it would not want to venture too far east of the City, not on foot anyway.

Unemployment, deprivation and the need for money led to simple thievery, filching, muggings, indiscriminate promiscuity, prostitution and finally murder. In the scramble to earn a living in the wretched East End, human suffering had become a thing of everyday life. The local authorities, always turning a comfortable and well-off blind eye, took to alleviating the situation like a tiny ant might take to laying siege to the largest, most secure fortress.

With his head down, Jakob continued, passing the thousand-year-old curtain walls of the Tower and into a new beginning.

Once past Aldgate, Jakob trod carefully over animal innards and waste that spattered every corner of the streets, discarded carelessly from the many slaughterhouses. Had he not been almost bereft of feeling he may have got all excited at the sight of blood as it soaked away into an ever-increasing grime of nooks and crannies.

Leaving the stained cobbles and offal behind, he weaved through the thin crooked lanes passing any number of doss houses and pubs. Here fresh animal giblets were replaced by ingrained dirt and grunge, shit-laden straw, piss and who knew what else, it was that unrecognisable. Irregular rows of men and scruffy young boys lined the streets — the dirty faces of the children skittering about belied their jocularity.

The narrow streets opened up into a larger carriageway. A tall moustachioed man leaned against an even taller lamppost, its bulbous round shade stretching high into the stale air. Another man, slim and wiry, broke out into a small jog as a muddied miniature-coach carriage, drawn along by an equally muddy horse, nearly rode over him, driving him into the grime.

The further east Jakob went the more piteous the stench and the more miserable the residents became. There were people everywhere, huddled together in groups, crowing, crying, singing, people with demented faces staring into space, with toothless grins. Mayhem. A heavy stench of human and horse shit and urine followed him.

London, or the East End in particular, was just as he thought it would be, as his mama had once accurately described it: 'an almighty hovel'. In saying that, it was the place he needed to be. In this bubbling cauldron of squalor the filth was manifest. He should be all but invisible but would still have to be careful. Here, the women, even children of the slums, may be inconspicuous but were still hanged for their petty crimes.

After traipsing around the slums for a while, avoiding the screaming kids, the solemn women, Jakob stopped to pat a horse at the side of the road. The ill-fed animal had a rickety cart strapped to it. With a rusting bit in its large teeth the cantankerous horse exhaled a misty brew and, shaking its head dismissively, it emptied its bowels onto the road. A man in a hat with black teeth stepped out of a crowd of other hatted and ill-featured men to leer at him, eyeing him disdainfully. *Oh shit, black bowler hats everywhere!*

Not wanting to draw any needless attention to himself Jakob nodded as politely as he could and carried on, stepping around the pile of steaming hot manure. An unsightly huddle of bedraggled women hung around on a street corner. One of the women turned and shouted something incomprehensible to a group of young men. To say she was not pretty was a grave mistake, the sight of her almost made Jakob jump. *Olyan ronda, hogy ha lemegy a bányába, feljön a szén - She is so ugly that if she goes down to the mine, the coal will come up on its own.*

Further still, a humble shop displayed its name above the door: ROSE. This definitely was not a place one associated with a beautiful bed of flowers. *Nincsen rózsa tövis nélkül,* Jakob reminded himself. *There is no rose without thorns.*

Jakob came to a halt on a corner by a three-storey building, a slight ornate chimney and clock decorated its façade. Below that, emblazoned as large as possible, the word TRUMAN'S proclaimed its superiority. *A true man? That's exactly what I am trying to be.*

He looked up at a smeared street sign, taking a minute to register its name. There he stood; he was a ghoul on Goulston Street.

Perfect.

ELEVEN

"But I am so fed up with it," he crowed at his companion.

"Well, it's not like you've got much of a choice now does it, Gregory. This is what you are, it's what you do. And, not to make too much of it but you are the best in the business."

The moaner felt no better for the compliment as the place was still charred and black. A fine persimmon glow filled the dimly lit hole, they were alone.

Why did we have to meet here, in this hovel? Uri was far more used to the finer things in life. He could almost feel his fine clothing being consumed by the pitch of the darkness, even with the warming glow coming from the fire.

"Thank you, but don't you think I know that, Uri," replied Gregory, unhappy.

Gregory's skin always seem to hold a grey tinge, even in the slight amber glow that reflected from Uri's bright clothes. Gregory was not unhappy really. Unhappy was not the word for it, it was simply monotony.

"It's just been so long, it's all so repetitive. When will it all end?" he asked.

"Who knows? Maybe tomorrow, maybe never. It's not for us to question the boss. You are clever enough to know that,

I shouldn't have to tell you." Uri was getting a little agitated at Gregory's banal questioning.

Feeling deflated, Gregory reached behind his back and began fidgeting; the weight on him feeling heavier than ever.

"All right then, but how do you know about this one?" Gregory asked.

"Listen Gregory, you know as well as I do, as well as we all do. Stop being so cranky. We have an important job to do. Now do I have to go and see Michael and tell him of your enmity at the situation?"

"No, no. No, don't be silly. He'll only report to the big man and then I'll really be in trouble."

"Exactly," said Uri. "I'm glad we finally agree on something. Only let's be honest, if that happens we'll all be in trouble. Especially if they get to him first."

Gregory nodded at Uri, saying nothing.

"As you know they've been quite active lately. All you have to do, Gregory, is keep your eye on the situation and report back as soon as you know anything. Now, off you go."

With that Gregory pulled himself straight and headed toward the bulky door. As it swung open brightness flooded in, lighting the room and Uri had to shield his eyes from the glare. The light diminished as the door slammed shut again behind Gregory. Extra oxygen from Gregory's exit fuelled the fire, the flames leaping higher in exultation. The place was no longer pitch dark. Waiting for his eyes to adjust, Uri was now alone.

Or not.

"I presume you know that we will get to him first, Uri?" boomed a low but powerful voice from behind.

Uri couldn't quite see properly, his eyes temporarily blinded, but he recognised the deep voice.

"Ah. Of course, I almost forgot. Always the dramatist. Why can't you ever simply enter the room like the rest of us?"

"Where would be the fun in that?" the newcomer asked, his muscular frame seemed cast from solid bronze in the fire's renewed glow.

It filled Uri's view as his eyes finally adjusted back to the dark. "I think your latest triumph may be misleading you into a false sense of bravado. Isn't this how it has always been between our two families?" Uri said.

"Well, yes, but it just feels so good to get one over on you and your boss. And even better to have one more out there. I mean, it's always good to get them on the shop floor as it were but to get another one in place, there . . . well, let's just say, it's heaven," he said, gleaming at Uri, content with his words.

Uri wasn't going to be upstaged by this infidel. He brushed it off. "Yes, yes. But, there's still a long way to go yet. He could go either way."

The irritating newcomer smiled. "A long way to go, indeed, but we have plenty of time to get there too, and I'm so enjoying all the killing. For me there's just never enough blood and guts."

Disgusted with his company and at the words Uri turned his back on the other man and walked towards the door. He could not look at that smug face any longer. Preparing his eyes for the onslaught of the light again, the light that he loved so much, he squinted.

"Come on, Uri. Don't go. We're just starting to get on and have some fun."

Slamming the door shut behind him, Uri left the gloating figure back in the room, alone in the darkness.

TWELVE

The long blade felt good in his wily hands. It always felt good.

Look at it. Such grace. He eyed it affectionately; it was his friend, his 'old mate', an extension to his whole being. When he was alone he often felt compelled to talk to them. Living on his own in the dross of the East End, he had to talk to someone — or something. He did not care who really, just as long as they would listen. In the end, they all listened.

Thoughtfully, he drew a finger and thumb through his moustache. He liked his facial hair, it made him feel genteel, proper civilised. There was no civility in this place, he knew. Whitechapel, Shadwell, Spitalfields, Poplar, Stepney, in fact the whole area, it was all just one giant cesspit. To him though it was home, what could he do?

Turning to his latest victim he amused himself. He held up the knife.

"Be a good un now and let Jacky give you a fine treat for what ails you."

The meaty body was still in the musty air.

"That's good, no backchat. I like that . . . but don't think you'll be leaving any time soon, not like that slag of a mother o' mine," he said, an obvious tone of anger in his voice.

His father had died when he was about six and he had few recollections of him. It was not so bad; he had thought afterwards, he always had his sister and mother. *Fuck.* Two or three years passed since his sister had upped and left; she was sick of their mother but she was much older than Jack and could go out and work, provide for herself.

So Jack was left on his own. His mother, however, now she had stayed and 'looked after' him, brought him up. *More like dragged me up — through this shit pit.* After his father had passed away his mother had been left with no income or means and so she turned to bringing men home.

"We need the money," she would qualify to her neglected son.

The money would soon be wasted, like her, on booze and so she had ended up bringing back even more men. In a drunken state she would then shout at him, berate him, and when he could not do whatever it was she had demanded of him or chose to ignore her, she would thrash him. Then she would lock him away in his tiny bedroom of darkened grime and unclean bedclothes.

His father may have been long gone but his leather belt and buckle remained, as did the raised welts on his skin. At first he would cry and cry until his eyes were arid like two small dried flower bulbs sitting in unison on his sorrowed brow. Too many years later he had not felt the beatings any more.

Now his time had come.

Twisting the knife over in his hands again he closely examined the polished edge. He liked to keep them sharp. Always. It made light work of things. He liked the efficiency of a keen edge. He had liked it better when he was thirteen, so much so that one night he took that keen edge to the not-so-keen edge of his mother's bed and calmly placed it to her dormant neck while she slept.

He had introduced them both in a whisper, so as not to wake her.

"Knife, neck. Neck, knife."

Thinking of all the times she had opened her foul mouth and raised her dirty hands to him he pressed hard, but not too hard. He let the blade find its own way almost, carving through her soft sleeping flesh. The selfish cow was too drunk to even feel it.

Fascinated, he could only watch, a strange feeling of reverence washing over him as her life drained away from her, leaving the bed sheets and the soiled mattress underneath soaked a vivid cherry-red.

At the thought of his beastly mother he lunged out at the swinging carcass that hung inanimately on the meat hook. His mind back at his work now, he carved with the skill of a master butcher, he sliced at it, attacking the fattier meat of the belly pork that hung in front of him. *Yes, no backchat.*

"Take that you swine," he said to the stripped body of the dead pig.

He liked his job. But he had loved killing his bitch of a mother. It was the only time he had ever killed. But he had decided that the animals at the abattoir were not enough anymore, were just not cutting it.

He laughed at the pun.

At thirteen, after he had snuffed out his mother, he had gone into the other room and bashed himself up pretty badly, wrecked some of the furniture and chattels. He broke a window. His mother's lifeless body lay in the bedroom, she couldn't tell him off, couldn't swear at him again.

He had sniggered silently to himself as he informed the police of 'the mysterious stranger' who had barged in and attacked him and his mother. Even his tears were convincing.

"Is . . . Is she going to be all right?" he had innocently chimed.

Yes, he had really liked that. He would do it again. *Soon*.

He hacked away at the ham, soothed by his thoughts. I'll get away with it again, too.

THIRTEEN

February. And it was cold. Not cold for Jakob, but it was still winter. Spring, for the year of 1888, seemed a long way off. This was the time of year that he had to be careful. Another problem Jakob had to deal with was the fact that because he did not breathe he emitted no vapour into the icy cold air, and he was worried it may arouse suspicion in the more discerning viewer.

It was something Lucinda had made him aware of. A hapless badger had wandered too close to them one freezing cold night. Lucinda's attack was swift and they had gorged themselves on the sturdy burrower's blood for some time. Had the badger been able to see their breath or even sense their heartbeats, it may have stood a chance. *I hope she's all right?*

The vapour from his breath in the cold was a lot like his pulse — non-existent. He took to putting a scarf around his mouth and then, by talking through gloved hands he would give the impression of trying to warm them. It was a terribly easy and natural thing to do when you really *were* cold, quite something else he had found out in pretending — and he was no actor either.

Sitting awaiting some custom in the shop on Cable Street in the small parish of Saint Georges-in-the-East Jakob browsed one of the exceptionally bad 'halfpenny' papers. Thumbing the tatty pages over was not without some difficulty — he could not feel his deadened digits.

He put it down when he saw a badly drawn bat and tombstone that proclaimed the stories and adventures of *Varney the Vampire*. He picked up the newspaper instead, the East London Observer, and flicked through, letting his eyes scan the pages. He found an article about the inadequate conditions that the workers of the East End were constantly at odds with — dire pay along with long hours and severe health conditions were contributing to 'White Slavery in London'. The rich got richer on the sweat, toil and imminent death of the poor and working class. *Typical.*

He shook his head. *They think they've got things to worry about?* He was supposed to be a vampire, he was supposed to bite his victims' necks and drink from the tiny red rivulets that coursed through their mortal bodies. Even the rats he fed from had to be despatched quickly with his razor and drained of blood so that he could imbibe. *Pathetic.*

Each time Jakob raised the razor to one of the wretched rodents he would think back to the night his parents were murdered. He had already vowed not to become the taker of life that his situation of being a blood-drinking vampire demanded. It would have to be the animals or nothing.

He put his hand up to his mouth, grimaced, and poked at his teeth. *Should I not have fangs?* He could not get any sustenance with these measly blunt things. The rats really would have to do.

Lowering his hand again he clutched the edge of the newspaper and carried on with his reading. This time an intriguing article about a woman caught his eye. She had been attacked and stabbed somewhere north of where he sat now, in neighbouring Spitalfields.

The area of Spitalfields was well known for its large ivory coloured church — Christ Church. Built in the first early part of the sixteenth century the church dominated the appalling area. It had been designed by British architect Nicholas Hawksmoor, a student of Christopher Wren. Its graceful pillars and arches supported an impressive large white spire that acted as a sign, a ray of hope for all the dredges of humanity that buzzed around it daily. It reached high into the grey sky, in a vain attempt to reach the clear blue above. Salvation for all, it proclaimed. Except that in this particular area of the city there existed some of the most depraved and debauched types, all dwelling among some of the most dangerous thoroughfares in London. Any redemption for the poor residents would be a long time coming.

He read on. The woman from Spitalfields had been brutally hacked around her legs and lower body, her nether-region, by an unknown assailant — a man. Looking back now he had no idea why this particular attack piqued his interest. Perhaps it had something to do with his mama but either way he decided to keep a look out for this so–called 'man' during his nightly prowls.

Jakob had a steady job, and one that he liked. Being in London, and wanting to get on, he had started to work with a Polish fellow called Ludwig whom he had met one night outside a gentlemen's club. They had got to talking and Jakob had been hired to work as a general labourer and assistant at one of the many barbers in the area. It was good work, clean and dry, no lugging fish, and he even got to cut the men's hair sometimes — his skills at shearing the sheep with the old hand-shears shining through.

During the more quiet times he and Ludwig would sit around and chat. With both of them coming from Eastern Europe they soon found that they had a lot to talk about. Jakob told Ludwig about the fine inventors of Hungary, about their music and a little of their history. In turn Ludwig would tell him of his studies. It turned out Ludwig had once studied in Warsaw to become a surgeon and had worked as an assistant to a fine local surgeon for a while before coming to London.

Ludwig was a good man, passionate about everything he did. Even when he executed a haircut it was approached with the same exact measure of science and dedication. Ludwig was quiet, subdued, but good with his clients — meticulous. Jakob and Ludwig soon became friends.

The day had been steady; a regular influx of bedraggled customers all left the shop looking a tad more respectable and a tad lighter in the pockets. They had finished for the day and Ludwig had gone out the back, into his living quarters. Jakob stayed out front sweeping the remnants of the day's work and cleaning up, ready for a fresh start the following day.

When he was done Jakob called out to Ludwig that he was finished and would be off to bed at any minute. After a brief pause Ludwig had not answered and so Jakob knocked on the living room door. Again there was no answer. Gently he twisted the door knob, pushed the door open and stepped in.

Usually impeccably dressed in his dark grey suit, Ludwig sat there, a bared leg resting on another chair in front of him. He held a razor in his hand.

"Ludwig?" Jakob asked. "Are you all right?"

He stared back at Jakob, silent. *Is Ludwig mad at my intrusion?* Ludwig's eyes were intense. He had a wide face and sharp features with a bold and black moustache that fell thick and heavy around his steely mouth. He continued to stare at Jakob. Jakob was not scared, he knew Ludwig could not hurt him physically but the look in his eyes made him feel a little uneasy.

"Ludwig, I apologise for entering your private rooms but if you're not going answer me then I will bid you a good night," Jakob said calmly.

Again Ludwig continued to stare at Jakob. The finger-stained walls seemed to be reaching in on them both, strangling Ludwig's words. Jakob was about to leave when Ludwig spoke.

"Forgive me Jakob, but when I am in this state, I have to concentrate."

Ludwig looked down towards his bared leg and gestured to a freshly shaved bald patch. "There is always a connection between man and . . . organism," continued Ludwig with his strange explanation.

Mit mondott? What did he say? Organism? Lost at Ludwig's words, Jakob replied, "I'm sorry. I don't understand."

Pointing down, Ludwig twisted his leg around into the light. On his leg, stuck to a shaved bald patch, were three black . . . *What were they? Slugs?*

"Leeches," the Pole revealed. "Promote blood flow, keep me fit, healthy. Very good for you."

Jakob nodded as politely as he could and shut the door leaving the strange Pole and his leeches in his room.

The next day Jakob was ravenous. He needed to eat, to drink. The place was empty, no one around. Ludwig had gone out a little earlier in order to pay some bills or something — he was always off on his chores, disappearing here and there. Not knowing what to do Jakob went out into the rear yard in the vain hope that he might be able to take his mind off his hunger.

The sky was light, and although it was approaching dusk it was still way too early to go out on his nightly forage of the city. There was movement in the shadows to the rear by the old fence post. There, scurrying away, was a small rat. If only he could get to this rat then it might save him a lot of bother later. He would not have to go down to the docks, ferret around for another.

Staying absolutely still, a statue in the fading light, the rat could not hear or sense his lifeless body. Its animal instincts heard no sound, no breathing, no heartbeat. Edging closer, Jakob was on it. He pounced. Like the rabbit of before, he got it. Squeezing it hard he brought the razor down and swiftly cut. Lifting the dying rat, still squealing, he put it up to his mouth — and drank.

Ahh, that's better.

Leaning back against the fence Jakob drained every last drop of the life-giving stuff. Sitting down in the yard, satiated, he suddenly noticed that he was not alone. Someone had entered from the back of the house. *Shit.* Ludwig. He had returned and was now watching him, not-so-discreetly, from the doorway.

Blood trickled from the corner of Jakob's mouth, dripping onto his shirt front.

"What are you doing, my friend?" Ludwig asked, confusion on his face.

"Um . . . well . . . I'm hungry." Jakob passed it off as calmly as he could, putting the dead animal behind him.

"But you are eating filthy rat, Jakob."

"Well, yes . . . I just felt like it," Jakob said. "I like them."

"You like them?" Ludwig asked. "Is disgusting. But you not eat, you drink. What are you? Some type great big human leech? Overgrown mosquito?"

That's it, I'm done for. Jakob could not believe it. All these years of being careful, watching his back, he had now been careless. He thought he was alone and that the privacy of the back yard would be fine. Wrong. Immediately, an idea struck him like a huge stone in the back of his head.

"Look, Ludwig, I know you are a private person, but you are also my friend. I have something to tell you. I need your help. Please let us go inside where there are no loose ears," Jakob said, looking around.

Squinching his eyes at him, he could see that Ludwig was intrigued. Getting up from the hard damp flagstones, Jakob brushed down his trousers with his left hand and threw the rat into the crude bin that lay in the corner with his right. Once inside, Ludwig faced Jakob, eyeing him curiously.

"Ludwig . . . this may be a little hard for you to understand, so I'll just say it. I have an extremely rare condition. One where I must imbibe . . . blood. Something to do with iron deficiency I believe."

Easing up, Ludwig relaxed his face. He looked at Jakob as though he had just been told the latest weather forecast. All quite normal.

Did he understand? Maybe the drinking of blood was accepted in Poland?

"This is, perhaps, good thing, no? You save plenty wages not having to buy food, yes?"

Jakob was incredulous. His awful attempt at throwing Ludwig off the trail had worked.

"Yes, yes, this is good. Can you drink any type blood or is just stinking rats you like?" Ludwig asked, grinning.

"No, it's not a good thing, it's disgusting. But since you ask, it's *any* blood, I think, but the rats are simple. Have you ever tried bleeding a bull? It's not so easy," Jakob said, not knowing why he had said it or how or why Ludwig was being so accommodating, so calm. *At least he doesn't think I am a freak.*

"Okay," Ludwig said, pleased. "I see many bad things in Poland, you are good man, but what is you ask of me my friend?"

"First of all, don't tell anyone. You mustn't tell. It's . . . embarrassing, and secondly, about your leeches — I want you to help by using your leeches to extract blood for me, so I can drink. That way I won't have to kill any more . . . rats." Jakob said.

"But of course, will be pleasure to help you, my friend." Ludwig finished and turned to go.

"Please, Ludwig, not anyone. It must remain our secret."

"Of course, Jakob, of course."

Tentatively Jakob stretched his arm forward. Picking one up in his fingers he inspected the hideous little wriggling creature under the close scrutiny of his friend. As weird as the leeches were old Mother Nature had obviously intended them for something. Jakob on the other hand was not natural — a member of the undead, not natural at all.

As he took hold of the small blood-filled annelid and pried it away from Ludwig's leg, Jakob shut his eyes. Shoving it, whole, into his mouth he began to chew. The small rubbery body 'popped' open as his teeth clenched down, releasing more blood than he thought the small creature could possibly hold. Sucking on its remains for a few moments Jakob spat the leech onto a small plate on the kitchen table.

Ludwig laughed nervously. "Wait, wait, we cannot let you chew little heads off, they cost small fortune to replace," Ludwig said.

"I'm sorry, what can we do instead then?" Jakob asked, wiping his sleeve across cardinal-stained lips.

"We must find way to draw the blood out, save them for next time," Ludwig said, looking round the room for something. He was right, people might soon become curious as to why a barber and his assistant, in the middle of the East End would need so may leeches.

"It is okay," Ludwig continued. "I have many instruments, including trusty syringe."

"Perfect," Jakob said. "Look at us. It's like the old proverb, Pole and Hungarian — Two good friends.

"Yes, I seem to remember," Ludwig answered. "How does go?"

"Lengyel, Magyar — Két jó barát, együtt harcol s issza borát, or Pole, Hungarian — Two good friends, together they battle and drink their wine."

"Yes, yes. Only I not sure if I like drink *your* 'wine' eh." Ludwig laughed.

"No, I agree. Just make sure you don't get any of those leeches on me. If it sucks on my blood it may be poisonous to humans. It could kill you. Or worse."

Hearing Jakob, Ludwig sat down, staring out of the back window, a strange reverie across his face.

FOURTEEN

The woman in the smooth fine dress had finished with her report. She stood there regal, tall and dark, her almost animal-like androgynous features showed no emotion at all. Stolid, she now waited for a response from her comrade.

Extravagantly decorated the room was much hotter than even she could stand. The only light in the room came from the fire that raged in its sulky hearth, pouring out an unceasing infernal heat. She moved away. Like an exquisite apparition, her svelte-like body glided over to the decorated window frame. Osteoid hands emerged from elaborate sleeves as she flicked opened the huge elegant latch with unexpected ease. Letting cool air into the suffocating room, she turned and faced her superior.

Sitting high up on his grandiose perch, the man laughed. Oozing with sweat his skin glistened, the colour of ripe pumpkin from the fire. His expression of mirth echoed through the air.

He really quite liked this man — this strange Pole. There was definitely more to this man than met the eye — the assistant surgeon who was now a barber. *Never in all my life have I heard such a front.*

Lifting his powerful arms, Antonas smoothed a large hand across his bald head. Still smiling he turned and directed his words at the female who now, after releasing the window and leaving it propped open on its latch, sat opposite, toying with her long black locks of wavy hair. At length, he spoke. "Thank you for your insight Pura, my princess, it is always appreciated. He will be ours, one way or the other".

Hearing his words the woman dropped her hair, brushed it down gently and peered back at him through dark eyes. "Yes, but the other one, the Hungarian, surely you'll leave him to me?" she said.

"That I will, dearest one, that I will. However, he does seem to be taking his time does he not?"

Antonas loved to wind her up. He was a little wound up himself after Uri, the sickly-sweet good-looking-man-about-town, had walked out on their little conversation a few days before. But Antonas was used to being rebuffed by Uri and his mob. It did not matter. Antonas only cared about one thing.

Outside, night had fallen and it was dark. Through the opened window the moon peeked in on them shining bravely across the woman's blanched, almost phosphorescent skin. Peering back at the moon, a vacuous look on her pale and thin face, she glowed in the dark, her deep velvety dress shimmering in moonlit unison.

"I don't want to sound too patronising but there is another you know," Pura said. "And whether you get him or I do, it won't matter, he will definitely join us."

Arising from her seat she walked slowly, majestically, towards the man. She gazed at his strangely handsome features, his muscular body and stroked his potent face with unusual softness.

At the sign of affection Antonas stood and took hold of her. Wrapping two mighty arms around, he pulled her close to his bared, muscular chest. They stood for a moment, together, quiet in the darkness as the world continued, suspended in its continual yet ancient orbit.

Good, or bad, it seemed life always carried on.

FIFTEEN

The day had started out slow. With the revelation that a vampire ostensibly lived forever, each and every day was beginning to fade into one long day, a bit like a Sunday — dull and tedious, even in the largest city in the known world.

Having nothing to do, Jakob had tried to lie down and rest his head. It was something he had not done for many years; since waking up on that fateful morning for his day trip to Canterbury. Returning to the large house in Seasalter that evening now seemed so long ago.

For some time he lay in his primitive lodgings on top of a lumpy horsehair mattress, the lumps so large that even his nerveless body could feel them as they cannoned relentlessly into him. He knew now why he had not tried to lie in a bed since. Restless, as the undead always are, he got up and walked over to the wash basin. He leaned in and looked into the mirror that hung above, into his lifeless eyes, then at his face, his upper torso. He did not know what he expected to see but instead of his once innocent and naïve looks he was greeted by pale skin and darkened veins, a rambling maze of blue lines in a field of chalk.

Turning his back on the mirror with its thin crude layer of silver-backed glass he bent down, put on his boots, grabbed at his shirt and coat and went out.

The moon sat low in the sky. London in the month of March, even as it closed in on April, was still cold. Dim smog clung to the blackened buildings, a little thinner than usual. Walking silently, passing a line of disconsolate doss-houses, Jakob spotted the dark silhouetted figure of a man.

The man, wrapped up in long black coat and cap, kept on craning his neck about, looking all around as he trudged along the stark cobbled street. Something about him was peculiar, Jakob thought. The man, who was now further up the road, was too busy in his nocturnal search and had not noticed Jakob watching him. With his head down, the man's hands were cast deep into his pockets as he seemingly trawled the night stooped over like a wizened old man.

Jakob's mind cast back to the article he had read a little over a month ago in one of the local newspapers — the article about the woman who had been attacked in Spitalfields. He looked over at the man again. *What is he doing?* Curiosity got the better of him and so Jakob decided to follow the man. After all what else was a lonely vampire going to do on another irksome night in the piteous East End of London?

Like cat and mouse Jakob pursued the stranger along Mile End as he, the stranger, strolled on, unaware that he was being watched or followed, when suddenly the man took a brisk right turn. Holding himself back, waiting for just a few moments, Jakob counted to three and continued around the corner. It was darker off the main road here and it took a short while before Jakob's eyes adjusted. He spotted the man again.

Although it was still relatively early in the night, being just after midnight, there was nobody around. The East End was usually jostling with activity, with revellers and drinkers and women lurking around every corner who, wholeheartedly, wanted only to extract a little cash from an unsuspecting client or passer-by with as little effort as they could muster and, in doing so, keep a firm hold on their own belongings or whatever they had upon their person. But that tended to be back in the more commercial areas; out here it was quiet, deserted and dark.

Clinging to the black shadows of the buildings Jakob stopped in a corner and watched. The stench of piss surrounded him. He looked down at his boots. *Great*. Looking back down the road he watched as the other man stopped outside a small house, his actions skittery, nervous.

Erratically looking up and down the street the man turned and looked directly to where Jakob stood. The man could not see him in the dark recesses, Jakob was sure. *No, he can't see me, it's far too dark.* Clearly happy that he was still alone the man withdrew his left hand from his pocket and began banging at the door.

A few quiet moments passed and then the door creaked open. A woman answered and she and the man now seemed to be in deep discussion. From where he was Jakob could not hear what they were saying other than they were steadily getting louder. Trying hard to listen to their distant voices Jakob observed the unknown man as he began gesticulating with his free hand, pointing and waving, and shouting abuse at the woman inside the door.

In the commotion Jakob left the piss-stained niche of the building and crept closer to them, careful not be heard or seen

— or smelt. Before Jakob had taken three steps the man's hand flashed out from his other pocket to reveal a knife. Threatening the woman he lashed out at least twice towards her bared neck. She screamed, grabbed at herself in defence with both hands, and staggered back into the hallway passage of the house, wounded.

"Stop that man," she screamed, a gurgled voice rising up from floor of the opened door.

Realising that the man had viciously and frantically stabbed the young woman in the neck Jakob acted instantly.

"Hey, you there, stop," Jakob shouted.

Alarm registered on the man's face as he swung his own unscathed neck round. By the look of his widened white eyes, the man had heard Jakob and could now see him running — in his direction. In a nervous panic the attacker almost dropped his sharp implement, then regained control over it. He rammed it back into his pocket, cutting himself in the process, and scarpered. Cursing, he took off down the street. Already moving at a run Jakob slowed as he looked into the hallway of the house, the woman injured but still alive. He saw spots of blood on the ground and a trail leading off down the street to where the man was running. Jakob went after him.

The man swung right and left, in and out of the alleyways, trying to shake off his pursuer. *He must know this place well.* Fleeing for what seemed only minutes the man was already beginning to tire. His large feet, almost flat, began slapping at the stones beneath in a jaded, uneven tattoo. Jakob, who did not need to use his lungs anytime soon, was not tiring, he couldn't. He was almost on the man's heels.

Close behind the man now Jakob stretched and reached out and, grabbing at the running man, Jakob wrestled him to the ground. Together the two of them went down onto the street, hitting the ground like an ironmonger's sack, the stranger's weary body beneath his, breaking Jakob's fall. The man lay there stunned, winded, as Jakob picked himself up and stood over him.

Looking up from the ground the man breathed heavily, his moustache twitching.

"Who are you?" Jakob demanded of him.

"N . . . n . . . nobody mister. Who are you?" he managed to squeeze out through an exhausted grimace.

"What were you doing to that woman?" Jakob asked, ignoring his question.

"Sh . . . she owes me . . . money," the man stuttered, catching his breath.

"You liar. You attacked her with a knife," Jakob said, angrily.

The man on the ground twitched again, his face betraying his thoughts as his hand reached out with the knife.

"Ya . . . ya better stay back mister. I ain't got no quarrel with you," he threatened, still breathing hard.

Obviously the man did not realise his position. He was lying there, spent, on the floor, while his unknown assailant, a vampire who felt no pain was standing over him. All the advantage was with the man still standing.

Jakob kicked at the knife. The man on the floor may have been tired but he kept a keen and firm grasp on the blade's handle. Not letting go the knife cut deep into Jakob's ankle. He did not feel it — Jakob's ankle, foot and leg, had died a long time ago.

Ignoring the grievous wound Jakob drew his leg back and kicked again at the man's hand, harder this time. With a yelp of pain and a rattle of thin steel, the man let go, the blade hitting the ground and skidding off some feet away.

"Get up," Jakob said.

The man, doing as he was told, stood as best he could. Catching his breath he leaned over slightly, his hands resting upon his knees. "Okay m . . . mister," the wheezing man said. "You got me."

"Who are you, I said?" Jakob continued with his interrogation.

"I'm . . . I'm Jack . . . mister. Who are you?"

Jakob was not prepared for the question. He peered down at the cut in his trousers and socks. It should have been bleeding profusely. It was not. Instead, a blackened stain started to congeal around the top of his boots.

Jakob thought. *Should I tell him? Would it really matter?* "Well, my name was . . . is, Jakob," he answered. "Are you the same man who had a go at that woman in White's Row last month?"

The man, Jack, still regaining his breath, hesitated, the tic on his face quickening — he had given himself up as the culprit instantly.

"N . . . n—"

Jakob frowned.

"Well, yes, but she . . . she was all right," Jack declared.

"She's all right at the moment. Believe me, some things take longer to heal than others," Jakob said, as a picture of

Emma cutting the ghastly heart shape into her own arm flashed in his mind.

"Why do you care?" Jack asked.

From the other side of the road a couple walked by, eyeing them suspiciously. The couple said nothing, just huddled closer and quickened their step, eager to be away. Clutching at Jack's long coat, Jakob walked him further into a secluded alley, adjacent to where they had crashed to the ground.

Alone once again, Jakob continued. "Why? Why did you attack her? You had better speak up or you'll be sorry." Jakob was growing impatient.

Looking around for an escape route, a concentrated but panicky look on his face, Jack spoke. "B . . . because they deserved it. Women, I mean . . . they're evil, they all need . . . they all need to die."

What is this man's problem? "My mother was killed by someone like you," Jakob said.

"I'm sorry . . . so was mine," Jack lied. "But I ain't the one who killed your mother."

"I know."

Images lingered in Jakob's mind:

Like savages the rogue soldiers attacked the crying woman as she struggled to reach the man she loved. Three soldiers stepped forward, grabbed at her, holding her still. Raising his sabre high the Russian soldier took a step towards her and swung it down.

"Szeretlek," she said defiantly. "I love you."
Papa gurgled. "No!"
A thud.
"Mama. Noooo!" the young boy screamed.

110

The rest of the men lashed out at the man who still refused to fall, even with the sword passing straight through his body.

"Papa."

"Go, my son . . . Jakob, go!"

Snapping out of it, Jakob was mad. Grabbing at the Jack's collar he raised his fist. Jack pulled away. He was strong but Jakob was stronger, the temporary stiffness that had set into his limbs during *rigor mortis* had given his muscles an extra rigidity and strength.

"I'm taking you in," Jakob said.

"N . . . no, mister. Please . . . please, I'll do anything. Just don't take me in."

Jakob, the meek and mild vampire, stood there holding this would-be killer, thinking. He was irate. But he had really had enough of the rats. And the leeches? — they were only a stop-gap to the real thing.

Real blood. He thought long and hard: the rats in London were endless, there was no excuse. But it was disgusting. And Emma's blood had tasted so . . . so good. *Could I use this cowardly cretin for my own purposes? No, it's wrong. Rats and leeches?*

Jack tugged at his collar. Jakob was unmoved, holding on tight. *I would have to be more careful than ever. But if I was?*

He would have to select only the lowest and desperate drabs. *Would anybody miss them? Maybe?* But most likely not. The East End could be the perfect hunting ground. *Oh, and Emma's blood.*

Jakob had made up his mind. Yes, enough was enough. The dregs, there were plenty of them, they could be his targets, it would be an act of humanity, like taking out the garbage. His mother had been healthy, had everything to live for, but she had been taken for no good reason. He would take them for a reason; after all, Jakob's dead nose could literally smell the bad in these people: the death, decay, the disease. Yes, this man could help him. Jakob knew he was no killer himself, but he also knew he needed blood more than ever, the good stuff that only humans could give him. It went against everything his parents had taught him as a boy. It was inhuman. But then he was no longer human, was he? *Bocsánat — Sorry.*

Seeing his captor in deep thought, the man, still held firmly by Jakob, stayed quiet, awaiting an answer to his grovelling and pleading.

"So, you like killing? You want to kill do you Jack?" Jakob asked, betraying all that he stood for.

"Yes," Jack said. There was no hesitation this time.

"All right. But from now on you will only do it for me," Jakob instructed him. "Is that understood?"

"But—"

"Like I said, I can always see what the local constabulary has to say about your improper night-time activities. Or you can kill . . . for me. But only who and when I say. We could be friends."

"Wh . . . what do you mean?" Jack asked, curiously.

"You'll see, Jack . . . you'll see."

Look at those two, thought the veiled woman. Typical men, always bickering and fighting. Peering hard out from the hidden depths of where she stood in the corner of the blackened alleyway she watched them quietly and carefully. Having slipped in there during the two men's altercation she had remained deathly silent.

After arriving in this fine metropolis she had soon felt the presence of another. *Yes, another.* On that single whim, only a trace of feeling, she had traversed the city, wandered high and low looking for the other of her kind. *But is that really him? And if it is, who is the other man?*

She could not make out the taller one's features from the Stygian blackness. Or what the two were saying to each other. She was close to knowing — she could feel it. And she would find out sooner or later. For now, she would have to wait, plan her next step with extreme care. After all, there were two of them now.

SIXTEEN

God, I hate this job.

No, that was not fair, or even true. But why had he ever decided to do this? He had been in an irritable mood all morning. Dragging himself up onto weary feet Ernie snatched his coat from the solitary coat-hook screwed to the back of the door. He pocketed his pen, together with a small notepad.

The office was cold, bland and stuffy. A grubby beige stained the walls. He needed to get moving and generate some warmth in his bones before he could even contemplate work and, to help wake himself, he badly needed some air in his lungs — even if it was tainted by the foul stench of the East End.

Yes, he liked the fresh air, that was real reason why he did this job. There was no way he was going to work in a grubby factory or down at the docks. That was too much like hard work. He was not a salesman either, but even if he was, the Jewish quarter had that line of work tightly sealed up — they were master businessmen.

Still young at twenty-nine Ernie had already promised himself he was going to make the world a better place. He relished the art of a good yarn, keen in the knowledge that the reader was being rewarded with a good story. If he couldn't give them money he would give them joy in the form of good narrative prose and a great ending.

After all, Charles Dickens had started out small and, with increased fame (and ever fascinating plots), had become friends with noted philanthropist Baroness Angela Burdett-Coutts. She was the one who held the purse, the one to make a difference, the richest heiress in all of England and as such had established the National Society for the Prevention of Cruelty to Children.

Yes, that appealed to him. Happiness for all and, all things being equal, for himself. If he was going to put the long hours in, he would want to take something out. Journalism, he had reasoned, was going to be big one day. So was he — and besides, the money was not too bad either. *If only I could get the next big scoop.*

Ernie had finished sliding into his grey overcoat and buttoning up the front when he heard his boss's sharp voice bellowing through the office.

"Ernest? . . . Ernest, where are you?" he boomed in a loud, Irish lilt.

Ernie dreaded these moments. The newspaper was relatively new and his new boss was always fervent for big news stories in a bid to place himself as the top newspaper in London. Also, the boss was not bothered whose feet he stepped on to do so. Or who got sacked if they were not pulling their weight.

"Er . . . it's Ernie, sir. I'm here sir," he replied through the gap in the open door.

A square-faced man with greying moustache and matching grey hair stepped through the aperture. Smartly dressed and trimmed, with his chest out and shoulders back, he stood perpendicular to the wooden floor of the office, a human plumb-line.

"Well Ernest, what are you still doing here?" his boss asked, his face beaming like a contented yet perplexed Cheshire cat.

"I was just on my way out when you called me back in, sir," Ernie answered.

"That's because you're supposed to come and see me before you go. Don't you listen to Henry, he works for me, remember? Now, am I or am I not the current editor of this newspaper?"

"Yes sir, of course you are and I'm sorry. I just thought that—"

"Ah now, that's your first problem there, young Ernest. You just *thought*," he said, in a less than patronising tone. "Now leave the thinking to me, lad. For now, you do what I tell you. It really is quite simple."

"Sorry sir, yes, but why did you ask me what I was still doing here if you wanted to see me first?" Ernie grovelled.

"Hmm, yes, well, never mind that. I need you out there on the streets. Do your research, interview all and sundry if you have to. Get me news, not hearsay, like giving me and the rest of London a first-class report on the stabbing of that woman on . . . where was it? Maid . . . yes, Maidman Street, by some damned madman," roared the bossy Irishman.

"Okay sir, but how do you know it . . . er, he was a madman?" Ernie asked. "Or even that it was a man?"

"Leave the sensationalism to me, Ernest. You'll get your chance soon enough. Just get yourself out there and get me a story . . . please. I tell you, there's something afoot here and by crikey we're going to be the paper to get it out on the streets."

"Yes sir," Ernie conceded and left the office, his boss hot-footing it to the next unfortunate soul who happened to be in his way.

The air was fresh as Ernie trundled off, heading east. The air seemed to drop a degree or two as he passed the Tower of London. A herd of onlookers were bantering with a street hawker in front of him. He could not quite see what was for sale but, cautious not to get caught up in the chivvying, Ernie crossed over the small courtyard, avoiding the group and the strange putrid odour that seemed to emanate directly from their circle.

On reaching the far side Ernie tried ignoring an inebriated prostitute as the pinch-cock waltzed straight towards him, her skirt a dirty two-tone grey.

"Fancy putting old Nebuchadnezzar out to grass?" she whined. "Only cost yer free pennies."

"Give over, you old bunter," he said.

"Oi, I'll give ya old bunter, mister. What are ya, some sorta mandrake?" she said.

"No, I'm working," Ernie told her as he stormed on past.

"Well, if it 'elps ya any, I'm only doin' me job an' all ya know," she shouted after him. "Ya finks I like doin' this for a loaf o' stale bread?"

Feeling guilty for ignoring the 'fallen' woman, Ernie tossed her tuppence. "There ya go darlin" he said, smiling at her as she raced after it. As Ernie ducked through another thin alley and out onto the other side he realised that he would never make any money if he kept on giving it away.

Feeling the cold Ernie pulled his collar up around his neck; he would soon get warm again. He hastened his stride along Aldgate High Street. He nearly fell as half-a-dozen young boys with blackened faces, dressed in not nearly enough clothing for the weather, charged through. With sticks firmly in each of their grasps, screaming and shouting, they were chasing a terrified tabby cat up the street. *Bloody urchins.* He laughed as the cat shot up and over a wall.

Soon he was at his destination on Leman Street, the Divisional Headquarters for the Metropolitan Police. He knew the police were not at all forthcoming with any of their information — especially to a reporter from the local press. *The police have any information?* Now that's a laugh, he amused himself.

Back at the office Ernie had been told by some of the older, slightly more cynical reporters that good old Sir Robert Peel's Metropolitan Police Force in their blue frocked coats with their bold brass buttons probably only knew as much as *he* did, which was next to nothing. But then Ernie was a good judge of character and could read between the lines.

Anyway if all else failed he knew he could talk to a few residents, fill in a few lines . . . or just make something up. Either way, Ernie would keep his boss happy. He was good at that.

SEVENTEEN

Springtime, 1888. Unsettled weather was plaguing London —
along with the unemployed, the thieves and the feckless. April
was seeing heavy hail, sleet or cold rain, or all at once. In the
freezing grey air Jakob pulled up his high-collar in pantomime
once more and took to the streets. Deftly, he dodged the
diminishing carriages and loiterers on Whitechapel Rd and
made his way across onto Commercial Street.

Earlier that day he had entertained some of Ludwig's
unpleasant leeches so he was fine for food, not needing to drink.
As Jakob strolled he thought of what he had suggested to his
new ally, the skittery and fidgety Jack. After their forced
'meeting' a few days ago, Jakob had established where Jack
lived. In fact Jakob had only just left his new associate's bleak
home after paying him a visit.

He wasn't surprised to find Jack at home. Jack was a
loner; he had no family from what Jakob could make out. A lot
like himself. Maybe that was why Jakob had originally
suggested, let himself agree readily, to what they were now
going to do.

Why had she turned him into this monster? He could not
stop thinking of Emma, the only woman he had ever loved, and
why she had done this to him. He knew he would never see her

again; like a coward he had left her screaming in the basement to meet with her fiery death. Torn, Jakob's semi-emotionless body was somewhat pleased, yet beleaguered with guilt.

Further along Commercial Street Jakob could see the great white church spire glowering in the night. The crowd had thinned, the day closing in. A muffled scream shot out from the half-light.

Jakob froze, listening. *Cannot be Jack.* Instantly he ran towards the noise, heading along Wentworth Street. He reached the corner in time to see an uncouth gang of men assaulting a young woman. One of the gang looked to be in his late teens.

In their hasty attack the gang had not yet spotted Jakob, their look-out clearly not doing his job well enough. Snaffling her up as one, Jakob could only spectate as they brought the lone woman down to the ground and began mauling and kicking at her. Again she screamed as one of the grotty gang's hands brushed up and covered her mouth, repressing her painful calls for help. It was almost the same situation his mama had been in, history repeating itself over and over in this barbarous world. Only this time Jakob would not run, he would do something about it. He had caught Jack easily enough, he would approach the gang.

"Leave her alone," Jakob said, categorically.

On hearing the threat one of the gang turned to stare him down. In his roughened hands, he wielded a long stick. "Ere, why don't ya just fack off an' leave us be, or you'll be gettin' it an' all, so help me Bob," he said, calmly, as if he had become accustomed to saying the same well-worn sentence.

"Look," Jakob said, "leave her alone, she's only a woman. There are five of you."

120

"Me an' this Rory," said the man with the long stick, pointing at the helpless woman in the hands of her four assailants, "we got's some unfinished business."

The gang leader took a step closer to Jakob.

Defiantly, Jakob stood his ground.

"Oi, Freddy, just take this fellah out, we don't wants 'im doin' a runner an' informin' the old garden gate," suggested another of the gang in a gruff tone.

Ignoring Jakob for the moment, Freddy, the man with the stick, turned back to the woman and started tugging at her clothes, pulling up her dress and under-skirt. The two men at her front grabbed her ankles, and spread her legs apart. As she struggled, Freddy casually rammed the blunt instrument deep into her.

"No!" Jakob screamed, and he leapt at them.

Jakob caught the first, Freddy the talker and assailer, nicely on the end of his bulbous nose with his clenched fist. Jakob's forward momentum helped in dislodging one of the other men who held onto the woman's left leg, and he butted him free of her. The three other men, now in disarray, let go of the injured woman. She tumbled to the ground, wincing, crying. The gang now came at Jakob from behind as he struggled to get the collapsing form of the butted man away from him.

Jakob crumpled to his knees as a blow came to the back of his head from a hard leather boot. He careened forwards, hitting the wall hard with his face. Fists and feet exploded into him — his back, his arms, his legs, his head. It was not the pain — as he felt none, even as his face hit the wall for a second time — it was simply that he was overcome by the many limbs that lashed and crashed into him, blow after blow after blow.

All five of the gang were now on top of Jakob and had a firm hold on him. In his bravado and haste Jakob had only succeeded in replacing the woman with himself. Looking through several ragged legs Jakob noticed the woman, now ignored by her assailants, getting up. Clutching at her abdomen, he saw the pain in her face as she looked him in the eye before running off down Wentworth Street, making her get-away.

"Right lads, 'old 'im real tight," Freddy said, rubbing the end of his fat, bloodied, clobbered nose.

Tearing his gaze away from the escaping figure of the battered woman Jakob focused on Freddy. The man, now firmly brandishing the stick out in front of him, was coming right at Jakob — *for him* — a malevolent glint in his eyes. With a dry thud, like a blunt rod into stale bread, the stick hit Jakob square in his chest and threw him backwards and down onto the roadside.

The five thugs stared at him from above, in simple victory as Jakob lay fatally wounded in the grime. The stick had entered at a slight angle, to the right side of his sternum and pierced straight through his skin, shimmied past his ribs, through one (now-unused) lung, coming to rest with its sharpened tip in his heart.

Jakob closed his eyes. *I'll be seeing you soon mama and papa.* There was a clang of feet as the five men ran off leaving Jakob on the cold hard stones to finally face his demons.

"Köszönöm," he managed to whisper, before his head fell back onto the cobbles. *Thank you.*

EIGHTEEN

Uri entered the strangely gaudy yet impersonal hall. Bland décor inside a huge tawdry space, the room was vapid. He did not really expect anything grand, tidy even, but this place, so lacking in any liveliness or spirit was quite depressing, was even more depressing than the black hole where he and Gregory had met before.

Gregory stood silently now having resolutely informed Uri of the events earlier and, in reaction, Uri was furious. Together they faced the bald man, a look of impudence surrounding his face as he waited to be addressed.

"There was no need for that stupid stunt in the alleyway earlier, Antonas. Five men onto one woman? That hardly seems fair play to me," Uri accused the smug man in front of him.

Antonas, unmoved, sniffed at the putrid air. "Is it me or is it a bit cold in here, Uri?" he asked, dismissing the initial statement.

Uri stared at Antonas. *God, he gets more difficult every day.* "This really is just a game to you isn't it? Uri said.

"Uri, Uri, if those five men want to do as I wish, who am I to complain? Am I not the one with the power anyway?" Antonas asked. He liked to see Uri angered. "And I didn't even ask them, I merely *suggested* it to them."

Uri looked up to the ceiling and shrugged his shoulders in silent defeat. He turned to Gregory who was fidgeting again, looking nonchalant. He turned back to the large malignant figure of Antonas. "You know the rules Antonas. Why can't you just stick to them? There won't be any need for these little meetings," Uri said, looking the place up and down. "I do not like it here . . . and I do not like you."

His calm demeanour gone, Antonas strode up to Uri, fixed his jaw sternly and stared deep into Uri's blue eyes.

"And I don't like you much either, but we don't have any choice, do we? Our families must meet and that's that. As for rules it seems to me that the rules are always changing to suit. I am well aware of what I can and cannot do. The interfering man who was trying to save her was . . . unexpected — it was not my fault he strayed into our business."

Uri responded resolutely. "I was talking about the poor girl. You really are just an ignorant animal. And the man, the one who got caught up in your wrongdoing, he's far too good to want to join you."

Antonas was happy with the term animal; he had been called much worse, and on more than one occasion. "Yes, you're probably right. You can have the girl, she'll want to join you soon anyway, I'm sure. As for the man, well, let's just see what he is capable of, shall we? That is, if he's not already dead."

"That's what happens when you get too clever Antonas. Your plans, they sometimes backfire," Uri said.

It was his turn to gloat now.

NINETEEN

Voices.

He could hear distant voices, echoing around the room. Slowly, Jakob opened his eyes, pleased in the knowledge that the injured girl had got away after he had intervened. Where was he? *Heaven or Hell?* Lying still, he flicked his eyes around the room. Oppressive greying walls hulked inwards, tomb-like. A dim light swung overhead.

Voices again.

He heard a man in the room saying his farewells, a door shut with a dull clonk, then the scrape and scrub of shifting footfalls. The click-clack of footsteps grew louder, the man walking towards where Jakob's supine form lay, still, his eyes wide.

"Good Lord," the man spurted out, shock on his face.

Laying flat on his back Jakob realised that he was not dead at all — now twice over.

"Er, hello sir," Jakob said as he leaned up, resting on his elbows. Looking down at his bare body, the stake projected out of his chest like a large fork from a *Weisswurst* sausage.

Jakob regarded the man as he stood, mute. He looked to be in his fifties, he was stout and strong with big bushy side burns. He wore outmoded, almost ancient clothing — his suit —

as though he had only yesterday peeled it straight out of a portrait by the famous 18th Century painter, Thomas Gainsborough.

Clearly in some shock and distress the man sat down. Seeing him sit down rather clumsily Jakob thought the man might be having a heart attack or some kind of seizure, a panic attack. Unsure though, Jakob waited. Finally the man brushed his sleeve across his forehead.

"Good Lord, I've just pronounced you dead, young man," he said, shaking his head slowly. "How can this be?"

Jakob knew where he was. "Aren't you a doctor?" he asked.

For a moment the man's blank stare and grey pallor made him look like a statue.

"That does not mean I'm prepared for a dead man to sit up in the middle of . . ." he trailed off.

"But you are? A doctor, I mean?"

"Yes, yes. Doctor Phillips, at your service, although I'm not quite sure what that service is at the present moment. This is rather irregular." A faint look of worry crossed the doctor's face.

He jumped as Jakob spoke abruptly. "Well doctor," Jakob raised his hand out towards him, "nice to meet you. My name is Jakob."

Doctor Phillips carefully raised his own hand and, clasping the hand of the man who was dead only a minute ago, they shook in the confines of the clinical room.

"You're still cold," he told Jakob.

"Yes, sir. I've been cold for a long time now."

"But . . . what do you mean?" Doctor Phillips asked. "How?"

"Erm . . . well, I'm glad you're a doctor. You may understand."

"Understand what?" Doctor Phillips asked as he got up from the chair, trying to stand.

"No, no, please stay sitting doctor, this may come as a bit of a shock," Jakob said. "You see," he stalled, a smile of friendship on his dead lips, "I'm a vampire."

Shocked further, Doctor Phillips looked on dumbfounded and scanned the room as though for some reasoning, some practical joke.

"Goodness me, that may explain why I incorrectly diagnosed you, but . . . oh my, please don't hurt me."

Doctor Phillips looked around again — this time Jakob was sure it was for a quick escape — he was totally bewildered.

"No, no, it's not what you think. Look." Jakob started pulling at his lips, revealing stained yellow but quite blunt teeth. "I don't have any fangs or anything like that and I'm not going to jump up and attack you any time soon. Look at me," he pointed to his chest, "I'm not much good at fighting, let alone killing."

A moment of silence passed. Letting the doctor take in what he had just heard, Jakob glanced round the room. Next to him on a stainless steel tray were some small tools. It was like a miniature torture theatre; the pruning-type shears, hideously curled at the end, sat innocently as though waiting to open up his ribs. Next to that the scalpel appeared to wink at him, its lethal edge passive as it lay on its side. Finally, the dolphin-nose of the big bone saw seemed to sniff at his body.

There was a bang at the door. The doctor jumped.

Startled, Doctor Phillips said, "Quickly, lie down again . . . and . . . well, just play dead for a minute."

Jakob obeyed as he heard the doctor go to the door. He then heard a different voice say that he had brought another body, the body of a policeman who had been brutally attacked whilst out on duty. More commotion ensued as the deceased PC was carried into the exam room and laid next to Jakob. After a short scraping sound followed by a thud and fading steps there was silence.

As soon as they had gone, the place clear again, Doctor Phillips cleared his throat. Taking it as his cue Jakob opened his eyes and sat up again. The doctor was clearly more composed now.

"Right. So . . . a vampire, you say?" Doctor Phillips said. "Then why are you not as dead as a dodo? What, with that stake through your heart?" he gestured at the obvious.

"I'm afraid I really don't know sir, but I've been finding out a lot about myself lately. I suppose the only explanation would be is that I'm already dead. But not, if you understand. So my heart is just a useless dead muscle left over from my living days."

"We live in strange and vile times," Doctor Phillips said, still in some shock.

"We've always lived in vile times, sir. Here and now is no different," Jakob said, not offended.

"Yes, indeed, but how? Why?" Doctor Phillips directed his gaze upon the fallen body of the Sergeant. "He was a brave man."

"I'm sorry if you knew him Doctor, truly I am, but we have more pressing matters at hand. I need to get out of here without being seen," Jakob said, a little urgency in his tone.

"Yes, I knew him. He was a good honest fellow . . . but yes, you're right of course. We must get you out of here."

"And keep your reputation intact," Jakob offered, rather emptily.

"Listen here, young man — I know I keep saying 'young' because you do look young — but how old are you exactly?"

"Not as old as some of the legends suggest but old enough to know a precarious situation when it occurs," answered Jakob.

Doctor Phillips looked around the room for inspiration.

"Yes, quite. . . let's get you some clothes first. Right, got it."

Apologising profusely to the deceased Sergeant, Doctor Phillips started removing the man's uniform. Understanding what the doctor had in mind, Jakob got up from the table and stood, naked, next to the sadly beaten and utterly broken Sergeant. He wrapped his hands around the end of the stick that still stuck out of his own chest and slowly eased it out of his body. He threw it to one side. It landed on the table with a clunk of wood against steel.

"What about your assistant? Hasn't he already seen me?" Jakob asked.

Lifting a pile of blue clothing, Doctor Phillips offered them to Jakob. "Don't worry about that, he's a simple enough and agreeable old chap — I'll tell him you were still alive, barely, and we had you immediately shipped off to the hospital."

Slipping into the woolly clothes of the dead PC, Jakob thanked him. The clothes were a little on the large size but he was certain that Ludwig would help him tailor them a little — Ludwig was good with a needle and thread.

Standing fully kitted out Jakob turned to the doctor. "Right, how do I look? Convincing enough?"

Doctor Phillips stood and admired the blue uniform, his integrity for what it stood for only too apparent.

"You look like you're good and ready for Her Majesty's Service," he said, nodding with pride.

"Thank you again Doctor Phillips, but . . . to pass this off, surely I'll need another identity?"

"That's easy young man, you're the long arm of the law — you're Johnny Upright."

In silence, Jakob twisted left and right, squeezing his lithe body into the heavy clothes. Stretching his arms forward he regarded himself for a moment. He looked down at his warrant number — 49889. *Rendőrség - Police. This could be fun.*

"Now, you must be gone. I have my dear colleague here to respectfully address. Oh, and please come back to see me when you can. The uniform will give you passage to come down here whenever you want. I'd be interested in learning a bit about how that body of yours works."

"No problem, I'll be seeing you Doctor Phillips."

TWENTY

The woman had been waiting on the other side of the road for most of the night. Without looking suspicious she had passed herself off easily as a prostitute with her haggard dress and dusty brown boots.

Seeing the police pathology department door open she dropped her head, hiding her sullen face. With her head tilted to one side she watched as the door slammed behind . . . *a policeman*?

Looking harder, she let her instinct take over, seeing him for all he was. *Yes.* It was definitely him, the man from the other night who had chased down and caught the creepy, weird-looking man with the twitchy face.

Yes, it was the vampire, the one she had been looking for all this time. Satisfied that it was him she turned away and calmly walked the opposite way up Commercial Street heading towards the market in the early morning light.

Approaching the market the woman ducked through the cut. There she stopped. In front of her another woman blocked her way. Her long black hair swung gently over her upper body, her perfect breasts.

The newcomer, blocking the way, mewled from her cat-like mouth. "Hello, my dear."

"Oh . . . hello, Pura," she said. "It's been a long time. This is. . . unexpected."

Not interested in small talk Pura got straight to the point. "I believe you've just seen him. Isn't he simply handsome?" she asked.

"Well, yes, but . . ." said the woman, unsure of where the conversation was heading.

Pura's voice always commanded attention. "But nothing, my dear. I'm glad you've finally found him and identified him for us but you must now leave him to me."

The woman simply listened, standing in the dawning glimpse of sunlight.

"There is something I need you to do. You know of his knew friend I take it? Yes, yes, of course you do. Well, I need you to make him disappear for a while. Don't kill him. You see this new friend of his might be a bad influence and we need him to face this alone, fulfil his destiny. Not as a silly policeman though — although he did look rather good in his new uniform," Pura teased her. "No, not as a policeman, but as the killer that he really is."

TWENTY-ONE

Where, for the love of Mike, is Jake?

Jack shook, his whole body seethed; he had no idea of his new friend's whereabouts. He stamped his feet, fidgeted wildly, restless. Instead of waiting for his next instructions as they had agreed, Jack had taken it upon himself and decided to explore the night. He was sure Jake would not mind, he was his friend now. Yes, he finally had one and had immediately, in his head at least, began calling him by his shortened more intimate name: Jake. He smiled. *Jake sounds so much like Jack!*

Happy with himself Jack traversed the dank streets alone, his mind working overtime. He thought of the stupid (and lucky) woman who owed him. She would survive the messy neck wound. Maybe one day he would go back for her, finish the job. Maybe she deserved getting away with it; he had been sloppy, had been seen by Jake, chased down and discovered. Perhaps it was a blessing in disguise; after all, he would still be friendless, unwanted, without the careless mistake.

As he plodded, no particular destination in mind, he wondered why Jake had agreed to let him go — what did he really want him for? Something struck him; Jake had frantically chased him and caught him in the alley but he had not even been breathing heavily, not even slightly? Jack realised that he, himself, was not the fastest person on two legs but he did have a certain stamina that others did not possess and yet he had been completely breathless. *Just what did Jake mean when he'd said I can kill for him? Who is he?*

He did not care really, just trudged along, blissful in the thought of being asked to kill; someone to approve of his misdeeds. He rubbed his hands together as he sauntered south along Leman Street. He stopped, grinned. *Look at that.* The woman he spied was standing on a desolate corner — alone. He padded his hands against his upper arms. *Blimey, it's so damn cold for spring.* He looked up and down the road, his face fibrillating excitedly. *She's close to a police station.*

He watched her for a moment, battling to resist his urge. *Sod it, I can't wait for Jake.* His hand darted into his pocket, feeling for his trusty friend — yes, he was there, resting quietly like a death's head hawk-moth. *Patience, my friend.* Turning his attention back to the single figure of the woman, he saw her wandering off down the road towards the river area. The docks, he supposed.

Jack followed.

The woman kept on walking south, ambling gently. *She's not going to get too much custom this far down the street.*

Not far behind her, and being careful not to stand out, Jack passed over into Wapping. The main road to his left, The Highway, was his kind of place. It was the site of the Ratcliff Highway murders where in 1811 at least seven people had been barbarically slain. The suspected murderer had been caught and his corpse dragged through the streets, with a stake through its heart. It was then buried at the crossing at Commercial Road and Cannon Street Road. Less than two years ago a gas company doing some work had dug up the remains and found the body, the stake still driven through it. Jack fussed over the details. The moral of the story basically was not to get caught.

The woman carried on, stealing further into the narrow constricting passages, heading towards the embankment of the river, surrounded by lousy alleys with their scabby tenements. Still Jack followed her through the dimly lit confines. Excitement welled up inside him. This place was ideal.

Theft and looting had long since tainted the 'Pool of London' further west at Billingsgate, but here, here murderers and pirates were part of the shabby furniture, all hiding out in the mire. Jack would add to its notoriety — soon. He would be on her in next to no time.

Stopping on a soiled corner he eyed the grimy straits, could not see her. *Where's that dollymop gone?*

There was a creak behind him and he knew instantly that he had been outmanoeuvred – and that she was probably not a prostitute at all; she had been too quick, too cunning for a pinchcock. Pivoting on his heels his face met with the full impact of the wooden beam that she had picked up and slammed into her would-be attacker's face. Seeing sparks, Jack hit the greasy, hard ground.

And passed out.

Jack woke some time later. The room was almost pitch black — or was that his eyes? The place smelled damp, reeked of shit. He sniffed, had no idea where he was except that he was freezing. Jack lifted his hand to his split lip — it stung, badly. He liked it. His tongue interrogated the swollen wound, the acrid taste of copper slid down his throat. He had been beaten up by a woman and it angered him. *The bastard bitch*. Only one woman before in his life had beaten him but his mother had paid for that, dearly. With no other option Jack decided he would wait. He sat down in the dark.

Ferreting around, Jack felt bars, some of them metal, some timber. Sharp splinters roughed against his fingertips and he pulled his hand back. The movement caused him to sway gently. *What is this, a fucking giant bird cage?*

Evidently her victim was awake; the sound of creaking steel and timber meant movement. In the dark she stretched out.

"Ow," Jack yelped, lurching in the darkness. He had not been prepared for the sharp needle point that she had thrust carelessly but forcefully into his calf.

"Stay still you wimp," the soft almost dream-like voice said from the blackness below him.

The woman. In sudden pain and panic Jack writhed about, beating at the steel and timber that imprisoned him.

"I said 'stay still', it will hurt you less," the voice said again.

Another stab of pain jolted him, his other leg this time. Grimacing, he flinched, and furiously rubbed his lower leg.

"Who . . . who the hell are you?" he asked.

"Never mind that for now, I'm drinking."

What?

A faint drizzle of liquid echoed through the silence, tinny yet obvious. It was followed by an obvious and loud smack of lips.

"Ah, that's better," the voice said. "Your blood ain't half bad for a scrawny weasel."

"What the . . . What the fuck are you talking about?"

Ignoring him, she continued, her question catching him unexpectedly. "Do you know the vampire, you blubbering fool?"

What is this? He did not recognise the voice that affronted him. *What is she talking about? Vampire?*

"Do I know you?" Jack asked the woman in the dark.

"Not like you'd like to, you pervert!" the voice shrieked back at him and she jabbed him again.

Jack screamed, louder this time.

"Now, I shall ask you again. Do you know him?"

"What? Who?"

"The man you met the other night? Or should I say the man that ran you down and caught you like a squealing pig? What's his name?"

How did she know? "You mean Jake?"

"Ah." The sound of relish left her lips. "Jakob."

"He's not a vampire you crazy whore.

"Really?" It was a curt reply.

Lost in the darkness Jack was now lost for words. He rubbed his head. Jake wasn't breathing hard — at all. *But how the hell would she know?* After a while he spoke again, directing his voice down into the pit. "Let's say I believe you, does that mean . . . you're a vampire as well?"

"Always so stupid. Why do you think I was sticking you? I just drank your blood you fool, what do you think?" she said. "What does Jakob want with you?"

His new friend, a vampire? No way.

"What does he want with you?" she asked again.

Jack appeased his captor. "He . . . he said he wanted me to kill for him."

The revelation had not surprised her — it happened to some of them from time to time. It was a natural human need; not to let go of one's soul and become something that, in all traditions and cultures was eternally damned, could be difficult to comprehend. Some took to it immediately — usually the benign, the gracious — others took their time. But it would happen, sooner or later. She knew the true human condition was one of rage, deceit and murder. The transformation from dead to undead and the need to kill for blood — at least for her — was inevitable, and instant.

"So that's it. He's a vampire who won't kill, I should have known," she said. "He will be needing you then. To kill for him, provide him with sustenance — because he is coward."

Agitated, Jack started shouting. "There's no such thing as . . . as . . . vampires, you crazy mollisher."

She laughed quietly. *I'm crazy? Maybe I should cart him off to Hoxton House?*

Codding him some more, she said, "no such thing as vampires eh? Then what do you think that body was, the one they dug up a while back on The Highway? The stake was still sticking out of the dead man's chest?"

It was an infamous story, everyone knew.

"Okay, okay," Jack shot back at her. "I . . . I'll kill for you, then. Just let me go," he pleaded.

"Ha. I don't think so. No, you will do just fine here. I need blood and yours should be plenty for now. Either that or I will have your sorry hide marched into the nearest asylum, you idiot."

"But, if Jake needs me . . ." Jack said, his warped sense of allegiance assuring him, "then he'll . . . he'll come looking for me."

"He'll not find you. Not here and anyway, he needs to learn how to kill for himself . . . Jack."

Jack's senses pricked as she said his name aloud. *So, she knows Jake caught up with me the other night but how does she know my name?* He was worried now, stuck in this cage, crammed into this prison against his will; he was free fodder for a fiend — and a woman fiend at that. Repulsed at his predicament, he reassured himself. His friend, Jake, would find him. Soon.

"He will come," he said to her. "But . . . but how do you know my name? Who are you? What's your name?"

Hmmm. She mulled it over; it was a fair question. Even Elizabeth Báthory had known who her captors were.

"You can call me master or ma'am, but you may be here for some time so, oh I don't know." She paused, feeling contrary, thinking for a moment, going through names at random.

Jack waited, scratching at his calf muscle.

"I tell you what, why don't you call me Mary."

TWENTY-TWO

Jakob heard the news. He was disappointed that the woman had died. Four agonising days had passed since her attack, the same attack he thought he had saved her from. She had died though, finally succumbing to the injuries that the gang of cowards had inflicted upon her frail and only-too-mortal body. It was little comfort, but he had tried his best.

The tragic event had put him in touch with the good doctor at least and given him a surprisingly respectable and constant supply of blood. His *acquired* police uniform, too, was being of enormous help; it had given him entry to everywhere and anywhere that he wished to go.

Which was all well and good but he could not find Jack. Jakob had been to Jack's house and had found it empty. There had been no answer, no Jack, no evidence that he had even been there. He admitted to himself that he had perhaps made a grave mistake in stating his intentions of killing to Jack, a total stranger — a stranger who had now gone and disappeared.

Jakob put it from his mind — safe in the knowledge that he had not told Jack *what* he was and, anyway, who was going to believe a belligerent hothead over a newly-uniformed policeman that he was indeed a member of the undead?

Jakob continued with his search. It was Sunday and Jakob had no work. Ludwig would cover if needed; fastidiously attending to anyone should they so wish to part with a few hard earned pennies in return for a respectable hair cut in the onerous East End of London.

An angry smell assaulted his senses. He was down by the far end of the docks, parallel to the northern bank of the river Thames. Jakob now found himself on Wapping Wall and he stopped to check the view — or lack of it. Thick green debris littered the sodden banks; the few buildings there were steadily being suffocated by the dirge of the river and its viscose contents.

A faint murmur of water rippled against the edge of the bank, the only characteristic that gave it away as actually being water; it composition making it look more like thick brown gloop. Jakob could have walked into the water, bathed himself ragged and emerged dirtier than when he had entered. Looking at the river he recalled the beauty of the Danube, himself as a child, swimming with Miklós until both their fingers and toes resembled shrivelled prunes.

Standing by the Thames he inspected his hands. They were full of lines and crinkles, an effect that death had freely bestowed upon him as a young man. An odd feeling suddenly washed over him — as if someone, or something, was following him.

Acting as casual as a vampire could he lowered his hands and walked on. Keeping the river to his right he tilted his head to the left, eyeing the line of buildings. He quickened his pace. Eventually he stopped and waited near a corner to see if anyone came out. Waiting for a bowler hat to appear.

He waited. Ready.

Nothing, no one.

He wondered how a vampire could be so paranoid. *Surely, I'm over that?*

Checking further down the side of the road, he spied an old looking pub. The sign said it was The Devils Tavern. It was a forbidding public house that was over 350-years-old, and it looked it too. However, much like himself, Jakob wondered what would be left of the ancient pub had it been in its original state. Jakob had passed it many times on his nightly prowls for unsuspecting dock-side rats, but had never gone in, always giving it a wide berth.

The ominous pub was said to be the perfect meeting place for moon-cursers, smugglers and cut-throats. *Maybe Jack would be in there after all?* It was a building surrounded in mystery and legend had it as being the once-favoured place of Hanging Judge Jeffreys. Two-hundred years earlier in the Pitchfork rebellion The Duke of Monmouth had attempted to overthrow James II. Monmouth was defeated and executed for treason but it then fell upon Judge Jeffreys to exact the sentences and subsequent executions of Monmouth's remaining followers by hanging nearly two-hundred men.

Jakob treated the legend with some scepticism; he knew they could be embellished. After all, were vampires not supposed to die when exposed to sunlight or by being staked through the heart?

Not too long ago even Charles Dickens, a writer whose works Jakob liked, had enjoyed a tipple or two in The Devils Tavern, no doubt in his quest to find the perfect antagonist or shady character to pen into his latest book. He wished Mr

Dickens was still alive, he had read a good many of his books during his quest in learning the English language that he now spoke so well. What a story a vampire in the heart of London with a potentially crazed murderer for a partner would have made.

Stopping outside the pub Jakob paused to peer through the window into the dungeon-like drinking hole. Hole was appropriate although not accurate — it was more like an oubliette, dark and damp, with unspeakably cruel patrons. Without entering the famed drinking establishment Jakob moved on, wondering quite how a crude version of The Black Hole of Calcutta had somehow spawned in the East of London, alongside the River Thames.

Where could Jack be? Was it possible that he had visited a relative or something? Jack had never mentioned any relative's and, anyway, how well did Jakob really know him? *I'll just have to keep an eye open for him.* It was not urgent, Jakob knew he always had the doctor and even Ludwig and his parasites to help in his quest for blood.

Summer was coming — the killing could keep.

TWENTY-THREE

'Mary' had no idea that Jakob had felt someone watching him as she followed him in the inky darkness. But his actions, his snooping around the docks, made her feel uneasy. Why was he still searching for the imbecile Jack? Why did he not just get out and do it — kill for himself? On mentioning it to Pura, she had dismissed it, only telling her to keep Jack for a little while longer yet before letting him go. Only then was Mary to move deeper into the East End area, find somewhere else to hole up and wait for more instructions.

"There are many places you could go to get lost but perhaps you'd feel more at home there, in the vile pit that is the East End?" Pura teased her. "It is by all accounts full of people much like yourself."

"Oh yes, and what's that?" Mary asked.

"Unconscionable killers of course," Pura said.

It was indeed true but after all these years Mary was growing impatient, fed up with being told what to do, where to go, the constant orders and the waiting.

Pura looked at the woman called Mary; she liked her feistiness. When Pura had 'recruited' her, the new recruit had known then to obey orders and as such she had risen quickly through the ranks, much faster than many of her male counterparts.

"Be patient my dear," Pura said.

She would be patient, would bide her time and obey — once again — for now. She might even do things on her own. Was that not what the big boss had done all those years ago — to be where he is now? Her time would come but for now she would just have to do what Pura, her superior, had instructed.

TWENTY-FOUR

The last few years had been hard on him. Hunting was the only thing George knew — really knew. Yes, he had done some building, had even done some decorating. But they were mindless chores, a way of making some quick money. It was in finding the church that had really lifted his cause. His initiation into the Lodge had been a good one and had also lifted his status. The Lord and the Lodge had made him a fearless man, rooted to his cause. Only death would stop him in his tiresome journey — to hunt down and kill vampires in holy benevolence.

The death of his sister troubled him. *Why wasn't her husband a stronger man, wiser? How had he let that weak and evil woman in? Been so gullible?* It did not matter, his brother-in-law was dead now, but then so was his sister. He asked himself the same questions over and over. Finding her in the basement, in that hideous state, had put him close to the edge. He had picked up the bottle again.

Members of the Lodge and his church had consoled him, had told him his sister and her family were at peace and were where the good Lord wanted them to be, with Him in heaven. Their faith was obviously stronger than his own. Anything was now possible, the drinking would have to stop, he needed to be alert, fresh. He was no stranger to the dangers of the world, evil creatures skulking around every corner, waiting for the chance to take an unsuspecting victim.

The building work he had done had the added bonus of also building up his strength and resolve, particularly in the incessant cold weather. His rough leathered hands might not be that of a gentleman, but they helped in vanquishing the terrible fiends that haunted him. Even at the end, when the last one was dead, he knew he still would not rest. Sleep brought with it dreadful images that cursed his dreams.

A screech of brakes and a hiss of steam meant they had reached their destination. With a jolt he jumped, a bead of sweat racing down his forehead. Picking up his bowler hat at his side he blinked and looked at his three companions. All four of them sat together in the rickety train coach. Just over twenty miles south of London, they had now pulled up and stopped. He looked out at the sign through condensation upon glass: REDHILL JUNCTION.

The monotonous grey of the platform summed up his thoughts. On the other side of the aisle, to his left, a big burly man with a bulldog face took up two seats. *Just as well he's sitting on the other side of the coach.* A lanky wisp-like man sat opposite the bulldog. Opposite himself a third small and quiet man with flossy hair sat twiddling his fingers nervously, a blank look on his face. All four of them wore black. *Fit for a funeral.* Getting up, his bowler hat tilted onto his head, he gesticulated to the three men with him. All were staring out of the windows taking in the dull sights. They were here as novices.

Heading for the door George threw it open and took in a deep nose-full of the cool, fresh midday air. It was good to get away from the oppressive dearth of the city — the stifling air. He had learned many years ago that it did not matter what time of day it was once the decision had been made to take one out, but having longer daylight hours always helped — and he did not like carrots.

The hard platform was deserted. It scratched and scraped underfoot as he placed his black leather shoes down onto the gritty concrete and started off. Bustling along behind him his three 'apprentices' looked uneasy, all unsure of what to expect. He too was uncertain of how they would react when it finally came down to doing the deed. Staring back at them he stretched his neck, pushing hard at his chin. The two men in front of the other younger man looked like an enormous walking 'number ten' — the tall man to the left, the large round man on the right. George wondered if any of them were truly ready. No amount of training and reading books would help them in committing the heinous acts that were necessary. It took strength, it took faith.

The town of Reigate, sitting below the ancient castle ruins and gardens had been mentioned as *Cherchefelle* in the Doomsday book. George was not sure why the town had once been called that but he liked to think that *Cherche,* coming from the French verb meaning to find, and *felle* being Latin for venom, meant he would soon find the venomous creature that he was searching for. The thought greatly pleased him, in his black bowler hat — it was the reason he had come.

Finding their way slowly the four men passed the diamond-shaped tiled house fronts, rows and rows of orange-brick daggers cascading downwards, literally pointing out the Devil's lair. They were in the right place.

Walking through the quiet High Street they soon came to the Red Cross Inn. It was never too early for George, and a strong liquor would steel the nerves of his three assistants — his walking 'number ten' and the smaller faint-hearted third man who always lingered at the back. Ordering drinks at the bar they each downed a swift ale and discreetly asked the landlord for directions to Lesbourne Road — and how it was pronounced exactly. The ones they were looking for were purportedly using the new invalid home on the same road as a safe-house.

It was late in the afternoon by the time they found the place. The new sign on the front proudly stated: THE GIRLS' FRIENDLY SOCIETY.

The men set to work. Talking steadily and clearly George went through his concise instructions one more time. The three others listened intently, only now grasping the horrid situation that was so close at hand. Taking their positions around the house they fell back into the trees and undergrowth that surrounded the home.

They waited.

After some time dusk began to fall. George was certain that a myriad of unsettled thoughts would be trailing through each of his three apprentices' minds.

Another hour went by.

Then, a distant sound.

A perceptible drone of quiet laughter, voices and steps slowly etching along the rear path, heading towards the back of the house — directly towards the heavy figure of a man struggling to hide his bulk in the bushes.

In his bowler hat George stood in the darkness on the opposite side of the rear gardens. He watched patiently as two figures came up the path, stopping near the back door. Had one of them reached out with a stretched arm they would have touched the big man.

The big man's decimal partner, the tall man, was lost perfectly among a line of trees watching the front of the house, his stoat-like eyes darting about.

Unaware, the two figures chatted, giggling for a few breathless minutes. One of them said goodnight and trundled off into the house, closing the back door, leaving the other — a woman in the garden — alone.

As the door clicked in its frame the men acted instantly. Stepping away from the bushes the big man seized the prey in his massive arms. Watching from his hideout, and safe in the knowledge that it would take a train to prise apart those solid limbs, George quickly skirted back around the house, emerging at the front. Whispering to the taller man he relayed his instructions. Then, taking a head start, George headed off towards the High Street again looking for the church, picking up the third man, the one with the flossy hair on his way. The tall man slithered around the house to aid his big friend, reuniting the 'number ten'.

Under cover of darkness the two assistants bundled the pale figure of a woman back towards the castle gardens. Dragging her by all fours, a cold arm and leg in each hand, the novices were now in full swing of their initiation.

Number 'One' was almost crowing with unexpected glee. 'Zero' looked decidedly grim. To look at them one would have thought it the other way round but, sure enough, the tall gangly man seemed to be enjoying himself. The gagged woman squirmed, letting out stifled muffles. Nobody was coming to aid her. At the castle grounds they halted. The grass was fine, freshly cut. They let go of her, dropping her down in front of George and the other man.

The woman cursed at them as her gag came free, her hair flailing around as she shook her head. Elongating a bony leg forward the tall man stepped viciously on her throat.

"That'll keep her quiet for a bit," he muttered.

George and the flossy-haired man stepped forward. A unique and special gift had been prepared. George had asked for it some weeks in advance after visiting the local warden at the Methodist church. Pulling the cumbersome thing towards the woman he and his young helper lined up the heavy object. They let go, dropping the metal frame forward, its weight encompassing the vampire. The naked iron maiden-type device was laced with long pinpoint tendrils.

With a series of chinks, the spikes entered the woman's long undead body and pinned her to the clay-like soil beneath, leaving her head with her mass of curls free. Leaning forward the big man lifted his almighty foot and gently rested it upon one side of the lattice, pushing down to drive the spikes home. She was pinned.

Unable to move because of the spikes that arrested her body the vampire cursed at them.

Standing at her head now, George leaned in closer. He looked her straight in the eye and smiled an upside-down grin.

"Good work men," he said to his apprentices before turning his attention to the immobilised woman. "Now, where is the other one?"

The vampire hissed at him.

"Where is the other one?" George repeated.

The woman twisted her head. "Who?"

"You know perfectly well who, you woolly-headed monster."

"If you mean God, I think he left us all a long time ago."

"Now now, it just won't do to take the Lord's name in vain," George said calmly, before kicking her in the side of the head.

The vampire shook her head wildly. "Who then? The corset-maker?"

"Stop being so cagey, my tall colleague here saw you both. Anyway I remember that old seamster, he fell out with the church — literally. I told him not to lose his head over it but he just wouldn't listen."

The doomed and trapped woman did not care anymore about the dainty tailor and how he had met his end, but she did care about her old friend from the windmill.

"I don't know who you're talking about, you prat. Old Neddy over there didn't see anything — his head was too far up in the clouds," she shouted.

The tall man eyed the others. "I'm sure it was boss, the one you're lookin' for."

The woman screamed again. "It wasn't him."

George nodded. "Ah, so there we have it. She said 'it wasn't him' — meaning, of course gentlemen, that there actually is *a him*," he said before turning back to the vampiric pin cushion. "He's in London is he not?"

"No. No."

"Oh, I think your vehement denial speaks volumes."

The writhing on the floor continued.

George turned to his three colleagues and spoke slowly and clearly. "Now, this is where we have to make one of only two choices. One is to burn her dried out 'living' corpse of a body. The other, and best method, is to remove her vile head. Rest assured this is the only way that I know of to thoroughly rid oneself of the beast. And believe me I've tried many times."

The three novices looked on, tentatively awaiting the grim decision.

"Now, I suggest that burning is out of the question as we are outside and may attract unneeded attention to ourselves, so we have little choice but to remove that wicked head from its shoulders," George said, passing the spade to the youngest and smallest of them — the flossy-haired man.

The vampire, finally realising her predicament, started to writhe violently, and thrash, but was held fast by the needle sharp spikes and the gangly foot on her neck.

Nervously flashing his eyes about, the small young man hesitated.

In an act of bravado the tall man stepped up and snatched the spade away. He placed the blade directly above the vampire's neck. Then he, too, hesitated. Shaking her head for all it was worth, the tall man ignored the vampire's distress, blinked away from her and turned to the bigger man. The big man had already turned to face the other way, had shut his eyes.

George's voice rang out. "Do it, do it now. Send her back, lay her body to rest. Finish her."

The tall man slowly lifted his foot, wobbling like a drunken snake. He slammed his foot down. The thin end of the spade did its work well. A tiny plop of severed bone and divided disc was the only sound heard as silence fell around them. A gentle brush of wind tickled the leaves of the trees that hovered above their heads.

All four now watched as the headless body, bone-dry after years of walking the earth without any water, surviving only on thick globs of blood, gently oozed a blackened liquid from the neck stump. The small man bent over and gagged, bile burning at his throat as he puked.

The breeze continued to blow through the trees and gardens as the four men stood alone in the night — judge, jury and executioners. Retrieving his hat, George tipped his bowler to them all. In recognition of a job well done he spoke calmly and quietly. "Well done. That's one down, now there's at least one more to go."

TWENTY-FIVE

The meeting had started well between them. Gregory was present as ever and, as ever, was restless. His witness statements were always invaluable and indifferent. He stood there mute, next to Uri and together they waited for a response.

Both Pura and Antonas were furious. It was apparent the two families would never, ever agree.

"What do you think you're doing?" Antonas spewed, his face ruddy with belligerence.

Emotionless, Uri faced the verbal onslaught with aplomb.

"You had her killed in . . . where was it?" Antonas raised his large hands in submission.

"Reigate." Uri was unmoved still. "Listen Antonas, was it not you yourself who started all this? After that ill-fated young woman you had accosted by that silly gang? I told you to back off then. The boss — he's not happy with you at all."

"That 'ill-fated young woman' as you put it, is yours. You can have her, she was a mistake. Sheesh, what's your problem?" Antonas chided him.

"The problem is that you had her killed at all. It's all about balance," Uri said calmly.

There was a flash of dark velvet as the only female in the room stepped over in support of her companion.

"Antonas, come away. It'll be all right." Pura comforted him, gently brushing her lips against his ear, slowly soothing his fury. "I don't think the others know as yet but we've still got the other one you were so eager about — you know, the one who's safely locked away," she whispered in triumph.

Antonas turned his back on the others and strode across the heated room. On reaching the far wall he turned and addressed the room.

"Uri, you can tell your superior, Michael . . . hell, you can even tell your big boss that we understand and will play by the rules. Is that fine by you?"

Uri silently questioned the honest outburst. He wanted to say more but bit his lip. His eyes narrowed. "Yes, I suppose, but you'd better not just be saying that to appease us, Antonas."

Opening his arms out wide Antonas gestured with his hands. "Who, moi?" he said.

"Cut the crap, Antonas. If not, we'll be seeing you soon and rest assured we will bring reinforcements next time," Uri said as he motioned to Gregory, who had stood by him silently throughout the whole proceedings.

Together Uri and Gregory left the room, leaving the others alone; evidently they were still angry. Pura turned to Antonas but before she could open her mouth, Antonas spoke.

"We need more time Pura. Just make sure you keep him locked away for a while yet. We still need to know whether the other one will join us. At least he's still alive after my gang skewered him. But if it turns out he'd rather join Uri's self-righteous band of pretenders then I'll have no other choice but to kill him — only this time I'll do the job myself. And let me assure you, he won't be getting up from that anytime soon."

TWENTY-SIX

Had it not been for the bizarre weather, summer would have passed uneventfully. Coming from Eastern Europe Jakob had seen more than his far share of the cold, hail and sleet. Being a vampire prepared him to expect the unexpected in all things now. It had not, however, prepared him — and the rest of southern England for that matter — for snow in July. In many ways he was glad that Jack had gone missing, he did not fancy leaving any tell-tale footprints in the snow.

He had since met the charming Doctor Phillips and had Ludwig for his liquid diet. The red food had never been so plentiful. Jakob put away his uniform and he and Ludwig busied themselves cutting hair and, of course, leeching. With little else to do Ludwig had become obsessed with harvesting blood, for his new 'rare blood-needing' friend, from his damned leeches. He now had so many of the critters for the job and fed Jakob as well as he could. For that, Jakob was grateful but he had found the blood from the tiny rubber specks was never enough. To that end Jakob had taken to visiting Doctor Phillips whenever possible.

Jakob still was not sure he should have told the amiable doctor that he was a vampire. It was not a particularly good idea but then he had had to tell him something once he had found himself laid up on the doctor's examination table, a crusty cadaver with a stake sticking out of his chest cavity.

With the deprivation and crime in this part of the metropolis anything could happen — so why not a vampire?

A pornography of disabilities, the travelling freak shows were relatively new to London and were commanding macabre attention from the locals, particularly in the East End. A man who looked like a pachyderm, a lady with a beard and a camel woman whose knees turned backwards so she could walk on all fours; these had all become commonplace in the unscrupulous district — it seemed Jakob was more normal that most of them put together.

Jakob rounded the last corner on his travels and came to a halt at Jack's front door. It had been more than three months and although he had kept a look out all that time Jack was nowhere to be seen. Again, he tirelessly knocked the flaking door, and waited. Again, nothing.

As he turned on his heels to go he thought he heard a noise, a shuffling coming from inside. Jakob tried the handle. The door was unlocked. He was sure he had locked it last time. Slowly, cautiously, he stepped into the small entry. A small brown box of a hall with nothing but dry floorboards and crudely plastered walls. Skimming the floor like a soft dust-cloth his feet traversed the hall in silence, stopping at the door to the tiny back kitchen area.

On the floor, crammed into the corner, covered in grime and smeared in black, dried and crusty blood, sat a man. Semi-naked and looking overwrought the man was banging his head slowly against the wall and staring off into the distance, almost through lath and plaster.

"Jack," Jakob said.

Bemused, Jack turned his forlorn face towards Jakob, his eyes glossy and glazed.

"Jack, are you all right?" he asked the dumbstricken face. "Jack?"

Jack's eyes blinked and there was life, a hint of comprehension. His reticence faded. "J . . . Jake?" he whispered.

"Yes Jack, it's Jakob. Where have you been? What happened?"

Jakob got up and fetched a small towel, running it under the tap. Stretching down, he mopped some of the crud from Jack's face.

"Thanks," Jack said, his voice a little louder, stronger.

After some time Jack managed to drag himself up. Jakob ran to his bed and scraped together some cleaner clothes for him. As Jack struggled to pull on his clothes Jakob noticed several blackened puncture wounds dotted around his body, his arms and legs. *Where the hell has he been? What's happened to him?* Once dressed, Jack sat down and slowly but surely started talking. Gradually, Jakob coaxed his disjointed story from him.

Jack had been caught by surprise, attacked, beaten into unconsciousness and kidnapped by a woman. But the woman was more than that; she was a vampire — a true-to-life vampire who had kept him holed-up in a run down and unused building down by the docks, in a barred cage. As her helpless prisoner she had fed from him, sticking him with sharp objects to extract his blood. It had been horrible. His mother had beaten him, he told Jakob, but this woman, this blood sucking beast, had a malice that few possessed.

The room went silent. Jakob instructed him to stay put while he ran out to get him some food — Jack was clearly weak.

Collecting his thoughts, Jakob skidded up the road. Jack was back, weak but alive, and chanting on about being held captive, about cages and indiscriminate blood-letting. Had not his Emma used a similar method? But then, maybe it was a common enough way for a female vampire to get the blood that their frail bodies required? They were just as weak as humans after all. *How many vampires are there in London?* The thought that there were perhaps others soothed Jakob in an odd way — it meant he was not the only one.

It was a constant struggle learning to live with the damnation that Emma had bestowed upon him. *Anyway, where can I get some food?* He spotted the Hope and Anchor and ducked inside. He was sure he would at least find some basic human sustenance in the pub even if it did contain poisonous chemicals.

Back at the house he sat down with Jack and watched him shovel the bread into his mouth, taking a large lump of cheese with it, his weakness subsiding.

"Did she tell you her name?" Jakob asked him urgently.

Jack shuddered as he remembered the shrill of his captor's voice.

"Yes. Yes, she did . . . Um . . . It was . . ."

Jakob waited with baited breath — or no breath.

" . . . Mary."

Dejected at the mention of the name, Jakob stood at the window taking in the pitiful view of a rear yard, cobbled and begrimed, barren of any colour, any flowers. *I'm just being silly.*

"She said she'd been watchin' us," Jack continued.

Great, but who was she? — and more importantly, what did she want? Jakob's thoughts perturbed him. If he could, if his body was not thoroughly dried out, he would have broken out in a sweat, a headache would have racked his skull.

"Why did she let you go then?" he asked.

"She . . . d . . . didn't, I managed to get away, broke the timber with my feet. I'd been working on it for a while, like a confined beaver," Jack said, pleased at the thought of his bestial escape.

"It may have ended differently had you not managed to get away," Jakob comforted him.

"It still could. I mean, you're a vampire an' all," Jack squeezed out his last sentence through pursed lips.

Jakob assured him. "Jack . . . if I was going to eat you I would have done it the night I caught you, wouldn't I?"

Devils and demons were one thing, vampires were something else — something that came from myth. But then Jack had just been held against his will by a female of the species — was it really so hard for him to conceive that Jake, his new-found friend, was also a vampire. After all, it was not your average everyday citizen that just turns around and asks you to kill for them.

Jack faced him. "Well, yeah, but . . . I . . . I had to get away. You said you needed me to kill for you."

The idea was deplorable, Jakob knew, but he thirsted, lusted for human blood, sweet and satisfying.

"Yes Jack," Jakob said, ashamed as the words left his mouth. "So I can have fresh blood, I'm sick of the other stuff."

"What other stuff?"

"Never mind," Jakob said. "Let's get you cleaned up first and then you get some rest for a few days. We can start soon."

"Yeah, no floozie's gonna put Jacky down for long."

"Good, now let this be a warning to us both. Keep your eyes open, we don't want to be getting caught," Jakob said, pleased at Jack's sudden recovery.

"No problem, but if I . . . If I catch that trull of a vampire, I'll cut her fuckin' heart out, just you see," Jack shouted, jumping up in crazed delirium.

"No. No, you won't," Jakob shot back at him. "You'll bring her to me first."

TWENTY-SEVEN

"You're still here," Jakob said as he entered the doctor's morbid lair.

Aside from the current residents, nothing had changed. The doctor jumped. Recognising the man clothed in the ill-fitting blue uniform Doctor Phillips relaxed. "Unless I died and reanimated, much like yourself, then I'd say yes I am still here."

"Very funny. I meant. it's late," Jakob said, his face straight.

"Is something wrong, my lad?"

Jakob looked at the doctor, said nothing.

Reaching over to his special refrigerator, Doctor Phillips opened the door and pulled out one of his saved jars. "Here you go."

"Thanks Doc," Jakob said taking it from him. He watched the contents as he swirled the jar round a little as if it were a fine and expensive scotch whiskey.

"I won't show you who it came from," Doctor Phillips said, waving his hand in the air, motioning towards a thinly disguised and covered cadaver, "but I'm more than certain you can guess. Now what is the problem?"

"I think my old girlfriend — you know, the one who turned me — I think she may still be alive."

"You mean undead."

"Well, yes. Not alive then, but like me."

"What makes you think that? Have you considered that it may be some form of belated grief?"

"No. Yes. Oh, I don't know. It's just a feeling I have."

"But I thought you told me she perished in a fire."

"Hmm . . . I did. Do you think a person could survive a fire?"

"Well, it depends on the size of the flames. A person may succumb to carbon monoxide poisoning quite quickly or just suffocate. If not they would no doubt die from heatstroke and shock, or loss of blood. But that's a real-life person shall we say, a living human being."

"Yes, but what about us?"

"It's difficult to say. Your bodies haven't seen water for so long, they must be quite dry and so, in theory, would burn rapidly. If that was the case then she would have suffered from immediate thermal decomposition."

Jacob did not like the word decomposition — it was the process of decay and that spelled the end for the vampire.

"So?"

"So, the conflagration would have been disastrous. I'm sorry Jakob."

Hanging his head Jakob looked at the concrete floor. There were dull brown stains everywhere, the methods of cleaning and scrubbing evidently not rigorous enough. *That's all that would be left of her now?*

Jakob held up the jar and nodded appreciatively at the doctor. "Thanks again Doc," he said, as he made his way towards the stone steps.

"It's not the best I'm afraid but it's all I've got at the moment. You wouldn't credit it but it seems to be getting harder and harder to come by, my dear fellow. It appears we live in a remarkably ordered society. Who would believe that, here in the East End?"

TWENTY-EIGHT

Several days had passed since he last saw the doctor. Jakob was low on supplies but forever grateful of being able to go out in the sunlight and had enjoyed the balmy day. It was August bank holiday, the first Monday of the month. Apparently an Act had been passed in 1871 declaring four days during the year on which employed people would get an extra day's holiday during the working week, allowing, in particular, bank staff to attend and participate in a game of cricket.

A game of cricket? He could not help thinking that the English were all mad, but then he had not minded the day off to get away from Ludwig and his strange fixations for a while. The weather had been brighter for a change but now the unremitting drizzle had returned and it was raining yet again — it seemed the London rooftops were permanently besprent with raindrops.

Paying the rain no attention he made his way to meet Jack. Despite the mizzle, in the last month or so the weather had righted itself and summer was getting warmer. Jack, too, had shrugged off his imprisonment, his wounds and scabs had healed but deep inside, along with other emotional discords, Jack still harboured a deep hatred for the one who had wronged him.

Tonight they had decided to first meet in a public house, that way they would be seen by regular folk and, the idea was to blend in, not seen to be acting suspicious. Walking up Commercial Road towards Whitechapel High Street Jakob spotted the seedy pub. It was on his side of the street. He was glad; it was always a chore to get through the rabble that cluttered the filthy thoroughfares, forever hanging out in the roads.

Jakob had reached the establishment when two revellers, arm in arm, pushed past him as the door swung open. Apologising to him as they barged on by the couple gagged with vulgar laughter and swaggered up the road, no doubt looking for their next shot of cheap liquor.

Dodging through the brawling crowd of drinkers inside, he spotted Jack sitting at a table talking to two older women. The bigger woman looked a bit rough; a reddened complexion surrounded her cheeks. In an artificially high-pitched voice the younger of the two was pestering Jack for another drink.

All sitting at a small round table on the sawdust floor, they had saved a seat for Jakob and he slid into it.

Joining them, Jakob nodded. "Good evening."

"Evenin," Jack said. "You took your time. This ere's Polly an' Emma." Jack pointed to the two obviously slattern women that accompanied him at the table and grinned. Jakob, always mindful of his upbringing, kept his manners and nodded politely at them.

"Where's you bin then, you looks as pale as a ghost?" the one called Emma said.

Emma. Jakob paused.

Aware that he was under scrutiny from the two women who sat opposite Jack, he spoke. "I need a holiday."

Nudging her friend with a fat elbow the older one cut in. "Eh, fink 'e needs a bit more 'an that." Like two slovenly witches experimenting with grisly ingredients over a cauldron they cackled to themselves.

Jack slammed his drink down excitedly, spilling the brown liquid across the table top. "An' you'll get more than that, you see," he said to them both, making them think he promised them money and a good time.

Again, they cracked up and wooed. After another drink the girls got up and headed for the door. Jack put his lips next to Jakob's ear. "'Ere, I've told 'em we're soldiers, out in our civvies. They like stuff like that."

Suddenly Jakob did not want to be there, he wanted to crawl away, back down into Hell, explain to the Devil that he was defective. How could he choose which one of the two would be on the menu tonight? Again, he withdrew from himself. But he knew he needed blood.

Outside, the faint drizzle persisted. And so did Jack.

He watched Jack take the younger, more low-set one, Emma, to one side and whisper into her ear. She sidled up close to him giggling beneath her black bonnet. Jack had already chosen — the predator had picked its prey. *Am I really going to go through with this?*

Polly came up to Jakob and touched his arm. "Reckon we should leave 'em to it," she said, pulling him away in the direction of Angel Alley.

Claustrophobic dwellings cowered above them, unknowing witnesses to the vampire and the killer's despicable plan. Losing sight of his accomplice as they trotted through the large red-brick arch Jakob felt uneasy.

Polly turned to him. "Come on then darlin', a girl ain't got all night ya know," she said in her low voice.

Thinking hard and fast, Jakob responded. "Look, Polly, I . . . Er . . . I don't know what my friend has been telling you but I . . . Well, I don't like women."

"You's not one of 'em queers is ya?"

Jakob ignored the bleating woman. *Jack's probably doing the deed right now.* Jakob didn't want all that blood going to waste — she would have died for nothing. He needed to dump this woman and get moving. Find Jack.

"I . . . I suppose I am . . . Sorry." He handed her a shilling.

She eyed the money closely and beamed. "Don't be silly mister, I'm probly a tad too old for yer anyways," she chortled. "Least my mate's gorra bit tonight."

Oh, she's got it tonight all right. Jakob reproached himself. Polly turned and whisked her body away, back towards the pub, towards the continuation of her dull and hard life.

"I needs me a drink," she called back to him without bothering to look.

If she had looked, the spot where her possible 'client' had stood only seconds before was now empty. Jakob had gone, was on his way to find Jack and the other woman. He knew the streets well but these nooks and crannies were more like a demented rabbit warren.

He headed north.

It's nearly two in the morning, where could he be? Turning into Wentworth Street, hurriedly looking about,

Jakob bumped straight into someone — a policeman. Glancing up, Jakob briefly spied his badge through the murk, the numbers two and six ruffled in the darkness of his uniform. The policeman lifted his Bulldog Lamp high. Jakob averted his eyes — and face

"Excuse me . . . officer," Jakob said.

"You there, what are you doing?" the policeman asked, demanded.

"I'm looking for a mate . . . A chum. He went off with a girl, sir," Jakob said. "You see, we're on leave for the night and, well . . . you know us guards."

The policeman on duty frowned, looked him up and down, considering what best to do. "Okay then, but you mind your step next time," he said, "and get yourself off home now."

Relief passed over Jakob as he heard the words.

"Thank you officer," Jakob said as the policeman let him by. Like a naughty child being let out to play again Jakob skulked away. Ignoring the policeman's statement to get off home, Jakob carried on with his late night hunt. Evidently the police were about. *Jack had better know what he's doing.*

Confident that the P.C. was out of sight Jakob headed back towards George Yard, retracing his steps. Stumbling on some loose stones he saw the building in front of him and at once remembered the large arch. On reaching it he disappeared into its hulking shadow — and stopped. Listening carefully Jakob could hear faint dull noises, the sound of a chunk of meat being prodded, poked and carved.

He nearly tripped up the rough grey concrete steps at the back of the yard. In the crude light he saw Jack, bent over the woman, repeatedly bringing his hand down onto, and into, her.

For a moment Jakob closed his eyes, then opened them. Nothing had changed. *What have I done? Please God, forgive my unholy soul.*

"Where've you been?" Jack whispered as he spotted him.

"Looking for you. And trying not to get caught. What the heck are you doing to her?"

"Well, I stabbed her once in the neck, look," he pointed blithely at her fallen figure. "And she went down dead, straight off. Then, when you didn't turn up I began to play a little counting game while I waited for ya — I'm up to thirty-nine."

Jakob could see Jack was visibly shaking with excitement, an infernal devil dancing on the hot embers of Hell.

"Don't worry though, I got yous some of the good ole red stuff." He handed Jakob an old bottle of what was once ginger beer, now overflowing with a dense ooze. Jack chuckled. "Yeah, I had trouble tryin' to catch it in that."

Brimming with fresh blood Jakob lifted the bottle and took a swig. It was not quite what he had expected after all this time. The 'fresh' blood was already starting to congeal — but he did not care, he was not letting it go to waste.

Jakob's eyes now fell upon the woman who lay on her back, her blood smirching the concrete flagstones like carelessly spilled liquor across a table. The same flagstones were now supporting her dead weight like a butcher's trivet. As if in anticipation of some final and exciting news her fists were clenched tightly together. Other than that she looked asleep.

I'm so sorry.

As the city slept in ignorant rest, the locals, the officials and the police, in fact the whole world, had little knowledge of the terrors that were about to befall the small East End area of Whitechapel.

As late as it was, something that miserable night had seen it all — the only witness to the tragedy that had taken place just a few moments before. Several yards away a shadow silently shuffled forward and peeked down from the vantage point it held high up on the decrepit roof tops. Two unswayed yellow eyes, barely discernible in the darkness, blinked as the two men left the murder scene.

TWENTY-NINE

"Well, well, well," declared the man in the centre of the ornate room.

Sitting alone, his mouth upturned slightly before a large smile appeared on his broad face. Antonas was happy. Or as happy as he ever allowed himself to get. He had anticipated the next move from the man and his friend. It was not really the outcome he had wanted but it had been a small victory in the scheme of things.

Jack was unrelenting, unflinching — a real malefic force. Jakob, the man who was in league with Jack, had at least gone along with him even if he had hung back in the shadows after chasing around the streets for a bit. He had stepped forward when it mattered though — and openly taken his offerings.

Obviously there were always others to consider but if Antonas could get Jack *and* Jakob to join him as well, then the world may be a different place. After all, it was Jakob the hungry who had been the instigator to the whole demented partnership.

There was still time.

Plenty of it.

THIRTY

Ernie was not used to being housebound but he now had not left the house for several days. The horror he had experienced in Reigate was enough to send him straight to the lunatic asylum or, worse still, the hangman's noose. At least he had not used the spade when it was initially passed to him. If he had, he was certain he would have been doomed to a life of eternal damnation. Even so, no decent jury in the country was going to believe that the four of them had done society a favour by ridding it of an unnatural blood-craving vampire.

"Yes, your Honour, my colleague here simply decapitated her with this crude digging implement while I held her down. Not guilty," he snorted out loud.

Technically they had not killed anyone — at least *he* knew he had not — simply because she and her fine rosy-coloured mass of hair were already dead. The lead man, George, was a pious but rigid man, deep in his beliefs and . . . well, Ernie had to admit it, he was scared of him.

Never mind any of that for now. It was time for him to focus; he had to get his head straight. Ernie looked around his paltry room with his few belongings, its clumsy chattels. He needed some money, and quick. *Will I ever get my break?*

Here was a great story of good triumphing over evil, where evil had been spiked, its head severed from its hellish body and yet it was useless to him. George, the capable Mr Lusk, was well experienced in covering his tracks. There would be no evidence left to find and even if there were, Ernie was sure the police in their hastened clumsiness would miss it — they were about as much use as tits on a whore.

Perplexed, Ernie knew he could not write it up as a major scoop, a London exclusive, no matter how fantastical — and true — it was. With over 150 newspapers in the London area, competition was fierce but finally he had a story where sales of newspapers, *his* newspaper, would soar. *If only.* He laughed at the insanity of it all.

He had to clear his head, finally get out of the house again, and relax a little. He slammed the door behind him. *Right, where to?*

There had been a murder off the Whitechapel High Street. He knew where to go to find tongues that would wag, fast and with monolithic imagination. To the poor and worthless of the East End it was tantamount to becoming a celebrity. By giving over some tiny piece of information, to get quoted in the newspaper, they would see their name in bold black print and brag about it for days. More often than not that is all they would see, their illiterate eyes barely recognising anything other than their ignorant scribbled signatures.

It turned out there was not much in the way of any news and Ernie was beginning to wish he had not bothered. Two women, both of them prostitutes, had been seen drinking with two men. Not exactly pinpoint evidence or very helpful, or even riveting reading, but one of those prostitutes was now dead, stabbed an unhealthy thirty-nine times, and was lying still on a post mortem examination slab.

Ernie headed off, first to the White Swan, and if he found nothing there he would try the Two Brewers on Brick Lane. Both women had been spotted drinking in each so it was a lead if nothing else, and if Ernie supplied enough alcohol he would eventually filch a story from one of the patrons — even if the police had no other leads other than a well-perforated cadaver and a pool of blood.

Ernie did not have much luck in the first pub so he moved on. On entering the second he immediately overheard a simple conversation about the two women and a couple of supposed soldiers. *Soldiers?* He thought hard. The day was fast running out and he needed a story, something. Anything. He knew anybody could buy up used bayonets on Petticoat Lane for a few pennies. No doubt some of the local children even owned several of the pointy things, and if they had not purchase them they had certainly nobbled them. He sat at a free table, placed his half-pint down and within minutes he was scrawling down some notes.

"Hello young man," a voice said from above him. "I . . . Er . . . saw you writing and was wonderin' what you were up to?"

Ernie looked up to see a shortish man with a moustache — his moustache still sporting a line of creamy white froth from his pint of pale.

"Oh, hello," Ernie answered, staying seated. He shrugged. "I'm a journalist. I'm writing up a story on the unfortunate woman-of-the-street shall we say, the one found brutally murdered in George Yard."

"Nasty stuff that," the man said, shaking his head. Froth fell from his moustache. "Do you mind if I sit with ya, my name's Buckie."

"By all means, sir. I don't suppose you happen to know anything that may be of interest?" Ernie jumped up. "Oh I'm sorry, how rude of me. I'm Ernie." He offered up his hand.

The two men shook and sat down at the table.

"The only thing I know is it's 'orrible times we live in nowadays," Buckie said, taking another swig of his ale.

"Yes, I'm afraid it is. Can I ask, did you know the woman?" Ernie said.

"Think ev'ryone knew Martha, although some liked to call her Emma. She was always wiv her mate, Old Pearly," Buckie said, smiling, obviously pleased that he could at least think of some details on the spot.

As he talked Ernie scribbled down some more notes.

"Right. Emma. Mmm-huh. Got it. And, you said Old Pearly. On second thoughts, it's probably better if I just leave the names blank until the police identify the victim for definite," Ernie said.

"I can't think that's gonna 'appen any time soon. You already know more than the old bluebottles do," Buckie said.

Ernie shook his head. It was hopeless. "Maybe I should just rustle up a report on the Queen's grandson," Ernie said, laughing grimly to himself. "In the grime of Whitechapel a woman lays brutally slain, and poor little old Prince Albert Victor has hurt his foot — Oh, how very newsworthy."

THIRTY-ONE

The screams began around half-past-eight. It was late August and a heavy storm was brewing — rain, coming straight down from marbled-grey skies. Adding to the misery and drama of the event that was unfolding at the south quay of the London docks, lightning struck. It leapt vigorously out of the dappled sky, followed only seconds later by a loud clap of violent thunder.

Away from the gathering crowd smoke could be seen steadily leaking through a cracked window from one of the large warehouses. It filled the air with a heavy black smut, only adding to the *London particular*. Huge blue and yellow tinged flames were billowing out from the first floor. The night sky lit up, the whole of Shadwell was aglow. The warehouse was well known for its prohibited medicinal contents; it held crates of spirits such as gin and brandy. The fire was toasting itself, literally — and feeding.

Feeding. Jakob was hungry, feeling weak. He needed blood. He needed blood now, tonight. Knowing Jack, he would revel in the idea that innocent people may be burning to death, caught up in the flames, and Jakob expected he would soon enough venture down to the docks to sniff out the burning flesh, gleeful in the anticipation of the death toll to follow.

Straightening his musty uniform Jakob followed the screams southwards and made his way toward the docks. After his cowardly actions back in Seasalter when he had ran . . . He shook off the morbid thought. Tonight, Jakob decided, he may be able to help. He ran towards the flames.

The closer Jakob got to the river area the more people there were. Gathering in huge crowds, watching the awesome sight as the fire raged through the dock, they were hindering the local emergency services' attempts at extinguishing the fire. He shouted at people to move, to grab a pail, anything. The ignorant and uncaring mob only looked at him bemused. It did not take Jakob long to realise he was only shouting to himself. A fiery red glow now feathered the sky. Fire Brigade steamers from all over London were turning up.

Jakob really wanted to help and get stuck in. Fire had been his friend in his younger 'life'. His father had taught him to love it, to trust it, to take a piece of metal and let the flames deliberately caress it — decide in its ancient wisdom how to mould it. It was different for Jakob now, fire was fire and if he was caught in it his body would burn up like dry kindling. He recalled the doctor's words: *Thermal decomposition.*

Absolved from what he still considered a moral duty Jakob let the fire brigade do its job. With the rest of the jeering, cretinous crowd he hung back and watched the alcohol-laced building continue to burn.

"Ere, that's gin that's a-burnin' up in that there fire," one old woman crowed.

"You'd know now, wouldn't ya?" a seedy man with a huge beard screeched above the babble.

The crowd erupted in demented laughter.

"That's the stuff . . . It's good for yer soul," another shouted.

"It's a sin."

"It's gin."

"Oh, such a waste."

"Rubbish," exclaimed a younger, and better dressed man. His face was clean shaven. "It's 'old mothers ruin' that, let the damned stuff burn."

"That's blasphemy my good sir," an older fellow chirped.

An argument ensued, exploding into a full blown slanging match.

Jakob turned wanting to be away from the crowd. It was only then that Jakob noticed Jack, dressed all in black, marvelling at the glowing sky and flicking his fingers at the floating embers as they passed his twitching face. As he neared, Jakob heard Jack sniggering away quietly to himself.

"Old mothers ruin, eh? — I'll ruin ya mother for ya. You'll see," he muttered to himself, to his own murderous ears, the only one to appreciate the statement.

Having given up his feeble yet valiant attempt at dousing the flames, Jakob went over to where Jack where stood, mesmerised by the combustive carnage.

"Come on, I need some food," Jakob said to Jack, the orange of the fire glowing its destructive reflection in both of their eyes. "Shall we go?"

"Thought you'd never ask." Jack grinned eagerly.

The East End would be quiet tonight. Taking advantage that the majority of the East End riffraff were likely to be gathered at the docks for some time, cooing at the impressive fire, the two men turned around and walked back towards Commercial Street.

This was to be their second official outing.

Just to be on the safe side, as there were still plenty of people up and about, they decided to go a little further east than they had yet ventured.

On finding their quarry, deep in the dark recesses of Buck's Row, one of the men stepped into the high-arched doorway with the ageing prostitute. In a flash he struck, her face bewildered and beaten. As the blood seeped from her split mouth she struggled in his grasp.

"Fear not my dear, this shouldn't last too long," he said. "Because . . . well, you won't know this of course, but my friend over there, well, he's starvin' hungry."

Still gripping her firmly, he thrust his excited face close to hers. He smiled at her contorted looks and swiftly spun her around. Her eyes widened in terrified realisation as his other arm came up, decisively. The poniard in his hand met her soft flesh, surgically slitting her throat.

She did not feel the incisive blade slice into her, only an odd numbing sensation as it cut deep into her nerves and, deeper still, into her vertebrae. Suspended in her attacker's arms she fixated upon the dirty gutter as her attacker let go of her and she went down, a strange warm feeling at the base of her head.

As shock took her by the hand and began to lead her slowly away from her pinched, hard life to the next, she looked up at the door. *That's one ugly door, spent many a year up against it but never noticed it before — how strange.*

She felt weak, her stricken body cold and tired. Her eyes began closing as small tears of salt fell against her whitening cheeks, gently caressing her to sleep. She could hear movement behind her, together with odd clinking sounds. *Sounds like someone rattling an old tin. Penny for yer foughts?* In her head she could hear herself perfectly, her diction almost flawless. *You see mister; I am a lady after all.*

Asleep now forever, she was dead. But there was still a little more work to be done. Warm blood sprang from the carotid artery in the woman's severed neck, a carmine jet coursing from a charged hose. Avoiding the rich ruby liquid with lithe dexterity the man took the tin and forced it into the flow, catching as much of the glistening red stuff as he could. *It gets better every time.* It delighted him.

Jakob had kept a quiet and vigilant look out in the street. His *vacsora — dinner —* was being freshly prepared while he waited, his doubts now irrelevant. Steadily, he approached the doorway trying to avoid looking down.

Passing the crude tin cup to him, Jack spoke first.

"Here you go".

"Thanks, I'm really hungry," Jakob said softly, and took the tin in his ashen hands.

Carefully, he raised the cup to his livid lips and drank, gulping it all down in one. "It's good. Another," he demanded.

Passing another, Jack, not yet finished with his knife, crouched over his latest 'triumph' and started stabbing at her guts. He cupped his ear and jabbered in a quiet, high-pitched voice. "What was that luv? I can't hear ya. You got a case of the dyspepsies? This should sort it for ya."

183

The body of the woman had ceased to listen but that did not seem to matter to Jack. Appalled at the sight that lay before him Jakob glared at his accomplice.

"Leave her alone you animal, she's dead," he said. *Mocsok diszn — Filthy pig.*

Standing up, the man with the knife pulled back his reddened blade and wiped it clean on his sleeve. He smiled wryly at his friend. *We're a match made in heaven, a partnership from Hell.* He was going to enjoy this — thoroughly.

Minutes later the two men stepped back out into the main thoroughfare. The smaller man paused and sniffed at the foul air. Without hurrying, they ventured back up the street, gradually garnished by the thick swirling smog around them. Before long they were fully consumed in its vast maw.

Gone.

The woman was left, sprawled, leaking in the gutter. Even in death the hapless victim was in the same position as she had lived and worked all her life — lying on her back.

As they skulked off, little did anyone know that the Prince of Darkness himself had taken up hammer and chisel to steadily record the horrors of London, etching them onto the eternal crimson pages of history — one word, and one victim, at a time — and at this Prince's will, the killing would continue.

THIRTY-TWO

The fire at the docks had not been much of a success. Rather, it had been a huge spectacle. Lurid flames had raged brighter and higher than most of the onlookers had ever seen in their drab lives, keeping them all entertained well into the small hours. It had kept them warm, too. But nobody had been killed.

In the centre of a huge threadbare room sat a woman, face to face, consoling the brooding man who sat opposite, motionless. His precise chin rested in his great hands, he looked glum.

The epicene woman looked on with doleful eyes. In brilliant imperial robes her long flowing hair draped forward covering her face, a childlike mischievous grin poked through the breach of her coarse hair.

Breaking the silence her expression changed as she opened her mouth to speak. "Come now Antonas, it truly was an awesome sight. A pleasure to behold."

Antonas stayed silent. Unmoved, he sat completely still, a grotesque version of Rodin's (started, yet still to be completed) Thinker.

Pura spoke again. "I don't want to state the obvious . . . but it really was impressive. It burned for hours, beamed into the night sky until the morning. We'll let them know we're not going away."

No answer came.

"I'm only trying to help. Let us concentrate on a different triumph then, shall we?" Pura asked.

"What are you talking about woman?" the grizzled Antonas answered.

"Well," she said, getting up and gently patting his back. "If it's any consolation, it appears our potential partner went out again last night with his friend on another jaunt."

The miserable man suddenly jumped up in excitement. When he had started the fire he had expected at least a few souls to burn — it had not happened. But news of the murder in Buck's Row was at least comforting.

"Yes, yes, but did he actually *do* it?" he asked the woman, anticipation salivating his fine lips.

Staying silent, she looked at him.

"Pura?" he asked again.

"Well . . . Um, that would be a no I'm afraid," she answered, averting her eyes.

He scowled and his nose flared as he clamped his lips in rage. Calmly, he spoke. "That's just it, don't you see? I'm not the one who should be afraid, now am I Pura?"

She couldn't look at him.

Antonas continued. "But you will be if he doesn't take to it soon. You, my dear, will find yourself surplus to requirements. I shall be forced to replace you and, I guarantee, you won't like what I have in store for you."

Pura bit hard on her lip. "I'm sorry, my master, but he is near, I know it. I didn't allow his creation for nothing."

THIRTY-THREE

It had been yet another dull day. Oppressive grey clouds masked any sunlight that may have tried to shine down on the desolate grey city.

It suited Jakob's mood.

As he travelled further north-east, the grim huddle of afflicted crowds began to thin. Jakob sank both hands deep into his pockets as he strolled solemnly up and away from the East End drear, and the sorry souls trapped inside. Miniscule parts of his humanity gnawed away at him. Like a hungry dog with an old bone he chewed over what he had done.

Why am I this thing, this beast? Was he paying for some atrocious act committed by his home peoples years ago? No, he did not believe in karma. He believed in action. His latest actions were the reason he was now here.

He must have walked for at least an hour. Jakob was finally at his destination. Approaching the worn and twisted cemetery gate Jakob pushed his way through and with a squeal of dry hinges he stepped through, standing silently on the other side.

Virtually out in the countryside, the City of London Cemetery in Little Ilford was made up entirely of old farm land.

Some thirty years ago a man named William J. Haywood had laid out the large site in an attempt to provide alternative burial grounds to the ever overflowing graveyards and church grounds of London. Conveniently, it met the heavy demand of corpses from the same place where Jakob had just come from. Ignoring the few murders each year, the cruel East End area delivered something like one in five babies and young children to the graveyards of London — all dead, thanks to unsanitary conditions that caused debilitating diseases like rickets, tuberculosis and bronchitis — before reaching the grand old age of five.

From where Jakob stood, he let his eyes patrol the area. Dozens of stones and memorials filled his view. Then he spotted what he had come to see. He set off towards it.

In the half-light, headstones bulged outwards and upwards around him, a steady stream of petrified soldiers all standing 'at ease'. Each one an eternal resting place for the sorry soul who occupied it. Jakob realised that rest was something he had since been denied.

His footsteps fell silent as he stepped onto grass and moved between the ossified 'comrades' of the headstones, some leaning half-wounded and staggering backwards, some semi-fallen and tumbling forwards. Strange Victorian symbols embellished the graves. At the foot of one a carved laurel wreath hovered above a small face, as if clawing its way out of the grave. He shook his head. *I know how you feel.* Upon another he spotted a circle — the sign of eternity. He frowned.

Early autumn leaves littered the ground, dappling the graveyard in bright sorrel and sienna. The grass fought its way through an ever-thickening cover of decay. Damp air engulfed

Jakob as he approached a freshly dug pile of soil, kicking up leaves with his boots as he went. From the broken earth below him the stark stench of death filled his vampire nostrils.

He remembered his days feeling sick from his voyage across the channel all those years ago, when he was as mortal as the sorry soul that now lay inanimate and slowly rotting beneath his feet. She was dead so that he could feed, he and Jack had absorbed the very liquid that gave her life.

What have I become? As dusk began its daily ritual of veiling the remaining light of the day, Jakob hung his head in shame.

Quietly, he stood for some time, his own respectful moment of silence.

"You know, the mourners came out in their droves," a female voice said from behind him. "She must have been quite popular."

Almost startled, Jakob turned to receive his unannounced and unwanted guest. Strange, with all the dry leaves on the ground, he had not heard anyone approach. He looked up at her to see if he recognised the intruder. She was curiously attractive with a blank countenance, her face quite asexual, neither male nor female. Only her voice and long dark hair gave her up as being a woman.

"Popular enough I suppose. She obviously had a great many friends," Jakob answered, angry with himself, and at the intrusion.

"More like a great many paying customers," the newcomer teased, standing like a teapot, with one arm on her thin waist she waved her spout hand about dismissively.

"It doesn't matter what she did in this life, she was still a human being," Jakob said as he took a threatening step towards her.

"You killed her," she said, prosaically.

Jakob said nothing. It did not matter that Jack had been the actual killer; Jakob had initiated the whole thing. Remnants of guilt chewed away at Jakob just as the worms, the maggots, were eating away at his latest victim.

She taunted him. "But, you see Jakob, that's the thing isn't it? You're not human anymore are you?" Pura did not like to make herself known to too many people but Antonas had been serious with his threats. She now had no choice but to try first-hand.

"Ah, so you must be the one who held Jack against his wishes," Jakob said, trying to figure out who, or what, she was.

"Oh no, that was Mary. And yes, before you ask, she is the other vampire."

"Who are you then?" he asked, staring blankly at her.

"I'm . . . No, let's just say I'm something entirely different."

"What do you want?" Jakob's pursed lips spat at her.

"I want what you want, Jakob. I want you to kill for the thing you need most — blood. Let the killer inside you loose. You see, the act of killing, it really is very, very simple. Your friend Jack has shown you just how easy it can be. And how enjoyable."

Jakob had already heard enough. He turned to leave the strange woman at the graveside, started walking away.

"How many years has it been now Jakob?"

He paused, stopping in his tracks.

"Whether you like it or not Jakob, you will become what you are — a true vampire. And when that finally happens, you'll be needing us," she said softly, her quiet voice carrying up the path and entering his ears as if she was standing right next to him.

He carried on walking as Pura called out to him again.

"Oh and Jakob, I nearly forgot. Keep a look out for the new inspector. He's particularly good at his job. You don't want him catching you before you get the chance to kill again."

Jakob turned, ready to confront the woman, but she was gone. Instead, all he saw was the pile of fresh soil. Without wanting to be reminded, he charged away.

THIRTY-FOUR

Jakob and Jack's second outing together had soon generated a frenzied reaction from the general public and the police alike. As the stranger in the graveyard had told him, the death of this woman had even drawn special interest from Scotland Yard, and as such an Inspector First-Class had been drafted in to Whitechapel.

By now it was early September and, donning his blue uniform again, Jakob decided to visit H-Division, the police station on Commercial Street, so he could 'inspect' the inspector for himself — after all, Jakob's strange visitor in the cemetery had spoken so highly of him.

Jakob hesitated outside the police station for a moment. He did not want to attract attention so he gripped the front of his jacket, pulled it straight and headed inside. He walked past a couple of other officers who ignored him. Jakob then walked around freely, quietly impressed with Doctor Phillips' insight. He spotted the inspector immediately.

Impeccably dressed, the inspector looked more like a chief banker or high-stakes investor, his hazel eyes burning through everything that he laid them on, suspicion attached to even the slightest action. He was a big burly figure of a man which made it easy for Jakob to keep his eye on him. Jakob watched him for a few minutes before leaving as briskly as he had come in.

Inspector First-Class Frederick Abberline's wealth of knowledge of the immediate East End area, its hopeless catacombs of repulsion and misery, made him an important member of the investigation team. Abberline knew firsthand the depths of crime, the poverty and hunger of the place, was only too aware that more than one in fifteen women prostituted themselves for a measly penny or two just so they could eat and get some shelter for the night. It was Inspector Abberline's new investigation team who had been given the job of looking into what was becoming known in a series of killings as the Whitechapel murders.

They were not murders, Jakob appeased himself. It was a simple act of survival. Nobody batted an eyelid at the guile of the carnivorous and wily stoat who would openly stomp and parade through a field of rabbits, brashly selecting a weaker specimen for its latest meal. That was nature.

The newspaper press, forever hungry themselves, were not going to miss the biggest scoop of the decade and as such were having a field day. In various reports the culprit was being branded a madman, a butcher, a maniac, a doctor, a deranged surgeon even. Jakob could personally vouch for the mad part, he had seen Jack in action, had witnessed his mindless slicing of human flesh.

As brash and manipulative as the press were Jakob knew that these so-called sensationalist reporters would have been only too happy to be shipped off to the nearest lunatic asylum and locked in a small windowless room had they known the real truth. Inside, they would be safe in their tiny cells while a killer and a vampire roamed the East End — a vampire who needed his regular helping of human black-cherry nostrum.

To add insult to injury, curious passers-by were now turning up at all times of the day to visit the two 'murder' sites, no doubt wanting to vicariously live out the victims' last moments while their own sickened eyes searched for tell-tale gore stains in a gruesome version of hide and seek.

Luckily for Jack and Jakob, the perpetrators of these evil acts, the police had not turned up any clues whatsoever. Even so, they would still have to be careful, especially with the new and diligent inspector on the scene.

In his new lusting for blood, in his cloak-and-dagger activities, Jakob had not realised what else was going on right under his nose. Something that would bring the new inspector, indirectly, right to his door.

THIRTY-FIVE

Jakob was dead, or undead, and his hair had long ago stopped growing. In all that time though he had never really done anything with it and it was now a bit of a mess. Wanting to appear the 'part' in his acquired blue police uniform, he had asked Ludwig to finally cut his hair.

The day had been quiet for them both so Ludwig decided to close up early and make a start on his friend and colleague. Ludwig beckoned for Jakob to sit in the brown chair. It was a warm evening so Jakob removed his shirt, revealing his strong upper body, lithe and ashen. Lowering himself into the chair Jakob felt unnecessarily vulnerable as Ludwig wrapped a towel around his frame. It would be easier to brush the hair off later, he decided. *It's not like it's going to make me itch.*

Approaching Jakob with the same vigour and professionalism that he approached all of his customers, Ludwig set to work. Jakob watched anxiously as the Pole reached for his scissors and started cutting. Comfortable with the sharp instrument in his hand, Ludwig moved deftly and efficiently around Jakob's head.

Since he had turned, Jakob did not like to look at his pale, wan face in the mirror. He closed his eyes.

Standing still, creating his art as his fingers busied themselves, Ludwig moved a step at a time and continued. His fluid movements making light work of the job.

Still behind him, Jakob had not noticed the leech that Ludwig had dropped onto his back, the parasite instantly sucking at Jakob's blood; the only action it knew. His vampire body, now a walking monument in honour to the Grim Reaper, had no live nerve endings and so he had not felt a thing.

Admiring his work when he was finished with the hair cut, Ludwig saw the gorged black · worm-like creature and plucked it from Jakob's skin, careful not to be seen.

Ludwig joked and pointed to Jakob's head in the mirror.

"Almost makes you look good, my friend," he laughed as he laid down his tools. Taking the leech, Ludwig popped it into his pocket.

"Thanks Ludwig," Jakob said as he turned his head to the left and then to the right, admiring the style.

Ludwig walked to his door; a PRIVATE sign in small bold letters decorated the front. As he stepped through he turned and spoke to Jakob. "Please, Jakob, just sweep and clean salon in exchange . . . I must go out. Good night."

Much later that night, in the exclusivity of his own lodgings, sitting alone by candlelight behind the small barber shop, a flickering figure of a man carefully lifted a singular dead parasite up to the acute needle point. Sticking the needle point into the wizened body of the leech, the figure began slowly and steadily drawing the syringe back, turning the tiny glass vial a deep rufescent.

Removing the needle, he threw the shrivelled leech into the waste bin and held up the strange 'poison' in the diminishing light of the candle. Happy with his work, his large moustache shifted gently upwards around the corners of his mouth as he moved towards his bed. He needed a good rest.

A loud rap drummed on the front door. It was early in the morning and the workforce of the East End buzzed around the grey streets in search of new earnings.

The knocking continued.

An internal door clicked open, and then creaked on its hinges as the man appeared. Bare and bony feet trudged sleepily across the shop floor. Ludwig opened the misty-glassed door, yawning as he went.

Outside, waiting patiently on the doorstep, the smartly dressed man in front of him was rather portly with a confident face that housed large sideburns. Hidden in-between a makeshift portico of police blue, two constables stood either side, flanking him.

"Ludwig Schloski?" the door-knocker barked.

"Er . . . yes, that is I . . . Who are you?" Ludwig evinced a smile and wiped his sleeve across his eyes.

"I am Detective Inspector Abberline of the CID. I'd like you to come with me."

As the hairdresser clothed himself in the back of the shop the three policemen waited patiently in the main shop. None of them saw Jakob returning from his nightly excursions and wait patiently out of view on the far side of the street. None of them, either, saw the sleepy man known as Ludwig Schloski slip the reddened glass vile deep into his pocket.

The disconsolate room back at the police station was sombre but clean, a single table commandeered the little space, a chair on either side. The two men sat, each looking the worse for wear after a long day of questions and interrogation.

The inspector had received reports of many witnesses claiming to have seen a man abusing young women in Commercial Road and the surrounding areas. A carbon copy of that described man sat opposite him now, carelessly leaning back on the wooden chair.

It was true, the ill-natured Pole, Ludwig, did have certain misogynous tendencies and had treated some women badly, even hitting them on occasion, but he had not killed anyone — at least not yet. He would need his poison for that.

"Do you mind if I stand?" Ludwig asked.

"Go ahead, it's been a long day," answered the inspector, raising his hands in mockery.

The station was quiet, a necropolis of so-called law enforcement. Every spare man on the force was out patrolling the area, eagerly searching for a killer, together with a potential promotion. More men were needed. The frightful murders had opened up an imaginary door where the low-life of the East End was mixing with the rich and influential — the two ends of the moral spectrum meeting somewhere in the middle. Public empathy was rife; it was good for the area, embarrassing the authorities by highlighting the squalor.

Public outcry was calling for a drastic change with improvements to the area, not just from the entangled burrows of Whitechapel but from high society itself. It was soon to see mourners lining the streets in sympathy for the miscreants who had been declined of their taking another breath — their throats, and abdomens, violently opened up.

Ludwig knew the station would be deserted and so took his chance now. He had been wrongly accused of being the murderer. So he had been out, treated a few of the opposite sex with disdain and perhaps beat on one or two of them, but kill? — no, the authorities would have to wait a few more years for that, until he had perfected his experimental toxicants.

Ludwig wondered whether the diseased blood that he had harvested from his friend, Jakob, would infect another — after all, there was something inscrutably wrong with someone who needed to drink blood to survive. *Who knows what could happen?* Perhaps it was not too late for Ludwig to get himself out of this mess.

It might be too late for Abberline, though.

Slowly, the suspected man inched his way around the table, inching towards the tired inspector. Reaching into his pockets Ludwig's fingers found what he wanted.

Abberline was tired. Rubbing his face with his hands, the inspector never saw Ludwig coming at him until it was too late. As he tried to defend himself, he stood, feeling the sharp needle point stab deep into his neck.

He squirmed. *Jesus.*

The wounded inspector grabbed at his throat as the needle was wrenched out again from inflamed flesh and he reeled. He could not quite grasp the fact that he had been caught unaware. *Unprofessional.* In twenty-five years of duty, Inspector Abberline had never even sustained an injury.

That had all now changed.

Pain flooded the inspector's body before he had time to call out, in vain, to an empty and desolate police station. The last thing Inspector Abberline saw before passing out was the man named Ludwig carefully putting away his emptied syringe.

The still-standing Polish suspect watched as the inspector fell. He was astonished, euphoric almost, at the rapid reaction to the tainted blood. *It was potent stuff.* Ludwig knew Jakob had warned him that it could be dangerous to others but this was impressive. *Really impressive.*

Reaching down to the floored inspector Ludwig felt around for a pulse. *Has it killed him?* If the inspector was still breathing it was very slight, barely discernible. Ludwig stood up, casually approached the door, opened it, and walked quite calmly out of the unoccupied police station, discharging himself — a free man.

THIRTY-SIX

Antonas was grinning. *So this Ludwig has a fascination with toxicants, does he?*

Pura herself had reported the information to Antonas as he sat in quiet reflection. He would have to keep a close eye on this one. This one, the curious Pole, could most likely be exploited by Uri and his lot if Antonas was not careful. *Maybe, maybe not.* It all depended on whether or not the Pole *would* eventually turn to killing for real and more so, just *who* he might kill when he did. It would be no good killing innocent people, that would only be defeating the object. *Like aiding and abetting.*

It was not that Antonas liked innocent people — he did not really like anybody for that matter — it was just that they were all simply a means to an end, a necessity as it were. It was always better if he could, as he put it: "Recruit the nastier ones — the more deranged, shall we say."

Antonas had his 'trusted few' around him, his devout and obedient acolytes. The rest, well, the rest could just rot in Hell for all he cared. However, if the Pole was going to kill innocents then Pura or one of the others would have to step up and take him in.

"Hmm. Let us just see what happens and not get ahead of ourselves, shall we?" he said aloud.

THIRTY-SEVEN

She had had enough of the big city; the mess, the stink. With so many people milling about the East End in great big packs it made it easy for her to fit in and mill about, unhindered and unnoticed, but also made it difficult for a female vampire to select her next victim. Safety in numbers, that was the saying — and at the moment it was proving to be true.

Frustrated as she was at her current situation she was still determined that she was not going to resort to drinking the blood of the lousy diseased rats that infested the place. No, only the blood of humans would suffice for her palate.

Returning late, famished, to her old den hidden in the depths of the docks, she spotted someone, or more importantly, someone alone, in the murkiness. Edging closer to the unsuspecting mortal body she saw it was a lady, rather tall, and clad in fine attire. The vampire eyed her. *Certainly better dressed than most around here.*

Staying well back in the shadows the vampire watched the well-dressed lady for some time. *What is she doing?* Something did not feel right. Way out here, alone, the woman was acting odd, most likely she was drunk, swaying on the shingle ground next to the deep water of the Thames. With a hungry vampire nearby the refined lady was in deeper water than she knew. *But why such a lady down here? On her own?* No matter, the woman was here, alone, and no self-respecting — and hungry — vampire was going to let such an easy meal get away, especially when so far away from prying eyes.

Seizing her chance, and her club, the smaller woman moved her vampire body and hands rapidly. She knew speed and surprise was the trick — together with a cold, hard blunt tool. Raising the stout wooden mace a whoosh came out of nowhere and in the still darkness she pummelled the back of the taller woman's head. A thud and a rattle upon the loose stones followed and the unknowing victim dropped down next to the used club.

Then silence. A quick kill.

Bending down, the vampire removed a small pocket knife that she always carried. It came in useful for a petite woman. She sliced into the dead woman's crooked neck, a fine neck that would never again support her bludgeoned, caved-in head. Leaning in closer still she crouched and put her lips over the warm perfumed flesh. She sucked at the newly created slit.

Fresh. Warm.

Good.

She let the blood flow through her, invigorating her in the darkness. She continued sucking. In her haste and desire for food the vampire had not heard the man stumble up the road and stop directly behind her.

"What . . . you . . . doing?" the man struggled to say through pursed blue lips.

Oh no. Caught in the act. She had to think quickly now or she was done for. Frantically, she wiped at her crimson lips,

204

smearing red down her chin. "I . . . I've just found this woman, I think she's hurt . . . or worse," she lied.

The man stopped in front of her, clutching at his neck. He stared at her.

She looked up at him. His clothes were creased, dusty, and he was shaking. His pale face seemed charitable, kind, yet his eyes relayed something far more . . . sinister. He had the look of someone who cared and yet hated at the same time. But there was something familiar about him. She felt like she should know who the wobbly man was; she was just not quite sure why at the moment.

He released his neck to rub at his chest. Coughing and wheezing, he was clearly finding it difficult to breathe. *Is he sick?* He stepped nearer. Up close now, in the gloom of the night, she could see his wan complexion. He was terribly pale. *Wait a minute.* She looked closer, then realised she did know his face, had definitely seen him before. Her senses pricked. *He's the new inspector and . . . he's now a vampire.*

Surprised at her deductions the vampire watched him from where she squatted as he tried to compose himself for a moment.

Abberline had awoken, or re-animated, back at the station. All alone, his suspect had vanished. In a blind daze Inspector Abberline did not know what had happened. The vampire blood from the syringe that had been jabbed into him by the suspected Pole had assailed the inspector's system instantly, voraciously. From the moment the leech-contaminated liquid had entered his system it had attacked all his living blood cells, metamorphosing, transmuting him from living being into another of the walking dead.

He had picked himself up, stumbled about in a befuddled daze, before walking out of the station in a lifeless state. Turning south, he just kept on walking, trying to piece together what was happening to him. He spotted faces in the street as he went; villainous faces that he knew — or thought he knew — once, in another lifetime. They all ignored him, leaving him to battle with his mind and traipse on alone. Had he not come across the grisly scene that now lay before him he would have walked straight into the slurry of the Thames.

From the floor she watched him as he staggered over to a wall, resting his back against it. Getting up from the supine figure of the deceased lady the female vampire walked over to the puzzled-looking inspector, emboldened in the knowledge that he would not hurt her.

"Tell me who did this to you," she demanded.

"Sus . . . pect," he said, his breath, or lack of it, fighting against his lips.

She nodded. "It seems Jakob has been a busy boy," she said.

He looked at her. "Don't know . . . any Jakob. It was a . . . Polish man . . . Ludwig," he stated, trying harder this time.

He looked down at the dead body on the shingle and an unusual desire welled up inside him, a craving shook his undead body, the evident metal-tinged aroma of blood arousing him. He needed something, but he was not sure what.

Not Jakob? "Well, I need your help," the female said.

"And I . . . think . . . I need . . . your help," the inspector said.

"Yes, but I need your help first. In return I will help you. You see, you're a vampire now, one of us."

The incomprehension that she had expected to see did not register on his face.

Inspector Frederick George Abberline was no fool. He had not risen through the ranks of the police force as quickly as he had because he was just any old dullard. No, stone cold and calm, he knew it to be true — he was not of the living any more. His senses flushed as the fresh blood pooled about them on the floor, congealing around him, filling his nostrils. The word 'vampire' went through his mind. He ignored it — it meant nothing. He knew only that he *was*, and whatever he could now smell, he knew by instinct alone that he needed it.

He looked down at the dead woman. "This is . . . your mess." It was not a question.

The female vampire in front of him now was silent, slowly shifting on the shingle, so he continued.

"What can I do . . . for you?" he asked his new sister-in-death.

"I'm too small to get rid of the body," she pointed blatantly at the large mass on the ground. "Can you help me dispose of it?"

The inspector stood in the quiet of the riverside for a few moments, deep in thought.

The female vampire watched him. Some of them turned immediately; others — like Jakob — took time. She had a feeling this one, the inspector, would act quickly.

"All right . . . I'll help you. You . . . wait here," he said as he started to walk off, his head clearer now.

She nodded, smiling in the darkness.

Agreeing to help his new vampire colleague, Inspector Abberline had told her to wait where she was while he sorted some things out. He returned in less than an hour with the stuff he needed. It was not long before she had coaxed some blood down him; it was congealing but he would feel the better for it, and he did need the energy. He gasped and sighed as he drank. All these years in his job, protecting the weak and innocent of society, steadfast in his integrity, his new vampire body actually relished it. As it did the idea of hacking a body apart.

In death he would now come alive.

The inspector hastily turned to his new work like a mycobacterial bug took to human lungs. Together, old vampire and newly-turned, they dismembered the despatched lady. The head was removed first, he had insisted — he did not want dead eyes watching them as they casually chopped her up.

With a louder 'pop' than Abberline would have imagined, the spine separated, the hairy-topped clump coming away clean. He then started on the legs. The female vampire stood by in awe. Rarely had she seen a newly-turned vampire take to killing and dismembering with such ease and determination.

Throwing the severed caput and loose arms and legs into the readily receiving river the heedful inspector began to meticulously wrap the limbless torso — the leftovers of the lady — in the brown paper that he had fetched earlier. When he was done, a neatly wrapped parcel sat innocently on the ground — a stiff and meaty gift for whoever came across it and decided to pull at the pretty little bow-string.

"Now what?" the female vampire asked, as the inspector picked up the recently-lightened package.

"I've got . . . the perfect hiding place. Scotland Yard basement — no one will ever look there," he said and made off up the street again.

THIRTY-EIGHT

The protector of life, unremitting in bringing the criminal element to justice, he upheld the law and sought the truth. And had done so — always. At least he had done so for the last quarter of a century. The inspector had now been reborn. As a vampire all that was behind him.

The few days that had passed since the Polish barber had stuck him had been a little difficult, he had to admit. But with all his powers of deduction he still could not figure out what had happened, and why, only what his new hench-woman had told him *had* to be the truth.

He supposed in hindsight he had expected the Polish serum to be some kind of sleeping potion or mild poison at worst. Instead of killing him outright though it had immediately terminated his bodily functions and allowed him to walk the earth in the form of an undead Inspector First-Class. First things first — he had to pay someone a visit.

The loud knock on the door startled Jakob. Alone in the shop he did not know whether or not to answer it. Only a few days before, Ludwig had been hauled away by the police, a suspect in the latest murders. Jakob always knew that Ludwig was an odd character — he did not even know if Ludwig was his real name — but since then Ludwig had not returned to the shop.

The banging continued in earnest. *What do I do?* Jakob approached hesitantly and grabbed at the door handle. He threw the lock and started to open the door. He backed off as it came in quicker than he expected, hurriedly followed by an irate and dishevelled looking inspector.

"Where's that bastard Schloski?" the inspector demanded.

Jakob stepped back further. He had not seen Ludwig for days.

"He . . . he's not here," Jakob answered.

Brushing past him the inspector barged his way through the room and headed towards the rear, Ludwig's private lodgings.

"That Polak's got a lot to answer for," he said, kicking at the door.

The feeble lock gave way instantly and the door flew inwards. Without looking, the inspector entered.

The place was bare. Only a few empty bottles, tiny vials, lay on the floorboards next to an old waste-bin and unmade bed.

"Arghh, where is he?" Abberline growled.

Again Jakob answered truthfully. "He's not here. I haven't seen him in days."

Disgusted and angry, Abberline stamped on one of the used vials, tiny glass splinters crackled underfoot. In a screech, the ball of his foot twisted sharply on the wooden floor and he pushed past again, out onto the street, leaving Jakob alone and baffled.

In the privacy of his own home Abberline paced up and down. He was not happy. Not only was Ludwig Schloski nowhere to be found, the inspector had found out he had to re-learn almost everything again — from scratch. *God-damn that Polish pig.*

It was strange to not have to eat regular food, to not have to go to the toilet for his ablutions; to not have to wash (he did not sweat anymore). Above all, he found that although he was not hungry for normal food, he still craved something. Ludwig Schloski's neck — and blood.

The woman vampire, the mysterious Mary as she had introduced herself while they cut up the woman, had helped him understand his new role in the world — that of indiscriminate killing with a shameless and bountiful intake of a certain fresh metallic-tasting liquid.

He needed to get out of the house.

As an undead police detective, the inspector followed several 'possibles' in the small hours of the night, around the thin web of dirty roads and foetid streets of Spitalfields. He sucked in musty air, exercising his lungs as he went, practising his new-found speech. *I'll get you Schloski.*

Turning off from Brick lane in his long Macintosh he spotted a woman-of-the-street leaning against an old rusting set of shutters. She was stout and small, about five-feet only in height with a pallid complexion that showed up against her black skirt. Her brown bodice matched her wavy hair. He looked at her neckerchief; it was white with a discreet red border. *Soon it'll all be red.*

The ageing prostitute looked unwell. Inhaling the stale air, Inspector Abberline could almost smell her diseased mass, he snorted. Stopping when he reached her, the inspector addressed her. He knew what he had to do.

"Mornin' ma'am," he said to her politely.

"Ain't it still the night?" she asked him. "I still gotta make some money for me bed," she said, before adding, "and I need me some new boots."

The inspector looked down at her old laced-up footwear.

"Listen ma'am, I'm . . . sure you've heard that us, the police, are looking for . . . a murderer."

Obviously more startled at the term 'police' than the word 'murderer' the prostitute jumped. "Oh, officer, I'm a good sort really, there'll be no trouble from me."

"No, no, I'm sure, but . . . you see, we need to bring him, this murderer, out into the open."

"You do?" It was a question and a surprised statement.

"Yes ma'am . . . and we need . . . some bait," he implied as he gestured — meaning her. "We have reason to believe he may be in the area tonight."

"Oh my, those poor women what were killed," she warbled, evidently a little scared herself now.

"We need someone like you . . . to help us," he carried on. "Will you?"

Hearing somebody approaching from the other side of the street the inspector kept his composure. With his back to the woman as she passed by the inspector dug his hands deep into his coat pockets and drew his shoulders up. He was glad he had stuck his deerstalker hat on. Listening through padded ear-flaps he heard the woman scurry on past and leave the two of them alone again.

On impulse the stout whore said she would indeed help the police. "Yes."

Taking her lightly by the arm the Inspector led his 'bait' down a corridor, into the secluded yard to the rear of number twenty-nine, stopping near a solid but tired-looking grey-brown fence. The Inspector knew time was of the essence. Immediately he struck. Grabbing at the woman he brought out his thin blade, pushed it forward to her throat and swiped. Her neck opened up.

In a stupor, the ageing prostitute flailed her arms forward at him. The so-called inspector grabbed at her, forcing her arms down and away. She tried to call out. A gurgle of blood and expelled air leaked from her severed trachea. *What's our Johnny to do now?* She thought of her crippled son as together she and the grappling inspector stumbled into the fence. She felt herself go light, light as a feather, and then thought sadly of her daughter. *Look Emily Ruth, I'm floating. I'll be with you soon baby.*

Her head crashed to the ground.

With no other choice the inspector let her drop to the paved floor. *I'm sorry you unwitting creature, but I must. I need more. I need blood.* He looked down at the body, her tongue almost protruding, almost sticking out at him in defiance. Crouching down next to her and mindful of his clothing being stained by any evidence he stayed clear of the blood as it spouted forth. He bent further and started lapping at the increasing circle of arterial flow that was steadily flooding the paving.

Out of the dark someone else stepped into the yard. Thinking he was done for the inspector scrambled to his feet, his guard up, ready to run. He stopped, recognising the small female vampire — it was Mary.

"Do you mind if I invite myself in for supper?" she asked, her eyes wide at the sight of the fresh puddle of blood.

Relieved, he nodded.

"Help yourself," he said as he closed his eyes and blindly stabbed the corpse.

"I need to make it look like the Whitechapel murderer has done this."

"Clever," she acknowledged.

Snatching the knife from his fist, she said to him. "Come here, let me do that for you. You had all the fun last time. It's gotta look convincing and, besides, you can drink the blood while I work. You need it more than I do."

Absentmindedly, she attacked the lower body of the dead wench, scything her way through soft dermis and muscle. With both hands she reached deep inside the cavity she had created, pulling at the intestines, freeing them of their visceral attachments, and held the warm entrails to her feeding mouth before discarding them on the cadaver's shoulder.

She continued cutting, ripping, while Abberline drank.

THIRTY-NINE

The early morning sky was leaden and thick. Jakob had heard from excited and rabid mouths on the streets that there had been yet another killing. Another prostitute was dead. In Spitalfields this time. Jakob had only just left Jack back at his house so he knew it was not him, definitely not this time.

Jack had been acting odd for the past few days, fidgety. He had told Jakob how it was he who had killed his own mother and had never been caught. Knowing Jack for his over-the-top and overzealous hyperbole Jakob was sceptical at first, thinking it was another of his lethal fantasies but as the story evolved his conviction grew and Jakob knew it to be, most probably, true. *Barbarism begins at home, it seems.*

By the time Jakob arrived at the police station back on Leman Street he had made up his mind. He entered and was immediately met by the odd-looking inspector. The same man that Jakob had observed before now looked exceedingly ill. With no time for any formalities the inspector informed him that the two of them were to go out together to look into a fresh lead. Perhaps afterwards they were to join the other men taking part in a new house-to-house search of the immediate area surrounding the murder scene.

The inspector's plan from Hanbury Street had worked. Extra men had been drafted into the East End to search for a crazed killer, making a total of around eight-thousand Bobbies on the beat. After all, he needed to catch the killer and cover his own trail in doing so. Surely anyone would do, however tenuously linked to the murders.

Jakob wished he had not put on his uniform that morning. There were too many people to take statements from and therefore a lot of work to be done.

The concourses and streets were buzzing with news of the murders, an aura of death hung balefully in the grey air. As the two of them walked through the crowds, all around them was hysteria, a society on the brink of panic. It seemed everyone and anyone was being blamed for the latest atrocity.

Men and women, kids even, were all abusing and accusing each other. It did not matter to the masses, the person would be marked prime-suspect-number-one purely if they looked a bit different, had another religion, whether they acted in a certain manner, wore the wrong clothes or were in the employ a slightly dubious yet completely legitimate line of work.

Walking side by side, Jakob and the inspector turned down a quiet thoroughfare and away from the barking crowds. At last there was some peace.

Turning to Jakob, it was the inspector who spoke first.

"You know, you look decidedly familiar. What's your name, Sergeant?"

Since leaving the station Jakob had been reticent, apprehensive and was dreading any attempt at conversation made by 'his superior'. He now had to think fast. Looking up at the heavy grey clouds Jakob said the first thing that came into his long blunted head.

"Thick, sir," he answered as best he could, his police etiquette not quite up to scratch.

"Well, Sergeant, you and I have a job to do. We've information on a suspect who resides right here in the East End. It's our job to arrest him. He's a bit of a nasty chap by all accounts, so we'd better be careful once we get there. Firstly though, we'll have to survive getting through this rat's nest, eh?"

"Yes, sir," Jakob answered.

Relieved that he was not the suspect, Jakob — or PC 49889 as he was in his present attire — followed the inspector out through the next alley and into a dark huddle of sleazy streets, lined with barely habitable lodging houses. As creepy and dangerous at is was in this part of town the two policemen met no resistance. They headed north-east.

Obviously the inspector suspected the wrong man — they had turned and were heading away from Jack's home. Jakob was somewhat disappointed; it would have been the perfect opportunity to hand responsibility for his actions over to the dutiful inspector and his minions.

Jakob harboured too much guilt over the killings that he and Jack had done and wanted it to stop. *What better way?* If the inspector *did* suspect Jack then he would soon be stopped and Jakob could carry on with his undead life. Instead they carried on.

"If this is the man we want then I'll rid this parasite from society," Inspector Abberline stated, an icy vehemence rising in his voice.

"Yes. Of course, sir," Jakob said, agreeing with the inspector. "But shouldn't we ascertain that fact first sir?"

Frederick Abberline, Inspector First-Class and vampire anew, turned his head and glared at his new colleague. He looked deep into Jakob's eyes.

"Don't be telling me my job, young Sergeant," he snapped with bared teeth. "If I choose, I'll rip him a new hole for his backside and tie the noose around his neck personally, just so I can watch him shit himself. You mark my words."

What is with the inspector? Surely this was not the same man Jakob had seen the other day. He had heard from plenty of others back at the station that the inspector was a gentleman who in his youth was a clockmaker — a line of work that required a gentle skill and quiet patience, not brute aggression.

"I'm sorry sir but I meant . . . erm, you only *suspect* this man of being the culprit?"

"Well, yes, of course man, it's called police work, Sergeant," Abberline added, rather blandly. "Let us just get there first and make a simple arrest, shall we?"

Jakob paused, staying silent, unknowing of what to say next. In the end he decided to simply observe the inspector, to follow in thought. *He's only human. Perhaps he got out the wrong side of his bed this morning?*

Mutely, they continued up the street.

They were not far from the old Bell Foundry when the inspector abruptly stopped outside a small house. He started rapping violently on the stained wooden door. After a few minutes of incessant bashing, the door creaked open and Abberline kicked at the base, wrenching it back on its hinges.

The broad-set man that stood before them was small and stocky. He rubbed at his dark hair in nervous panic as his eyes frowned in either surprise or fright. Or both.

In seconds, the inspector had hold of the terrified man and began dragging him outside. It was then that Jakob realised he recognised the man, remembered seeing him when he had met Ludwig at a club some weeks ago. Jakob had even spoken to the man briefly and said hello. The man, like Ludwig, was Polish.

"Ere, 'e's got the murderer," a voice screeched from further up the street.

"Come quick, the police, they've got 'im. There's a nubbing to be 'ad."

Resident wagging ears all turned on hearing the latest and immediate 'news'; people started seeping out of the crumbling brickwork and filthy cracks, gathering from nowhere to fill the thoroughfare. Seeing the inspector hauling out what appeared to be a completely credible candidate for a murder suspect, it was not long before the bottle-headed crowds were baying for blood.

"You're coming with us Pizer, you and that old apron of yours," Abberline shouted above the commotion that was steadily building up on the streets.

More heads appeared as the crowd grew, curious, angry, and came towards them.

"You, Sergeant, keep these wolves away from him — at least, for now. He's ours."

Pushing his way through malodorous bodies with ragged arms, Jakob started up the street again, away from the growing crowd. Abberline followed closely, hauling the frightened Polish suspect along behind him.

The impatient crowd was becoming restless; they were convinced the man being dragged away in the arms of the law was indeed the killer, the evil slayer of prostitutes that had cursed their 'Chapel.

Winging from the hoard, a stone flew, low and hard, catching the suspect in the cheek. Pizer yelped at the surprise and the obvious sting of pain that followed. The cut on the man's face instantly opened up and blood ran from his flesh.

Abberline turned to see what the cry was about, and stopped. Eyeing the blood, he wanted it. But the situation did not allow it. The masses were already after the suspect, a man who had not even been tried, a man who in all likelihood was not the killer anyway. In their small and simple minds it did not matter, the baying crowd still wanted to lynch him, to blame somebody. Quick justice. How differently they would feel if the inspector revealed his new true self and began licking at the side of the wounded man's face.

Jakob looked on. The inspector's wide eyes bulged from his face, burning a deep red, his gaze fixed.

Perturbed, Jakob screamed at the crowd; he knew the man was innocent. "Stay back everyone. This man is entitled to a fair trial. And if I find out who threw that stone one of you will be coming with us to the station as well."

Jakob was met by loud jeering from the angry mob. The people of the East End were demanding an answer, an answer in the form of on-the-spot capital punishment. Discipline, as well as intelligence, had departed from here long ago. Jakob looked toward the inspector again. Putting himself between the herd and the suspect, Abberline had now composed himself, the blank stare gone, and was again performing his daily duty.

Tension followed the three of them like a bizarre street polka — as they stepped, the beastly hoards stepped with them.

Approaching the police station the crowds slowly dispersed, the realisation that they too may be taken in was now upon them. Two officers stepped out of the police station front door and started up the street towards them.

The two officers led the arrested man back to the station, leaving Jakob and Abberline with the easing crowd of wanna-be hunters.

"What was all that about?" Jakob asked.

"As far as the so-called good people of London are concerned we've just apprehended the Whitechapel murderer."

"You know this man is not the man we want," Jakob said.

The inspector studied Jakob in his uniform for a minute.

"Maybe . . . maybe not. What makes you so sure? You think if the Metropolitan Police can't catch him then you will, on your own, Sergeant? Or perhaps you have the help of those overbearing cods over at the Whitechapel Vigilance Committee?"

FORTY

"All those in favour of Mr George Akin Lusk in becoming the appointed Chairman of this, the Whitechapel Vigilance Committee, please say aye."

A loud chorus of ayes echoed around the stale, moth-eaten and smoked-filled room. Mr Lusk, builder and decorator, had been granted power initially by his lodge in 1882, so the outcome of this position was predetermined, simply a matter of pomp and circumstance.

Lusk liked the acronym: W.V.C. He laughed inwardly, sardonically. *More like Witches & Vampires Condemned.* Stepping down from his appointment to spatting applause he analysed the room, scanning each of the members present.

The Whitechapel Vigilance Committee had been set up to aid the search of the Whitechapel killer. A murderer was still on the loose — the police had no clues whatsoever and needed all the help they could get. Volunteers would patrol the neighbourhood at night, block by block. Amateur detective was now added to the ever-growing list of respective trades that currently included a cigar-manufacturer, a picture frame maker, a tailor, even an actor.

If, by chance, one of the volunteers did manage to seek out the murderer one lonely night, they probably would not know what to do with him but at least they could dress him nicely, light him a cigar, take his picture and border it artistically. They might even adapt a play to his evil character in a local morbid stage-show at the Adelphi, up west.

Trying to win over the humble residents of the East End so that together they could avenge the blood of these unfortunate women was going to be a tough call. The members did not all share the same moral and metaphysical ideals that he did — there could only be one Supreme Being, and it sure as hell was not going to be the kith and kin of Diabolus himself. If anything it was going to be himself, Mr George Lusk Esquire.

Organising patrols and reporting suspicious findings was the easy part but convincing the Vigilance Committee members to decapitate, wholeheartedly and harmoniously, the Devil's own spawn — to consciously kill something as inhuman as a vampire — was going to be an entirely different matter.

Convincing the police and covering up would be straightforward, that was the simple task of the lodge. Of course, George did always have the help of a certain flossy-haired young journalist with a vigorously passionate and imaginative pen — even if he could not use a spade.

FORTY-ONE

Going down the steps out of the gloom Jakob found himself in the pathology examination room at the local police station again.

Hearing his entrance, the man in the starched white coat turned around to greet him.

"Good day, my dear boy," the doctor said.

"Hello, Doctor Phillips," Jakob answered. "How are you keeping?"

"I'm well lad, at least a little more auspicious than any of the discharged souls that end up down here." He gestured towards a greying cadaver. "More to the point, how are you?"

Doctor Phillips was an old fashioned and tacit man — a little odd at times but a welcome friend and aide to Jakob in the harsh city. His broad face and dark curly hair belied his charming, almost wicked sense of humour. He needed to have a certain amount of jocularity in his profession. Being around dead bodies all day not only made a person face their own mortality on a daily basis but would, no doubt, make their view of the world slightly askew. For all the doctor's peculiar attributes, Jakob could not ask for a better friend.

The sight of the woman's dead body made Jakob shut his eyes. *Poor woman.* It was little consolation to him but he knew he was not responsible this time. *I was taught to respect life but I must eat.* He shuddered. Emma had been right all along. Here he was, a fearless vampire, the stuff of legend — undead and un-killable it seemed— yet, in close proximity to where the dead body lay quietly rotting away, Jakob was shivering in fear.

"I need some more," Jakob said.

The blood that his body craved, that his body needed, had to be fresh. A gloopy congealing mess was of little use. Without it Jakob's body would start to degenerate even further, his skin start to peel with the dermis underneath going pulpy — he would literally waste away, disintegrate to dust. He had found also that he could drink the blood cold, just as long as it was not too old.

Without Ludwig, Jakob had been visiting the doctor more and more for his dietary needs. Doctor Phillips was being extremely proactive, experimenting on Jakob's behalf. By using certain chemicals, such as sodium citrate, the doctor was attempting to prevent the blood he stockpiled for Jakob from congealing, making its 'shelf-life' longer.

If needed though, Jakob could go without it for a week or two — at a push. He had found that out the hard way, when the intervals between his feeding had increased by his early refusal at having to kill. Living in the East End of London and having met Doctor Phillips gave Jakob easy access to blood with a degree of a normal life — or as normal as it was ever going to get for him.

His co-conspirator, Jack, was becoming increasingly more withdrawn, obsessed in his crusade of death. Together they had chosen only the desperate ones, would–be victims who were old, destitute or ill. Jakob was already having second thoughts. *I have to tell Jack the killing game is over.* Jakob only hoped Jack would agree to it.

Another matter was the inspector.

Undead life was on the up — Jakob could go out into the daylight and observe the sun's sheer magnificent beauty without exploding into a ball of flame. The episode of the 'stake' in his heart had not ended him either as some of the legends had suggested. He could not let the inspector catch him — not now. He had to stop before it was too late. Jakob cursed himself for letting it get this far.

Doctor Phillips clearly did not know of Jakob's involvement with Jack, only that he was a vampire and, of course, thanks to the good doctor himself, he was now a policeman — albeit not a real one. The doctor was helping him, keeping him nourished. Jakob, in turn, could at least put an end to all the killing.

Jack was getting worse; there was no denying it, he was mad. *Oh God, how many has Jack killed? How many has he killed for me? Why did I ever suggest anything to him? I was desperate — the trick with the leeches wasn't working very well, there just wasn't enough blood to survive on and besides, it's disgusting.*

Just not as disgusting as the evil he and Jack were now perpetrating in the greatest city in the world.

"That is, of course, if you have any blood for me Doc?" Jakob asked.

"No problem young sir, I have some here that I put aside for you a little under half-an-hour ago," the doctor answered before reaching out and handing Jakob the clinical jar.

The guilt that racked Jakob's mind had left him overtly downhearted, looking depressed for a moment so the doctor interjected. "Please help yourself — it's better quality than last time," he said eagerly to Jakob.

Jakob took the jar, shaking his head, wandering what exactly constituted a good quality blood from a bad one — around here most residents suffered from a constant lack of nutrition mixed with too much cheap alcohol. Putting the glass to his lips Jakob reluctantly started to drink the gratifying red liquid.

Doctor Phillips tried to ease the mood and distract Jakob.

"You know, if you do ever . . . What's the word I'm looking for? Die? Pass on? Expire? Can I ask for your gracious permission to allow me to perform an autopsy?" the doctor said. "It would be in the interests of science of course my man, not that I wish anything were to happen to you — you being un . . . er, un-alive as it were." The doctor chuckled to himself.

"Only a madman would want to do that, but I suppose you do fit the bill," Jakob said. "That's if there's anything left of me," he added quickly before taking a final large and needy gulp.

Doctor Phillips looked on curiously like a large cat eyeing a fluttering moth around a light bulb. Jakob could see that the doctor, a man of science, still felt a little uneasy yet he was completely in awe as he observed the vampire's physical needs.

Blood. The stuff of life. A small glob dripped from the corner of Jakob's lips.

"The strangest thing, Jako . . . I mean, er, PC. On the Whitechapel Road, there's been quite a buzz going around, among us medical lot anyway. There's a chap who is half-human and half-elephant. It's true I tell you, I've seen him with my own eyes, sad wretch of man but, you know the most amazing thing — he's intelligent. Intelligent as ever a gentleman was! He's not one of your lot is he? Maybe that's what happens if you don't get enough blood? Perhaps you're not the only strange phenomenon in London today?"

"I know of him sir, but no, he is not one of 'our lot' as you so gracefully put it. He is far too gentle a soul for that and never a monster such as I." Jakob could feel his self-pity creeping through but Doctor Phillips just stood there, indifferent, listening.

"There is official news of more than one killer," Doctor Phillips stated matter-of-factly.

The statement shocked Jakob. *Oh no. Official? The police can't be on to us, we had nothing to do with this last murder.* But someone had slain her. *This other vampire — Emma? No, it can't be. Or the stranger from the cemetery?*

After a long pause, Jakob spoke. "I'm sorry Doc, I don't mean to be rude but I really must take my leave now. After all, there is at least one murderer out there, and I wouldn't want to be seen shirking my duties." He pointed to his blue uniform.

"Yes, ghastly stuff it is too but it does keep me in a job and you in good health, shall we say."

"You're a good man Doctor".

"Anything to oblige, young man."

Jakob turned, leaving the same way that he had come in. The stairs baulked his progress. The handicap, it seemed, was all his — he was a timid man, a vampire unable to kill, a monster who wanted his long-dead, undead love back.

Putting his head down he ran up the stairs, threw the door open and stepped out again into the night.

FORTY-TWO

Outside the police station Jakob went headlong down the street. Again, his mind reeled. *Emma.* He missed her. He missed Lucinda, his parents, and his simple life. But all that was long ago. So much had changed since . . .

He needed to concentrate, get back on track, stop Jack and get away from London.

Turning the corner he stepped straight into the path of a black hat. A black bowler hat, right in his face.

"A-ha, so here you are," a familiar voice said.

Jakob froze. After all these years he knew that rasping voice instantly. It was the man from the basement in Seasalter, it was Mister Death.

The man in the bowler hat stood fast, barring Jakob's way. His face stretched wide into a smug grin. Jakob noticed a small crucifix attached to the top of Mister Death's lapel and in his left hand he gripped a small glass vial. Absentmindedly, he was rolling it gently between finger and thumb.

Jakob thought hard and fast. *Holy water?*

"George Akin Lusk," Mister Death said, extending his right hand in mock greeting. He doused Jakob with the contents of his left.

"What the . . . ?" an angered Jakob said. "Don't think that stupid folklore is going to work in your favour, you fool." With his sleeve Jakob wiped at the tiny droplets rolling down his pallid face. "I don't need your acquaintance, you already know me — you killed my girlfriend."

"No, no, no. I only killed a parasitic fiend, a fiend that came straight from the depths of Hell." Lusk simpered, a contented grin stuck to his face. "Which reminds me; we exchanged pleasantries with your old friend in Reigate. You know, the one with far too much Barnet on her vile head. That's hair to you. We asked her to *stick* around but she refused and lost her head — with a garden spade."

Jakob thought of his friend. *Please not Lucinda. No.* He shook his head. Yet another woman in Jakob's life was dead. *Nyugodjék békében - Rest in peace.*

"But—"

"But, nothing," Lusk interrupted, eyeing his uniform. "But now you're a man of the law? Untouchable? I don't think so."

Jakob looked down at his police attire. *I do look silly.*

"Look, I never asked for any of this, leave me the hell alone."

"Hmm . . . Hell? Alone? Now that can be arranged my sacrilegious friend — your blasphemous contempt for nature can be easily . . . extinguished."

Agitated, Jakob threatened him. "You did your worst all those years ago, now back off or I may use some of my blasphemous contempt . . . and put out *your* lights."

"So, the true identity and bloodlust of the vampire finally surfaces. And no doubt it is you and your ghoulish ways

232

that are responsible for the awful murders on our streets?" Lusk gestured about him with open arms.

Jakob just stood there, defiant, unknowing of his next word . . . or move.

"Your reticence speaks volumes," Lusk said, nodding gently, the bowler hat exacerbating the pendulous motion of his head — his accusing eyes fixed on Jakob.

Turning on his heels Jakob did what he knew best — he ran.

"Don't worry," the man in the bowler hat shouted up the street. "I said I would find you, it will only be a short matter of time before we meet again . . . mister *policeman*. And rest assured, this time, retribution — or to be more concise, your coming annihilation — will be swift."

FORTY-THREE

It was during the quiet times, when there was little reporting to be done, or times of little inspiration, that Ernie had taken to meeting his new friend Buckie in some of the local pubs for a few sups. Together they explored various ales in each as they sat and chatted extensively about the murders.

During the autumn of 1888 the topic of the East End murderer was pretty much the only thing people were talking about — their poor living and working conditions temporarily forgotten in place of an anonymous killer. It seemed the whole of the East End had an opinion on just who the murderer was. Suspects were being dragged out and raked up from every bedraggled nook and cranny.

Pizer, a man who just happened to own a leather apron, had been mobbed in broad daylight and almost lynched in front of the police, even before a perfect alibi had been established.

"I just need a really, really good story. It's not enough just to report on the facts or hearsay of the events. I need something that will set my story apart from the others. Something big, bold," Ernie said to his new drinking partner.

Buckie looked about the old local, its sorry interior sapping any remaining inspiration out of him. He watched his jaded friend put his chin in his hands, gloomy as the pub's cheap furniture. "That could be a bit tough there, Ernie. Our mightily impressive so-called police force couldn't even find their own whirlygigs if their bleedin' trousies fell down." Buckie laughed.

Ernie agreed. It was because of that the police were not even a reliable source themselves — they had nothing to tell, and sure enough, they had no news to sell.

"My boss gets harder and harder on me," Ernie said.

"You could always come to work with me, if you're not afraid o' gettin' your 'ands dirty," Buckie said to his dejected friend on the other side of the table.

Ernie could not quite see himself doing manual labour. He jabbed his pen into the blank page of his notepad in frustration.

"Or, you could make somethin' up like you said before. Only somethin' real sensational," Buckie said. He thought for a moment as he took a gulp of his drink. "You know, somethin' like a letter that coulda come from the killer himself — now that'd make great news." Buckie nodded and sat up in his chair, brimming, pleased at his idea.

Understanding just what Buckie actually meant, Ernie's face picked up, a hint of mirth stretched across his cheeks. He lifted his pen. "Hey, that's not a bad idea you know but it's a bit improper," Ernie said.

"Bugger that, Ernie. You don't want the old bunter's to 'ave died for nothin' do ya? You could do it as an act of respect. Like an in-memoriam kinda thing. Let's face it, the police have probly already forgotten."

"You know what, you're absolutely right. But what should I write? It's not like I'm a killer or anything. I'm going to have to be really careful."

"Well yeah, careful'l help but they ain't gonna know your writin' from the next chap, not if ya fancy it up a little. Now all ya gotta do is use your imagination. That's what you're good at, you writers. Turn killins into shillins."

"It's not like I don't need the money. I've got a couple of ideas already but I'm going to need a false name to add to the authenticity. I'd look rather silly signing it Ernie the cheap trickster, wouldn't I?"

"Not really, but even Our Majesty's finest may soon catch up with you if you do put that. What about somethin' short and proper common-like? Somethin' so they don't catch on too quick," Buckie said, excited.

Ernie thought, his face blank. "Like what?"

"Think about it. What's anyone call anyone in these 'ere parts?"

Ernie shrugged.

"Why, Jack, o' course."

FORTY-FOUR

After his close shave with Lusk, old Mister Death, Jakob had laid low for the last few days. Jack was bored and getting restless, wanting to get back out on the streets as soon as he could — to satiate his desires, to find another.

Jakob was finding it increasingly hard to even have a simple conversation with Jack these days — he was clearly insane. Unwittingly, in his own selfish desire for blood, Jakob had fed Jack's deathly disposition, his proclivity for killing. Jakob should be the one to stop him, to reason with Jack, state that if they went back out on the streets too soon then they may well be caught.

Everyone in the East End was being accused of being the killer — if they said the wrong thing to pricked ears, if they wore something as mundane as an apron, if said apron had a little stain on it, or if they spoke with a foreign accent, sported a bigger, longer moustache than usual. Immediate capital punishment and public hangings would soon be in full swing — literally.

Jakob did not need Jack to support him any longer, he now had Doctor Phillips to sustain his cravings, he must stop Jack at once. He must also find out who this other vampire was — this female. *Why hasn't she revealed herself to me yet?* They were one and the same after all. *What is she waiting for?* Jakob had no idea.

There was something else troubling him. He had no idea what to make of Abberline, and now Lusk was on his tail. Jakob felt trapped, stuck in the middle of them all — the suspicious inspector, an unidentified vampire, the mad Jack, and now a steadfast vigilante vampire hunter.

Jakob despaired; he really did not know who to trust. *Is everyone in this city mad? Is that the reason behind the might of the English, their strength? The Empire built by madmen, back-stabbing and killing at will?* Jakob pictured his home — papa and himself working the land, feeding the animals, his mama indoors, cooking, reading, singing. He now pictured civilised London — a man with delirious eyes, sharpening his blade to a thin point, calling out to 'er-indoors': "I'm just nippin' out for a little refreshment — be back in a jiffy once I've killed half-a-dozen or so. What's for tea darlin', spotted dick?"

Outside, more rain patted the mire, the cobbles and flags etching out tiny streams that flowed between the cracks, the River Styx miniaturised and repeated, over and over. Earlier, there had been a torrid downpour which had only let up around midnight.

Turning up at the house, it had been empty, a burrow of loneliness. Jack had gone. He could not have gone far, Jakob knew, but would he find him? — the snarl of back-streets had culminated in the sordid creation of an eternal labyrinth as if right out of the belly of Sheol. Jakob expected he would end up there one day, in Sheol, or some other demented version of it — only not just yet.

Instinctively, Jakob let his feet take him off, into and through the grubby tangle of streets. At least forty-five minutes had gone by when Jakob turned off Commercial Road and finally spotted what he was looking for.

There he was. He could just make out two dark figures on the deserted street. Jack was pursuing another woman. *How predictable.* He had not seen Jakob and, thinking he was alone, the male figure (obviously Jack) grabbed at the woman.

Jakob winced.

The woman yelped something unintelligible before stumbling backwards and falling awkwardly to the soggy ground.

A clicking of footsteps close by brought another man into view, a reveller returning home from the Working Men's Club. Turning around, Jack saw the innocent man was walking towards him. Jack watched intently, ready to pounce, a coiled spring, as the man crossed the road and marched off, resolutely avoiding any altercation.

Following the man's quickened pace Jack now spotted Jakob, the unavailing vampire, with a troubled and questioning look trapped on his pale face. Jack shrugged his shoulders as the would-be witness scurried away. *Shit. What's he doin' 'ere? S'pose he thinks I'm bein' a bit hazardous. We'll see.*

Jack looked questioningly at Jakob, raising his arms wide, before shouting out loud. "Risky?"

Relieved that the man had scurried away, like a dockside rat and that they were once again alone, Jakob implored Jack to leave the woman alone.

"Leave her alone, you say?" Jack said.

In his eyes was a malevolence that Jakob had not seen before.

"Why should I? Ain't I always doin' what poor old *Jakob* wants?"

Jakob fixed his face and looked the mad murderer, his disturbed friend, hard in his eyes. Brushing past him Jakob bent down to help the woman up, her black skirt wet and smeared, her bonnet crumpled. Taking her arm, Jakob led her away.

Not far enough. Twitching furiously, an incensed Jack came at them both. Barging his friend aside Jack grabbed at the woman, dragging her beneath the archway, out of the main street, into a dark recess of no return. Before Jakob had time to reach out and react, it was over.

Jack's superbly practised hand came up to meet the soft flesh of her neck. There was a flash, a glimmer of cold steel — not a glimmer of hope for the toothless scream that she tried to emit. A gleeful glint shone in Jack's eye — a powerful mastery had taken over him.

The woman did not even have time to ponder on the newcomer, who he was or where he was going. The sudden attack had left her giddy. *Why all the commotion over me? I ain't never bin nuffin' to no one.* She felt herself weakening as she acquainted herself with the pavement and the piss-stained wall.

She managed to feel inside her pocket as she went down, felt the key, its round bow and square bit. *Maybe I shoulda stayed in, let Michael padlock me in again?* She squeezed on her prized bag of scented cachous, suddenly protective of her few possessions — mindful that at least, in death, her breath was fresh.

Jack let his victim's leaking body crumple to the floor, facing the wall. He turned to face Jakob who had only watched, helpless as the woman's blood and her life leaked away. "No blood tonight Jake, my boy, you's not been a good friend to me this evenin'."

"But, please Jack. I tried to tell you, I don't need it anymore, I can use Doctor Phillips now," Jakob said in earnest.

"Oh, *you need* . . . what about what I need? And anyway, who's gonna provide your precious doctor with bodies, eh?" Jack said as he started to walk off.

Defeated, Jakob attempted to follow him.

"Don't bother following me," Jack warned. "I'm done with this place. I'm off to the City."

Jakob watched as Jack paced away, steam billowing from his mouth as he seethed. *Why the hell didn't I stop him? Shit. What can I do?* Jakob raised his arms, looked at his white skin, his pale hands. He had to face it now. He was a vampire, a fucking vampire. After all these years he had finally given in to the need for good red human blood. *Things must change.* He could stop Jack; he had caught him initially and subdued him. Why not again?

Starting up the street, Jakob went in search of a killer.

FORTY-FIVE

Heading west towards the City, the culmination of the East End steadily narrowed around the old City gates to only a few thoroughfares.

He can't have gone far.

Coming along Duke Street, a faint aroma wafted in and hit Jakob's blood-sensitive nose. The blood was fresh. *No.*

He crept towards the square, scanning its ebony shadows, its darkened angles. In the far left corner the insane Jack was crouched over a prostrate form. He was thrusting and lancing wildly.

"Come on Jack," Jakob pleaded as he approached.

Alerted to his presence, Jack threw down the pile of innards in his hands. They landed with a wet slap above the dead woman's shoulder. Jack had shit on his hands — Jakob could smell it. The silk gauze of the woman's neckerchief was saturated; fresh warm blood flowed from a deep gash across the front of her throat. It gurgled and bubbled against her flesh and upper clothes.

"Leave me alone," Jack said to Jakob, wiping his hands up and down her once-white vest, turning over marbled streaks between his digits.

Ignoring Jakob, Jack bent and took his knife to the dead woman's face. Jakob watched aghast as Jack grabbed the tip of her nose and cut the fleshy point clean off.

"What the hell are you doing?" *Ön beteg házasságon kívül született - You sick bastard.*

"I'm cutting the nose off to spite the face, which is what you'll be doin' if you try to stop me killin' for ya — you won't eat," quipped Jack.

"But I will, I've got the doctor, he's got lots of blood for me. Come on, let's go, now — we'll both be caught."

"Yeah, but I got somethin' for ya first," Jack said, handing him a jar of freshly 'squeezed' blood. It was an act of appeasement.

Jakob took the jar from him.

"Hang on," Jack said, as he cut away at a piece of apron.

"Use that — no point in us both gettin' dirty."

Wrapping the jagged cloth around the jar, Jakob, in his vampire need, drank. It was too late now for Jakob to stop Jack. The woman was dead, her blood flowing down his throat like a fine warm claret.

"She's dead Jack, please leave her," Jakob said again.

"You go, I'll be along in a minute."

Satisfied that he, too, was satiated, Jakob left the small place, no longer a square, more an unbalanced and temporary charnel house dowsed ruby-red for all to see.

Safely along Petticoat Lane Jakob realised that he still had the jar in his hand. There were a few of people around now, alerted by Jack's first victim earlier, and he would look suspicious if the crowds grew, which he knew they could.

With any luck Jack will get caught in his deranged blood-stained state, putting an end to it all. Aware of the jar, Jakob stopped on the next street and dived into a large doorway. Wiping clean the glass jar, along with his grimy hands, he threw it across the rear fences, as far away as he could. In the distance, a faint shatter of glass broke the silence, a cat shrieked. Realising that he may have drawn unneeded attention to the sound Jakob threw the blood-smeared piece of apron down and spurned himself on.

He had tried to stop Jack but his attempt had been pathetic, for two more women now lay dead and mutilated because of him. As if things could not get any worse he had even accepted the glass jar filled with blood and drank it down willingly as well.

Depleted of any form of life, or undeadness, Jakob walked aimlessly, searching inside himself, pleading for the wrath that Mister Lusk and his holy crusade had promised. In death Jakob would find a way out of this Gehenna, battle onwards through purgatory and arise victorious, or at least — in peace by his parents' side.

FORTY-SIX

Mitre Square was pitch black. She watched intently as the taller man moved away, leaving the killer and his eviscerated creation alone once more. She would leave Jakob till later.

"Hello Jack," she called out from the blackness, stepping forward into the dull light, revealing herself.

The man jumped, the blade in his hand steady. Jack turned to see a face. Finally, there was a face to go with the voice that he recognised so well. A primal fear of the woman who had caged him all those weeks ago flooded through him. His hackles rose.

"Stay away, you bitch, I've . . . I've got a knife and I ain't afraid to use it." He shoved the knife out in front of him.

"Oh, I can see that," she replied, the evidence all around her feet.

Staring down at his handiwork, she approved, mimicking applause with her hands. "That's a nice job you've done there."

"What?" Jack said.

"It's a nice job, I hope you've not wasted any of that there blood," she said.

"Th . . . thanks," Jack said. Perhaps he could warm to this woman after all.

"Listen, I'm sorry for what I did. I needed you out of the way for a while. That's all. Nothing personal. I've got a proposition for you," she said. "That Jakob, he's no good for either of us. Let's get rid of him. You and I can carry on the killing. Together, we can polish off hundreds, thousands, till your heart's content."

In the dark, Jack contemplated what he had heard. Could he trust her? At least she wanted to kill, not like that weak-willed excuse, Jakob. Gleeful at the idea, Jack said, "That's not a bad thing. I . . . I s'pose I could forgive you for coopin' me up like that."

"I know, I'm sorry but I had to. But I knew you, us, we were meant for better things. That's why I let you go."

"I killed my slag of a ma 'cause she thought she knew it all."

"Yes, but I'm not your ma now am I? No, I'm a vampire who needs a partner — and one who just happens to approve of all this," she said, stretching a white finger out, directing it at the destroyed and bloody corpse.

In the dim light, she could make out a small fading tattoo of blue ink on the victim's left forearm, two tiny letters — TC.

Jack noticed her watching. "Stands for Terminally Carved," he scoffed.

"Very good. You're a natural artist," she said.

246

FORTY-SEVEN

A few days later, the East End basked in the spotlight of the world for all the wrong reasons. London had become a boiling hotpot of suspicion and fright; there had been yet another two killings.

Jakob knew only too well, for he had been there for both. The newspapers were harping on about 'a double event' this time; two undeserving and thoughtless prostitutes had been killed in the space of an hour.

This time though the journalists had given the culprit a moniker. Jakob gulped, his dry throat somehow seemed drier. He read on. Jack . . . the Ripper. *Jack? Did they know? Has he been caught?* Reading further about what had been penned in a letter to the press Jakob nearly froze as it spoke of: saving some of the proper red stuff in a ginger beer bottle.

If it was Jack who had written the letter to the press then his arrogance was going to be his downfall. But then would Jack even know or care? — he was, after all, a complete lunatic.

Another startling press release, this time definitely nothing to do with Jack or himself. A headless and limbless body of a woman, a torso, had been found in a small vault by the Victoria Embankment, beneath the new construction site of Scotland Yard.

Mohandas Gandhi, the man who was yet to become one of the most important men in history, leading India to its independence and inspiring civil rights and freedom movements throughout the world, had not been studying at the University in Bloomsbury in London for even a month, and was celebrating his nineteenth birthday on the day the gruesome find had been uncovered.

Jakob sat and wondered about Abberline. *What do I know about him? And where is Ludwig?* Jakob tried to assemble a time-line to the estimated date of death of the discovered body. *Was this the work of the mysterious female vampire?*

The newspaper articles that Jakob had read now gave him an idea. The crisp white paper lay blank, staring up at him, a pale and innocent naked sunbather against the browning table top. Jakob sat there in thought, he had not written anything for a long time, an age almost.

He had to get the pious and fervent Mister Lusk off his back. Jakob decided to send Lusk a message, a warning to leave him alone. After all, Mister Lusk with his trademark bowler hat had already made it his sworn duty to travel to the far ends of the earth and hunt him down.

Jakob's oral English was now good since learning to speak again, but the same could not be said for his writing and spelling. It was atrocious; he was Hungarian for God's sake. It did not matter, he reasoned — it would only make the warning seem more real, more threatening. Holding the pen, he continued writing:

. . . tother piece I fried and ate it was very nise. I may send you the bloody knif that took it out if you only wate a whil longer . . .

For all the madness and killing that surrounded him, it was a comical moment. Here he was, a vampire, a dangerous fiend of the underworld, wreaking death alongside a steady stream of blood, unless he could quietly get away with writing a discreet and threatening letter.

Glad with the result, Jakob signed it:

Catch me when you can Mishter Lusk.

Dropping in a small piece of ripe and raw kidney he had purposely fetched from the kitchen, Jakob went out and posted the small package.

FORTY-EIGHT

Stepping in from the drear of yet another grey day, Inspector Abberline and his blue-uniformed colleague, Jakob, descended the cold stone steps. Once inside, the doctor's charming voice could easily be heard as he stood talking to two strange men, their backs to them.

One of the two men, a bulwark of a man, stocky with no neck, had arms the size of rail sleepers, and probably as rough. The other man was tall and gangly, his form slithered around the floor, his body movements that of a creepy upright lizard.

Immediately Abberline recognised them. Not strangers anymore. On hearing the shuffling of feet on concrete behind them, the two men who were in conversation with the doctor turned and regarded the newcomers.

"Good evening, inspector. Evening PC," Doctor Phillips said.

Abberline stopped in his tracks. Jakob did likewise. They both nodded to the doctor.

"Do you know my two visitors, Mister Grand and Mister Batchelor?" The doctor pointed to the burly man first, his head directly atop his shoulders, before introducing the serpentine, lissome form of the other.

"Yes, good evening gentlemen." Abberline greeted them uneasily. "I think we may have met during a heated debate. Something about the Home Office and some kind of reward?"

"Sort of sir. We met at the Whitechapel Vigilance Committee a few nights ago. You were there telling us, well, telling our gaffer not to bother with his silly slayer hunt," the bulky man said, his gravelly voice deep and booming.

"Ah, so you are Lusk's men then?" the Inspector asked.

In a flimsy reed of a voice the tall man squealed. "No . . . Well, yes, indirectly. We work within . . . within our own capacity."

Great. More trouble.

Aware of his standing in the community and, of course, his rank, the Inspector First-Class took control of the situation. "Would you two 'pretend officers' then please leave of your own capacity. Myself and the doctor need to discuss important and real police matters." It was not a question.

Offended, the snaky man visibly shook, the tiniest of motions from his skeletal form exacerbated by the sheer length of his limbs.

He was about to reply when the bulky man interrupted.

"Come on Batch, let's get going, we wouldn't want to outstay our welcome — the inspector has lots of work to do if he's ever going to catch . . . Jack the Ripper."

"Just get out of here will you, or your guv'nor might find your bloated bodies floating in the Thames. Or better still, with your throats cut lying in a pool of your own piss and blood, the latest victims of 'the Ripper' as you say." Abberline laughed.

Mister Grand and Mister Batchelor eyed each other nervously. They made their way out of the room. Huffing and puffing, the two men brushed past an anxious Jakob. He looked up at the gaunt face of the lanky one named Batchelor. *Is this the man who had followed Lucinda?*

Mister Batchelor leered down at him. Obviously the fanatical Mister Lusk had not passed on to his two colleagues about his meeting with Jakob the other day. They were unaware of his real identity.

"Go on, get out and stay out," Abberline shouted.

"Real police indeed — they couldn't even catch a bleedin' cold," echoed a wispy voice from the top of the barren stairs before the door banged shut.

It was partially true — Jakob had not seen or heard from Jack since the night of the double event. And if Jakob did not know where he was, the police were going to have a hard time, particularly as Jakob knew that at least two of the murders were not Jack — that of the torso found in Whitehall and the unfortunate girl on Hanbury Street.

Either way, Jakob realised he was just as guilty as Jack was. If he had not tried to stop him, then Jack in his fever would not have gone on to kill the second woman, cutting and mutilating her so badly.

Standing slightly behind the inspector, Jakob raised his finger to his lips in an attempt to keep Doctor Phillips quiet about their friendship. The doctor's eyes registered the mute caution.

"What can I do for you two good gentlemen?" Doctor Phillips asked.

Abberline opened his mouth to speak.

252

Jakob interjected. "Well, my good Doctor, we . . . we need some blood."

"We?" probed the doctor.

Jakob hesitated and looked towards Abberline. "Yes Doctor, Inspector Abberline is a vampire."

FORTY-NINE

Annoyed, Abberline fixed his face, his hands curling up into fists. He turned to Doctor Phillips and then looked at Jakob, searching his blank face. He readied himself to run. Jakob stepped into the stairwell, blocking any attempt at escape. Doctor Phillips looked on, fidgety. He reached into a small tray and picked up a scalpel. Like a simple and deadly game of piggy-in-the-middle, the three men stood there waiting for one or the other to make the first move.

It was the always reasonable doctor who spoke first.

"Just what is going on Jakob?"

Without taking his eyes away from the inspector, Jakob answered. "Well Doc, it appears that somehow the inspector here has gone and got himself turned into a vampire. I'm not quite sure how at the moment, all I know is he's changed, he's different somehow."

"But how do you know?" Doctor Phillips asked.

"It was the other day when it dawned on me. We had apprehended the Polish fellow with the leather apron. His face was cut by a flying stone that some idiot had thrown and . . . the inspector's eyes were—"

"Were what?" Abberline cried. He was not going to just stand there mute while these two spoke about him. "Does it matter? There's not a lot I can do about it now, is there?"

"I'm afraid Jakob would know more about that than I," Doctor Phillips said. "Although I have been *trying* to understand."

"It appears I'm not the only one here who's infected, am I? You said 'we need some blood', Mister Jakob Sergeant," Abberline said, peeved not to have known that PC 49889, or whoever he was, was also a vampire. *And I'm supposed to be Inspector First-Class.*

"Yes inspector, I am a vampire. And the doctor here is a great help. He keeps blood for me."

"Bully for him — and you," Abberline stated.

At that, Abberline visibly relaxed himself, the thought of blood nearby soothed him.

Doctor Phillips put down the scalpel. "I'm terribly sorry inspector but I was a little scared."

"Rightly so doctor, what with two vampires in the same room as you."

"We're one of a kind inspector and I'm proof you don't have to kill for blood. It's all here on tap," Jakob said, pointing to the shelves.

"There's nothing wrong with killing. It's accepted here in the East End," Abberline said.

"Erm . . . No, it's not. That's just the perspective of a warped imagination, and the press. The people are up in arms about the murders," Doctor Phillips said.

"Inspector, I know all about you, your record is impeccable. I don't think you really mean that. You've always upheld the law," Jakob said.

"Yes, but that was before."

"But I also suspect you know more than you're letting on — like that body, or part of a body that was found in Whitehall the other day?" Jakob probed.

"A similar question could be aimed at yourself — like what do you know about the Ripper killings?" Abberline asked, ignoring his question.

"I will tell you inspector, but from now on we have to trust each other. The doctor here is our friend; you have no need to worry about him."

"Thank you, Jakob," Doctor Phillips said.

Abberline glared at the two men. "Well, thank you doctor, but I need to speak to my colleague here in private. I'll bid you good night."

Jakob and Abberline stepped out onto the road again. They checked the street for unwanted dawdlers. Mister Grand and Mister Batchelor had long gone. In the dark, outside of an unknowing police station in the midst of the East End, two vampires stood side by side discussing the murders, the deeds of Hell.

Jakob was not shocked when Abberline mentioned the other vampire. Abberline went on to explain that after he had turned, he awoke and was in turmoil, his body rebelling against all that he was. Of course, Jakob knew exactly what the inspector was telling him for he had been through the same anguish only a few years earlier.

The inspector said that he had met her, another vampire, feeding, down by the docks. There she was, quietly attached to the neck of a recent kill, a lady of good standing by all accounts if you took in her attire, taking her blood as freely as a dog taking a piss — both done on the side-walk. He told Jakob how he had felt good as he had tasted her blood for the first time and then went about dismembering the hapless victim, hacking through bone and gristle, pulpy globs of fat and gore surrounding him.

Jakob was horrified. "Inspector, you simply cannot kill like that," he said.

Abberline may have been a well respected inspector of the law and higher in rank but Jakob was definitely the more experienced when it came to the afterlife.

Abberline stared at Jakob. "I'll be the judge of that, Sergeant. I didn't ask for this but now that I am, well, let's just say that I rather enjoy the taste of blood."

"That may be so inspector, but just butchering anyone isn't an option, particularly if you want to keep a low profile . . . and keep your job."

"You're right. Are you willing to help me then?" the inspector asked, realising the truth.

"Yes. Believe me, I've tried many things. The cravings are hard and I'm not saying I'm completely innocent but we can survive on the blood of animals — rats, chickens, anything. Damn, I've even tried to extract it from leeches. None of that matters for as long as Doctor Phillips keeps up his good work we can feed on human blood without the need for killing," Jakob said. "But first I want to know who this other vampire is though."

"Honestly, I don't know. I didn't ask anything about her and she didn't say much. Only that her name is Mary. I just felt free . . . although I did notice she was beautiful, even in the pale moonlight."

Mary?

"Even in death, beauty holds us firmly in its grip. I knew a beautiful girl once. She was the one who turned me . . . and I let her die in a fire," Jakob said. "However, the fire was Lusk's doing."

"Lusk?" the inspector asked.

"Yes, that bastard Lusk is a vampire hunter and those two thugs back there . . ." Jakob pointed back towards Doctor Phillips' room, "they're his two trusty assistants — vampire slaying apprentices."

"Ah, so that's what they are. We'd best be on a serious look-out then," Abberline said, carefully scanning the road. "Mind you, I think we'd see those two freaks coming from a long way off."

"Come on," Jakob said. "We've still got to stop Jack before he strikes again."

"Jack? Oh, that. That's just a wild made up name from a stupid letter that the police received. I read it myself. It's just a fake," Abberline said.

"Erm, I think, my good inspector, you'll find it's not. It's now my turn to be honest with you."

FIFTY

"Meet me at number thirteen, okay?"

Ernie nodded.

"Number thirteen. And make sure you come alone."

Ernie nodded again.

"Now remember, it's directly on your right as you come into the yard," Buckie repeated.

"Okay, okay, I'll be there. I might be a little late though. What, with work and everything," Ernie said.

"Just get there as soon as you can. Knock on the door, real gentle like, and I'll let you in."

"But what's going on?" Ernie asked.

Buckie bent forward over the table, his head and chest hovering above their two half pints of ale. "Listen, you want your scoop don't you?" he whispered.

"Well, yes. But what's going to happen?" Ernie asked again.

"Nothin' for you to worry about. Trust me, all right? Just make sure you bring some paper and, whatever you do, don't forget your pen," Buckie said.

"Okay. Will do," Ernie affirmed one last time.

FIFTY-ONE

It was late; it had been a dull day, full of slow drizzle and bleak grey clouds, and still the rain persisted. Jack sauntered along the street, unseen in the late darkness. He was in a cheery mood — he was soon going to kill again. Only it was not about to happen the way *she* thought it would. Although he had fallen out with Jake, he had since accepted that these things were bound to crop up; it was exactly what friends did from time to time. Real friends at least — they sometimes argue.

Jake *was* his friend. Jack had come a long way since his fortuitous meeting with Jake, but he would carry on the killing, with or without his friend's blessing. He would do it for himself, not for anyone else, especially not for *her* — a detestable vampire.

Stepping into Dorset Street, Jack thought he could hear someone singing quietly in one of the rooms in the small courtyard of houses. *What they got to be happy about?* He listened harder, hearing the woman's words: Father and Mother, they have passed away. He grinned, his face twitching deliriously. Treading softly up to the front door he placed his small black bag on the flagstones next to him, knocked twice and waited.

The woman opened the door and greeted him. The light coming from the room was not great but it lit her enough so Jack could see her properly for the first time. He regarded her for a moment. In almost exact opposition to her obvious natural tendency for killing, she was exceptionally beautiful and had the most searing blue eyes he had ever seen. He entered the room as she backed away, beckoning him across the threshold. The squalid room was small, a single bed pushed to one side with an open fire burning gently to the other — the flames throwing their ominous shadows about the room, licking the greying walls in silent expectancy.

Confidently, the woman turned her back to her visitor and sat herself down on the bed. The springs in the mattress let out a high-pitched groan. Looking up from the mattress, the glow from the fire gave her skin a dancing faux orange pigment, the most colour her complexion had seen in some years now.

"Hello," she said.

Jack nodded.

"You know why you are here?" she asked him, his shadowy form above her.

"Of course. I know why I'm here — I'm here to kill," he said, a sly malice on his breath.

"Well, yes, you are. Just not yet."

"Why must I wait?" he asked.

"You killed your mother," she said, changing the subject.

"So fuckin' what? She got what she deserved. No more, no less. You'll get the same too if you don't shut up," he postured.

She ignored his threats. "It's not that I dislike killing, it's just that I don't approve of matricide, Jack or . . ." she hesitated, "or should I call you Buckie?"

He flinched. "Jesus Christ, don't you ever call me that. How the hell do you know? Buckie died the day he slit his mother's throat. I'm Jack now, geddit? Jack."

"OK, I'm sorry. *Jack*. I am of the undead and I know things you cannot possibly comprehend. And I've already caged you like a suckling pig in want of its mother, afraid of the coming spit," she threatened.

The mention of the word 'mother' again sickened him, incensed his hatred further. He leered at her. "Yes, but this little piggy got away, didn't he? Went wee, wee, wee, all the way back to Whitechapel."

"I told you, you didn't get away. I let you go. I need you for my own ends — for killing Jakob. Let me *turn* you, er . . . Jack. Become a vampire with me. Without Jakob, we can carry on the killing, forever feed and—"

There was a faint knock at the door. Surprised, the woman, the vampire, looked at the door.

"Don't worry, I'm expecting someone," Jack said.

Taking only two steps in the tiny room, he reached for the door and opened it. There stood Ernie, his collar high up around the sides of his neck, one hand stuffed deep into a pocket.

"Come on in, you're just in time," Jack said, his tone lifting, to his drinking buddy.

"I brought my pad and pen," Ernie said as he pulled them from his pocket and steadied himself, ready for the big news.

"Who are you?" the vampire asked from the bedside.

"I'm—"

"Forget that," Jack said firmly. "Just sit over there, get your pen out and observe."

Lowering himself into the rickety chair, Ernie obeyed and sat quietly.

Jack turned back to the vampire. "Where were we? Oh yes. *Turn* me? You're not goin' to turn me. I'm not surviving on blood, on that . . . that disgusting red slime. You parasitic slag. I'm never drinking that shit. Anyway, Jake is my friend — why would I want to kill him?"

Had he just heard that? From where he sat, Ernie could not quite believe what he was hearing. His friend, Buckie, had always seemed so placid. He shook his head, watching intently.

Behind him on the small table, Jack's concealed hand reached into his black bag. He knew exactly what it was he wanted to find in there. *Ah, there you are.*

The vampire spoke again. "Jakob is weak; he cannot face what he is. Why else would he have you as his crude partner? I . . ." she faded off, a twinge of humanity touching her for the briefest moment. "He's a coward, you simpleton — if you won't kill him, then I will."

Why was she talking down to him and calling him names? She reminded him too much of his mother. *Vile.* It angered him, inflamed him. *Yes, she might well be a vampire, but surely even the undead can be re-deaded?* In a mad frenzy Jack launched himself at her.

"You're not taking my friend from me," he strained through gritted teeth as he came forward. "You fucking bride-of-the-devil."

Still sitting, surprised at the rapid onslaught, the vampire was overcome by his brute strength. Gripping the haft of his knife, Jack threshed his arms around wildly, the sharpened blade catching her soft dry, sapless flesh.

Ernie huddled down by the wall at the side of the room. Petrified. *What is Buckie doing?* Ernie was more scared than he had ever been in his life, even more than his excursion to Reigate with Mr Lusk and his two pals. He did not know what to do. *Stay or go?*

She was a vampire, true, but more than that she was a woman, and half his weight. She did not have the advantage of bars this time, of staying out of his reach. Jack, on the other hand, was an adrenalin-pumped mad murderer. She had no chance. Her arrogance and over-confidence in the realms of the undead had backfired on her. It would be her undoing — literally. Quickly and easily Jack throttled her neck, stifling any screams that might flow forth from her dry lungs, her juiceless innards. *We'll have a look at those in a bit.*

After some time he realised she was never going to be strangled to death; his fingers were starting to cramp, badly.

How the fuck do you kill a vampire? He thought of Jake and his tale of the gang together with his mishap of the stake through his heart. *No good there then.*

Entrusting his fanatical butchering ability, he let the knife find its own way. To her neck. Cutting deep, she thrashed about the old mattress for her undead life to continue — his weight thrown fully behind his hand forcing her face down into the pillow and keeping her pale and pulseless throat exposed. Her eyes widened. He smiled morosely at her. Viscose and blackened blood seeped from her awful wound.

That's it, I'm off. Ernie could stand no more. If he stayed, he was certain he would be the next one in line to meet his maker at the hands of Buckie, or Jack, or whoever he might be. Ernie did not care much about vampires, as long as they left him alone.

Jack was in full swing by now, mesmerised in his fevered actions, stabbing, cutting, ripping. He never saw or heard the door open and close gently behind him as Ernie made off into the still night of Dorset Street.

Still the vampire writhed, unwilling to yield. Still Jack cut deeper. In a saw-like motion, he severed through her larynx, her muscle, not stopping as he hit the hard bones at the back of her neck. He looked her in the eyes. She stared back, fearful but defiant — still alive.

Pulling back with his deadly weapon, Jack used the knife as a soldier would use his bayonet. The last line of defence, he thrust it back into her neck wound, jabbing wildly, trying to find a gap between the vertebrae, and into her spinal column. Inching quickly forwards, he found it.

He pushed — hard.

The sharp point of the knife found its mark, enough to sever her twisted brain stem. Finally, she was still. The vampire who had once been known as Mary was dead.

Panting hard, Jack the Ripper was still unhappy. She was dead, yes, but she had taken a long time to die while he had probed and stabbed. She would have to suffer some more. He would live up to his name, leave nothing to chance.

Slicing and cutting at her limp cadaver, his hand reached in and pulled out her old heart muscle. Holding it up he marvelled at its wretchedness, just a shrivelled lump of desiccation, its former job of pumping freshly oxygenated blood around her body relinquished all those years ago. He threw it into the dying fire. Like dry grass, it burned brightly and quickly, the extra light aiding his abominable work.

Looking at her derisively, he realised he hated her, the way she looked. He would get rid of her looks. He merrily stripped the bones of her flesh, removing her face, her muscles, cutting sinews, slicing tendons and nerve-endings, withdrawing organs. In the hour or so it had taken him, his unspeakable trade had finally acclimatised to the evolutionary jump from animal to human in just a few strokes of the knife.

Satisfied, Jack stopped his bloody work and began to clean his blade. It was time to leave. Jack turned to scan the room. In his passion for his work he had not realised that Ernie had left. It was understandable, he was only a reporter. He shrugged. To witness a murder first-hand was probably not the best way to go about things. Jack, well Buckie, had only wanted to give Ernie a real-life scoop.

The hinges squealed gently as the door opened again. Jack turned, expecting his friend. *Never mind, that's obviously him returning.*

As the door flexed further open, a large bare-chested man appeared. The intruder's hairless body shone in the glow of embers from the hearth as the flames grew higher in renewed vigour. Large feet made no noise as the new intruder took one almighty pace into the room, closing the door softly behind him. Jack gaped at him.

"Good evening or morning, whichever you may prefer, *Buckie*," he said to Jack, his voice a mere whisper.

"My name is Jack," he said.

"No, no. You are Mr Buchan, and I have known you by that name since your birth. That is what I shall call you now."

Jack — Buckie — seethed. *Who is this man? How does he know me? Since birth?* Jack ignored all that for the time being. His mind screamed at him — *Don't leave any witnesses!*

"Who in Hell are you?" Jack asked the stranger.

The newcomer smiled wryly. "My name is Antonas."

"Antonas? What sort of a name is that?" an irate Jack said as he gripped the knife, preparing to despatch the fool. Jack stepped towards him. In one fluid movement, he thrust his knife savagely towards the intruder's stomach.

Stopping fast, the knife thudded against hard skin. The sharpened point did not penetrate. Incredulous, Jack fell back across the small room. The tic on his face raced as he tried to think. The blade was true, wickedly sharp, yet it was as if it had hit solid steel, and stopped dead.

"Well, I happen to like the pseudonym, the *nom de guerre* if you will. But Antonas? . . . No, Satan. Hmm? I think you already know me so there should be no need for shock or surprise. You introduced yourself to me the day you killed your mother as she slept. And now, Mr Buchan, you've successfully extinguished one of Pura's footsoldiers, or vampire as you people like to say up here. Pura won't be happy with you. I can't say I'm happy with you either. You see, all the wretched women that you are killing . . . well, you'd think that the lives they lead would send them straight down to me but, alas, it seems that their souls are . . ." he paused at the word, "pure . . . and so I miss out."

"Bu . . . but . . . I . . . stabbed you," Jack stammered; he clearly was not listening.

"Please, Mr Buchan, don't concern yourself with such trivial matters, it is what I expected of you. I can't have a killer who has any morals. You must be able to stab anybody, man, woman or even *Devil* in this case. And if you hadn't at least tried then I would have to question my own skills. You are what's known, quite simply and universally, as evil, my dear fledgling."

Since the day he had sliced his mother's throat and watched her bleed to death in slumber, Jack, or Buckie as he was then, had never been afraid. Now, he was visibly shivering. The adrenalin that had coursed through his body while he was in his murderous throes had left him, replaced now with sheer terror.

Although the voice was soft, dreamlike almost, it spoke with such command, such authority, that any mortal man was forced to listen — and listen in fear. Satan spoke again. "I can't have you filling His coffers up with innocent souls, you work for me. On my books, you will only kill the despicable, the iniquitous from now on. Evil begets evil," he instructed.

Jack sat, mute, dumbfounded.

"But first, Mr Buchan, you must pull yourself together. There's something I want you to do for me."

FIFTY-TWO

"Help, help, please, come quick," the shop assistant shouted, going pell-mell up Commercial Street, heading as fast as he could towards Leman Street Police Station.

Abberline's attentive ears picked out the sound from inside the cold building as he stood talking with the other men, including Jakob in his police attire. There were several rumours that Sir Charles Warren, the Metropolitan Police Commissioner, the big-wig himself, was about to resign. The police still had no idea where Jack was, but they would very soon have a good idea, at least, of where he had recently been and that he was, most probably, close by.

As the shop assistant frantically approached, screaming bloody murder, everyone hurried to the front of the station. Outside, the duty inspector was trying to fathom the shop assistants monosyllabic words, in-between his heaving breaths.

Behind Abberline and Jakob each man in turn shuffled forward, eager to hear what the shop assistant had to say in such haste. The words left the laboured man's mouth in slow motion, banishing entirely all thoughts of the Lord Mayor's Day celebrations (that were due to take place later on that day) in a solitary knife stroke.

"There's been another one," he eventually gasped as he panted, massive eyes bulging from his petrified head. "Jack the Ripper. Awful."

FIFTY-THREE

A loud crack echoed through the court. The timber flexed and split as the axe handle came down. Pulling back, he went in again, harder. The door gave, splinters flying. McCarthy, the building's landlord stepped back, the axe handle now at rest in his hands. Abberline stepped forward. Reaching through the fresh hole in the door, an intent hand tried the stubborn old latch. Seconds later, the door swung open, a hiss of rust against metal. He stood aside.

Doctor Phillips, along with another doctor, had been called and was the first into the room. Abberline followed, passing the landlord and his shop assistant. The unwitting man who had first reported the grisly scene after poking his inquisitive nose through the murky window — and seeing . . . well, he did not know what it was exactly, but the amount of red was enough to warn anyone of terrible danger — was still visibly shaking.

After scrambling through a sea of constables within the courtyard itself, Jakob pushed through and entered the door, finally stepping into what could have been the very lair of Hell itself.

The whole room was red; it was everywhere, as if a bad painter had suddenly given way to a tremendous fit in the confines of the four walls. Blood and viscera skirted the small room. Any attempt at decoration had now been blotched out.

What is that lying on the bed?

Someone in the yard was crying out a name. "Mary, oh dear God, no!"

A disfigured form lay on the bed in front of them. All eyes within the room, some outside peering in, fell upon the grisly scene as the doctor and inspector talked quietly among themselves. Two of the duty constables, now guarding the doorway, were pinching their thumb and forefingers together above the bridge of their noses and into their eyes, in disbelief, with the faint hope of squeezing away the bloody sight from their memories permanently.

Who, or what, is it? Jakob took stock of the room. *Mary? Wasn't that the name of the vampire who held Jack captive?* He stepped in closer to inspect the bed and its contents — stopping short.

Above the unrecognisable and pulpy mess of sliced skin and bared muscle was a sea of brilliant red hair – the same red hair he had first witnessed all those years before when he had lugged the day's catch about Whitstable harbour.

No, no, it cannot be. The left arm told Jakob all he needed to know. Scratched crudely into the pale and dead flesh for all eternity, was a small heart-shaped scar.

No. Jakob could not cry, could not really feel any emotion any more — after all, did emotion not come from the heart? — but something, deep inside, pulled at him. His heart had stopped a long time ago, had even had something rammed through it. The feeling of loss and the death of someone he had loved, however briefly, left him with a hollow feeling. *When will it stop?*

He kept a straight face as his innards raged. This undead person, the strange being within him who was trying to keep his soul intact, had now gone, had left the scene along with the murderer. The vampire within him sprang forth in all its glory. He was the walking dead, a vampire, a monster that the Devil had spawned. Yes, Satan, Old Nick, Lucifer, Hades, Lord of the Flies, whatever he called himself, would be extremely proud of him now. *Enough is enough.*

Walking out of the small grey courtyard Jakob pushed his way past the sick and twisted mob who were all trying to 'grab a butcher's' at the latest gruesome murder. As he went Jakob's eyes scanned the crowd. *Look at them all. Love, compassion? - It's all crap. Szia - Shit.* His undead mind yelled at them. *You're all scum; none of you give a damn about any of the dead women, just as long as you get a good look. I'll eat every last fucking one of you, drink your blood, bathe in it, till the Devil himself walks back into Heaven.*

Enraged, he pushed his way out of the baying crowd of vultures and despicable parasites, heading off down Dorset Street. At speed, he soon passed the Ten Bells public house. One of those bells was now tolling for the target of his vengeance. With fixed determination Jakob headed towards Brick Lane. He knew exactly where he was headed.

The killing stops now.

FIFTY-FOUR

Looking deep into the eyes of the familiar face sauntering up the street towards him, recognition hit Jakob like another stake through the heart.

I don't believe it.

Jakob did a quick double take. *Yes.* It was one of the gang members. On his own. *The* one indeed.

How could he forget Freddy? He would recognise that fat, foul nose anywhere. It was Freddy who had plunged the dirty wooden offcut deep into his chest with the firm intention of sending him straight to the morgue — which, of course, he had done.

This time, things were different. There had been five of them that night. *Fucking cowards.* As he approached, the man with the fat nose spotted Jakob looking at him. He noticed, too, the blue of his police uniform and began whistling, dismissing him in criminal arrogance.

Not this time.

Conscious of his uniform, and also of giving himself away for the blood-drinking monster that he really was, Jakob let the sauntering man walk on by.

As soon as Freddy had his back to him Jakob glanced up the street, then down. There was no one around. Why would there be? — half of Whitechapel and Spitalfields had congregated *en masse* in Miller's Court this morning. Were all still there. *Sick, pathetic bastards.*

Quickening his pace, Jakob walked up behind Freddy. Hearing his steps, the man took flight, and ran. Jakob rolled his eyes, looked to the sky, shrugged his shoulders and went after him. *No, not this time.* Ducking down this alleyway and that, the fat-nosed man soon started to tire. Jakob caught him easily, an arm looping around his neck, and dragged him to the ground. Jakob was not even breathing hard, but then he was not technically breathing any more since he was a vampire, having to suck air in past his larynx to speak.

Panting heavily, the man looked up past his fat nose at Jakob. "Cor blimey . . . geezer, I . . . I ain't done nuffink, blue," he gasped through gritted black teeth.

Jakob stood there, over him, contemplating his next move. His only move.

"Come on now . . . sir," the man hesitated. "I really ain't done nuffink, I'm a good 'un, me."

"What about poor Emma Smith?" Jakob said. He thought of his Emma, or Mary, as it had somehow turned out to be.

"Never 'eard of 'er," Freddy contravened as he tried to stand up.

Jakob seethed. "Seems you're a fan of sticking people with blunt instruments."

Freddy relaxed his face, his eyes widening as his mind resolved the conflict of exactly who his captor was. "But—"

Jakob's hard, taught fist hit the man like the butt end of an old *Crab and Winkle Railway* coach. Hard undead tissue — for it was no longer flesh in the real sense of the word —

275

smashed into living flesh, the gristle and bone of Freddy's nose. With a loud crack, it collapsed completely. Freddy gurgled, an incomprehensible bubble of snot and blood. Jakob hit him again and again.

Then stopped.

Jakob's fist was stuck, caught in the gaping aperture of what was once the man's face. To anyone watching, Freddy must have looked like a ridiculous parasite, his face sucking on the end of his arm. Jakob struggled to free himself from the creature's accidental suction. Pulling his hand away, Freddy's crushed nose was now an ugly hole of gore. Jakob released his truncheon from the 'special pocket' on his uniform. Raising it, he slammed it down hard, ramming it into Freddy's exposed nasal cavity — paying back the favour.

Like the fish that Jakob used to haul around at the harbour, the man's dead corpse slapped onto the cobblestones with a dull wet thud. Jakob pulled the freshly glazed baton from Freddy's seeping brain cavity, and held it up, regarding it. It shimmered in the midday sunlight. *Beautiful*. Putting it to his mouth, Jakob started lapping at the blood. *Mmm . . . Édes a bosszú - Vengeance tastes sweet.*

The warm serum trickled down his raw throat. After all these years of drinking it cold, it was good. It flooded his body, fuelling his anger. Jakob was going to need all the strength he had.

FIFTY-FIVE

Jakob had arrived. The small begrimed house was contaminated, not by the irreclaimable scourge of the East End but by the savage diabolic fiend within, a regular Mephistopheles — Jack. Jakob tried the door and, finding it free, he walked in. *Should have locked it. It's not safe here in the East End — there's a killer on the loose.*

Jack had to die. Jakob would rid the world of this lunatic. A lunatic who he, himself, had entered into a simple blood pact with, and who despatched his victims with a jubilant and gleeful malice. It had been Jack's job to find sustenance for a vampire — not dead but decaying, not alive yet living — but he had more than overstepped the mark.

Time to pay the piper. Long before now, Jakob had been afraid of even killing a lousy rat. His mother and father had taught him well, had taught him simple values, morals. Emma had taught him better though, and now he had finally graduated — a killer for real.

Jack would be asleep, his late night activities must have turned into an all night debauched butchery session. He had spent hours trying to kill Emma — *just when had she taken the moniker Mary?* — eventually succeeding by skewering and severing the spinal cord in her neck vertebrae.

Dear Emma.

Jakob knew he should exercise caution. Jack had already killed a vampire and that meant that Jakob, too, could die. He was going to have to watch his step. On the whole, Jakob had the upper hand, he did not need sleep; Jack would, or should, be exhausted.

Searching the first room proved fruitless. Jakob gingerly shuffled around and tried the other room. He did not notice the stale air as the door banged against its splintered frame in the cool draught. He crept closer, his fists on the ready, his senses alert. *Quietly now.* Quieter than a dead whore on the streets of Whitechapel, Jakob pushed through the door with all the force that his blood-enriched body would allow. *Nem - No.*

The room was bare. Jack was not there. *Maybe he panicked? Ran?* Surely not, reasoning was the luxury of the sane. Surely Jack had to rest, the doctor and the police had corroborated that the killer must have left in the early morning, well after spending hours hacking at the woman — the same woman who had made him, Jakob; the woman he thought he had lost all those years ago. Although he hated her, he had loved her. Once. *Truly.*

Killing was easy for him now. Jakob *was* Death. He was going to carry on his feeding, a natural act for an unnatural being. In a guise that would make the Grim Reaper look like a frightened little pussy-cat, Jakob would rid the world of the low-life, the immoral, the perverted, the real monsters of this planet.

This was to be his new cause. Roaming freely, he would take their souls and their blood until God, or perhaps even Lusk, caught up with him. Humans would be his preferred food, his sweet sustenance. Jakob was not from Hell, he knew, but for those few that now got in his way, he would be Hell on earth.

FIFTY-SIX

Ten days passed. Jakob and Abberline searched high and low for all that time. Neither of them needed to sleep and so had continued, unabated. Feeling weak, they had visited Doctor Phillips again for some much needed nourishment. The doctor, as always, was obliging in his most favourable of ways. This time he had pestered the inspector about performing a detailed autopsy on him, once 'he'd passed', of course. Doctor Phillips had not said or mentioned anything to Jakob about the woman at Miller's Court, obviously never realising that he already had a dead vampire in his possession, resting at that very moment on his cold slabs.

Afterwards, Abberline said his farewells and headed back to the station; there were things for the inspector to sort out there. A huge crowd of mourners, well-wishers and morbid spectators were expected to turn out to Mary's — Emma's — funeral procession as it made its way to the Roman Catholic Cemetery at Leytonstone. The same people who had crowed over her whittled and pared body in Dorset Street were now turning out in a huge display of public sympathy. Bootlickers and hypocrites, the lot of them. Abberline told him he would catch up with him later.

Jakob found himself back a Jack's house. The cold abode was devoid of life, just as it had been more than a week earlier. Angry at finding the place empty yet again Jakob stepped back out into the street. The tall thin figure of Mister Batchelor stood before him. Next to him — he could never be missed — the huge mass of Mister Grand invaded the space of the small thoroughfare. They had followed Jakob, and were waiting outside for him.

"We followed ya, thought you'd be 'ere. Now, if you wanna see your friend alive again, you'd better come wiv us," bellowed the big man.

"What makes you think he's my friend? And that I want to see him alive?" Jakob said, undeterred.

"You vampires, you all stick together," squeaked the thin form of Mister Batchelor.

"You really don't know anything do you?" Jakob taunted.

"Well, eiver way you're comin' wiv us," Mister Grand said as he took an almighty step towards Jakob.

Jakob pulled backwards, away from the big man's grasp. A faint gap revealed a stretch of road behind the two men and Jakob spotted a red-eyed Abberline pounding up the street towards them.

The inspector joined in the unsettled conversation. "Now now, Grand, Batchelor. What do you think you're up to?" Abberline asked.

"Shit," Mister Grand barked under his breath.

"If you're going anywhere, you won't mind me tagging along now will you?" the inspector said to the two morose men.

A mountain of muscles, Mister Grand shrugged. "Okay then guv, let's go. You can both come along for the show."

"Yeah, we've got a special treat for ya — a reunion for the masquerading constable here, and a treats for you, good Inspector, sir," Mister Batchelor skreaked.

Together, the four of them started up the street.

FIFTY-SEVEN

Stepping into the house revealed a strange scene. Lusk had Jack tied and bound to a heavy wooden chair. The captive murderer was still in ecstasy from his latest kill by the look of him — his head, off to one side, stared blankly into space, a fevered rapture spread across his face.

"Greetings, my dear fellows," Lusk said as Jakob entered the back kitchen. "You know Jakob, you didn't have me fooled with that silly piece of kidney."

"No," Jakob admitted, somewhat embarrassed.

Inspector Abberline entered next, followed closely by his two goons. He spotted Lusk. There was a man tied to a chair.

"Afternoon George," Abberline said in a dry and mirthless tone.

The new voice shocked the prisoner in the chair back to reality again. Jack scanned the room, seeing Jakob. "J . . . Jake, help me, this fool thinks I'm—."

Lusk slapped the face of the whining man. "Quiet! We caught him leaving Dorset Street earlier on," Lusk said, glaring at his captive. "It seems he liked his own handiwork so much that, curiosity getting the better of him, he just had to go back and have another look-see. Big mistake. This young man here," he pointed towards Jack, "he's the culprit."

Lusk turned to Abberline. "You see Inspector, someone can do their job correctly," he said, smarmily.

Yes, send a madman to catch a madman, mused Jakob.

Together, Abberline and Jakob stared at Lusk. Like a proud sentinel, Lusk waited, a newly sharpened cut-throat razor in one hand, a leather strap lay to one side on the brittle kitchen work surface.

The man strapped to the chair, Jakob's one-time friend, had gone too far this time.

"I asked you to bring her to me," Jakob said to Jack.

"B . . . but she wanted to kill you. I . . . I wasn't goin' to let her," Jack said.

"I don't believe you Jack, she loved me."

Both Lusk and his men looked on, confused.

"It turns out that you didn't finish her off back there in the basement, Mister Lusk," Jakob said.

"I don't know what you're talking about," Lusk answered.

Abberline interjected. "Is there something you should be telling me, George?"

"No, no, just something that me and young Jakob here need to sort out."

Mister Batchelor pointed his spindly finger towards Jack. "What we gonna do wiv 'im?"

"Well . . . he *is* the killer," Jakob said.

"What? What you doin' Jake? It . . . it weren't me, it was . . . it was you, your idea," he shouted, panicking.

"No Jack, it was your doing. You're a killer. You wouldn't stop even when I pleaded with you. I've tried for so long to do the right thing. Inspector Abberline will tell you."

"How very touching," Lusk said.

"I'm innocent, please," Jack cried, begging. "Let me go, it was Antonas, he made me do it."

Ignoring him, Mister Batchelor searched Lusk's face before speaking. "Like I said before — what we gonna do wiv 'im, then?"

Silence flooded the room as they all stood reflecting each other's glances, waiting for one another to speak.

Solemnly, in a low voice, Abberline addressed the room. "Look, I believe that we should listen to our suspect. Surely, as policemen and responsible citizens, we have to consider him innocent until proven guilty. We cannot condemn him in this little room. And you, George, you're certainly not judge, jury and executioner all in one."

"But Inspector—"

"I mean just listen to him. He's blaming another chap by the name of . . . Anthony? We have a duty to investigate further," Abberline continued.

"Further, indeed. This man is clearly insane," Lusk said.

Jakob nodded in silent agreement.

"Yes. L . . . listen to the Inspector," Jack said. "Just let—" he tried to add, his voice fading, muffled, as Lusk wrapped a cloth around his mouth to silence him.

Jack's eyes bulged, implored Jakob like a puppy dog in a shop, silently toting 'please take me with you'.

"I'm sorry Jack, you should not have killed Emma."

"Jakob, we don't yet know that he did?" Abberline said. "And I thought her name was Mary?"

"Oh my. A strange irony really," Lusk said, blandly. "Here we all are, on Robin Hood Lane, only we're not robbing the rich to give to the poor. No. Instead we find ourselves in a position to do the right thing — to rid the world of a killer to save the poor of the East End."

"Don't touch him Lusk," Abberline warned.

"Good Lord, my dear Inspector, did it ever occur to you that I don't care what you say. You have never been forthcoming with your help. You mocked me personally when I came to you to offer my services. You and the police have had your chance and you have royally cocked up. I, on the other hand, have succeeded where you have failed. Even your trusty Sergeant here agrees that whatever happens the Whitechapel murderer must die — today."

At that, Lusk stepped forward to slice at Jack's throat with his razor. With all the chatting that had been bouncing around the room, no one, not even the manic-eyed Mister Batchelor, had seen Jack shake loose of his bindings and slip out of the chair.

At speed, Jack rebounded off Mister Grand's huge belly, bundled through the doorway and found himself standing in the lane outside. Looking up and down the street, Jack scarpered, making off towards the river.

Abberline raised his arms in the room. "Let him go."

Jakob and Lusk screamed in unison. "No."

Mister Grand and Mister Batchelor looked at each other, waiting for their superior to move first.

"Come on you fools," Lusk barked at his two assistants.

Lusk turned and headed for the door. Jakob flew out into the road, this time it was him following Lusk.

"Who's he callin' a fool?" Mister Batchelor turned to Inspector Abberline.

"I think he means both of you. And if you want my opinion, he's exactly right," the inspector answered.

Unhappy at being called a fool twice, Mister Grand stepped up to Abberline and stuck his oversized and angry face into his. Like an eclipse, Mister Batchelor vanished from the inspector's view.

Undeterred, Abberline said, "All I'm saying is that you must be a fool following that madman around the country. Does he even pay you? I mean, as a detective, *I* get paid."

A whiny voice came from the back of the room. "He's got a point you know, Grandie."

Mister Grand's face relaxed. He growled. "Yeah. And if Mister Lusk calls me that again, he'll wind up swimmin' in the Thames."

"I'll happily look the other way," Abberline said. "I do that every day with most of the pinchcocks around here anyway."

"Sorry to break up your cosy little chat but haven't we got a murderer to catch?" Mister Batchelor said as he reeled past Mister Grand and Abberline.

"Yes, let's go. We don't want to miss old Georgie boy in his big moment," Abberline said as he left the building closely behind a now-running Mister Batchelor.

Like an unearthed mountain bouncing up the road, the big man with the matching big name — Mister Grand — complied and pursued the others.

FIFTY-EIGHT

Jack's blunt legs took him along the railway tracks behind Prestage Street — the shabby backyards of the twenty-five or so terraced houses all ignoring his fearful flight for freedom as he headed towards the East India export docks. Behind him, a smartly dressed gentleman carrying a small portmanteau suitcase waited alone on Poplar Station platform.

As Jack charged by him — nearly bowling the both of them over — he noticed the dapper man looked totally out of place near a working dock and appeared more depressed than bewildered. Jack glanced behind him again. There had been no train go by but the man had now gone. *He's at the wrong station if he needs a lift – bleedin' toff.* Jack's view was replaced by a man in a bowler hat and a fake policeman, both running, and the two were getting nearer. *Shit*. He put his head down and pumped his numb legs harder.

Moments later, Jack knew he had made a grave mistake. In just running blindly, he had gone and ran to the edge of the Thames. On reaching Brunswick Wharf, he had very few options.

Lusk and Jake were getting closer.

He ducked past the old hotel, now some sort of emigrants' lodging house for would-be New Zealanders. All seemed quiet. A couple of yard workers were having a tipple in the Tap, the bad ale they served distracting them from noticing the Whitechapel murderer as he slipped into the brick warehouse next door.

Jack slid on dry hay as he entered the warehouse, and made for the stairs. Up he went. On the first floor, boxes of Garibaldi biscuits blocked his way. He pushed at them, the hard cardboard casings screeching on the floor. He stopped. *Damn.* The noise might attract Jake and Lusk. Carefully, Jack crept by the boxes, avoiding the packets of 'squashed flies' — he hated currants. In the far corner he ducked down behind some discarded older crates. It was not long before he heard exactly what he did not want to hear — Jake and Lusk were in the building.

"You look along there, vampire," Lusk said, obviously talking to Jack's old friend.

"Okay Lusk, but be sure to leave him to me. You've had your chance," Jakob said.

"But are you prepared to do what is necessary when it comes to it?"

"He killed my girl."

"Your 'girl', as you say, killed my sister so I don't really care about your little tiff with your friend, the Ripper."

"I'm sorry about your sister Lusk but it had nothing to do with me. You may have scared me before but now things are a little different," Jakob said as he turned and glowered at Lusk.

Jack listened to the vampire and the hunter as they bickered, could see them as he peered through the various cracks in the biscuit crates.

"Come out, come out, wherever you are," a voice said. It was Lusk.

"Careful Lusk, Jack's not all there you know, if he does come out, you may be first in his firing line," Jakob warned.

"It won't be the first time I've stood face to face with danger, you heathen."

"You mean back in your builder days? I can imagine the terror of a poorly constructed wall falling on you, or the fear in your heart as your freshly hung wallpaper peels off in front of your eyes," Jakob shot back.

Jack felt a flush of pride as his friend, Jake, knocked Lusk and his chosen trade. *Why has Jake turned on me?* Jack puzzled over the obvious before realising. *Oh yeah, the girl.*

"You're not—"

"Shut your mouth Lusk. Just get the job done, I'm growing impatient. I'm not in the mood for any more of your crap," Jakob bawled.

Jack gulped. In the distance he could see two other figures rummaging around, kicking at the boxes and junk. *Damn it.*

His escape was getting narrower by the minute. He readied himself to go, to move his deadening legs before it was too late. Soon, the whole police force would be here. A shadow passed over him and he froze. Lusk stepped into his view, inches from where he was concealed. Luckily, the vampire hunter had his head turned towards Jakob. Jack held his breath as the world and the innards of the crate got darker; a deep rasping noise started up. *What the—?*

Agitated by what he saw in Jakob's vampire eyes, Lusk turned back to what he was doing, continuing to search the dusty warehouse without a word. A heavy panting sound, a noise like a human steam train, came up behind Lusk. It was Mister Grand; he had taken some minutes plodding his enormous bulk down the road in pursuit and was wheezing badly.

Mister Grand sat down on one of the crates, sweating and sticky. He was visibly shaking. Hoicking a thick glob of spittle from the back of his throat, he spat. In disgust, Lusk turned away. The sudden movement, as his giant head jolted down and forward, forcing the gob high into the air, caused his weight to shift. Like a colossal baby, rolling gently in his makeshift crib of rugged boxes, Mister Grand wobbled.

There was a creak, a tiny, barely audible note, followed by an almighty crack as the crate imploded, sending dust and biscuit crumbs into the air and covering the immediate area. Mister Grand went down like a stevedore's wages. The floor shook. Feeling the tremors on the far side of the warehouse, Abberline and Mister Batchelor came over to check out what was going on.

"For God's sake you idiot," Lusk screamed at his fallen comrade.

Abberline smirked. Mister Batchelor went to aid his friend although what help he would be seemed questionable — it would be like a feather lifting one of *Currie's Calcutta Castles* away from its resting berth.

"Get the big lug off me," came a voice from under the crumbs.

Mister Grand lay wriggling, his enormous frame on top of the crate and debris. Below him, Jack writhed, his hideaway unintentionally revealed by the exhausted fat man.

Jakob brushed past Mister Batchelor as Mister Grand made it back to his feet. He bent down and grabbed at Jack, hauling him up. Watching, Mister Grand brushed at his suit and picked a broken piece of biscuit from his lapel. He looked at it before popping into his mouth, crunching down.

Ignoring the hungry beast behind him, Jakob's attention was totally on Jack. He reached into his pocket. "I'd like to say I'm sorry Jack . . . but I'm not," Jakob said, before lashing out and cutting deep across Jack's Adam's apple.

Jack babbled and clutched at his neck, desperately attempting to stem the natural flow. He tottered backwards and Jakob lifted his boot, shoving him back further. The broken window did nothing to stop Jack, only aided in altering his centre of balance. He toppled over and hit the cold water below head first.

Jakob and Abberline stepped to the window and peered down. The body floated for a minute and then slowly sank from view.

The inspector, still looking down at the water as it pooled with crimson, directed his words at Jakob. "You cannot kill him like that," Abberline said.

Jakob turned to face the inspector, his eyes dark. "I'm not drinking from him."

At the sight of Jakob's delirium, Mister Grand and Mister Batchelor backed away.

"Get them, you fools," Lusk shouted at the biscuit-muncher and his tall companion.

Incensed at being called fools yet again, and probably more so at having his treat of Peek Frean's interrupted, Mister Grand looked up at Mister Batchelor. The tall man nodded back.

"Go on then, get them," Lusk said again. "Damned fools."

In silent unison, the human 'number ten' moved forward and lifted Lusk off the floor. Manhandling him to the window, Lusk struggled to free himself.

"Do as I say," Lusk screamed at them.

"Nobody talks to me like that," Mister Grand said.

"Me neither," Mister Batchelor pined.

In fear, Lusk shouted to the inspector. "Inspector Abberline, I implore you. Please, get them off me."

Abberline and Jakob were enjoying the show. It was comic relief after what had just taken place. Lusk deserved it.

"Oh, I'm sure I've got to attend to something a little more important. A beaten cat perhaps," Abberline said.

"I told you he'd wind up in the Thames if he said it again, didn't I?" Mister Grand said.

On the last word of his sentence, the 'I', Mister Grand flicked his mighty arms up and tossed Lusk out of the window.

"Noooo—" The scream got quieter before disappearing altogether at the sound of a deep splash.

Abberline looked out of the window again, saw nothing. "I think you may have killed him. Oh, no, wait, there he is."

The other three stepped forward and all laughed as they watched Lusk, scrambling through the shitty water, chasing his black bowler hat as it floated away.

"So, what now? We all walk away, deny any involvement, fabricate a   suicide?" Mister Batchelor asked Abberline.

"Yes, good idea," Abberline replied. "That's exactly what we'll do."

Abberline nodded at Mister Batchelor before turning back to the warehouse stairs. He and Jakob were leaving. "You know, you two should go out on your own," Abberline called out.

Mister Grand nodded, he was smiling now, and he had another of his biscuits ready to pop into his mouth. Mister Batchelor rubbed his thin hands together, they were both in affirmation.

As Abberline and Jakob exited the musty warehouse, the inspector looked up at the grey afternoon sky and spoke. "Well, that went better than planned."

"Yes," Jakob answered, shrugging his shoulders.

"What if they decide to come after us. I mean, once old Georgie boy has dried out from his afternoon dip in the river?" Abberline said.

"I don't think we'll get any more trouble from those two in there. Lusk is a different kettle of fish though. I suppose we'll deal with him as and when we need to. We are vampires Inspector, we are meant to kill."

FIFTY-NINE

The two men walked back, along the quiet and soiled walkway. They passed the triple pontoon of the floating pier at Limehouse Kilns and headed west, the water rippling against the edges, bubbling in grime. In conversation, the two policemen headed up Narrow Street.

Milling about on the shale of the docks below and trying to look as inconspicuous as they could for the supernatural beings that they were, another two figures spotted them go by.

The fidgety one gaped and turned to ask his companion. "There they go, sir."

"Yes, thank you Gregory. I think I can see them for myself," Uri said.

Gregory was a Watcher, despatched to the earth to watch over the humans. He would report anything out of the ordinary to one of the four Archangels, including the one who currently shared the same patch of Thames real estate, Uriel. The others, Michael, Gabriel and Raphael were busy doing other things. Particularly Michael, it was he who commanded a legion. God's armies were at his beck and call in the event of an uprising from Satan's forces.

"Do you think we've lost him sir?"

"Unfortunately Gregory, yes, I do. He seems to have released his grip on his humanity. I think Jakob will now concentrate all his hatred on the vile souls that roam the planet. A strange paradox really — in one way, he's doing the world a favour by ridding them of the wicked, but at the same time he'll be filling up Satan's loathsome coffers. In a way, it's a shame the Whitechapel murderer is now dead — at least his victims have good souls and are now with us," Uri commented as he kicked at a small pebble, watching it skate into the Thames. It disappeared with an uneventful splash.

"Should we not help Mister Lusk out of the water?" Gregory asked.

"No, I'm sure he'll be fine. It might sober him up a little."

"Of course. I'll keep an eye on him . . . and Jakob and the Inspector. I'll keep an eye on them all."

"Thank you Gregory. At the end of the day, it's all about balance."

SIXTY

It was hard for Jakob to comprehend, but around one-hundred years had passed since his human birth, his real birth. Yet here he stood, still enshrouded in the same body, the body of about a twenty-something-year-old man, albeit one in need of a good suntan.

Jakob had returned to the place that he had always felt most comfortable: Whitstable. He enjoyed its anonymity. When the English holidayed in the south-east, they tended to miss Whitstable altogether, heading instead for towns like Margate or Ramsgate.

Maybe one day he would go back to his beloved Hungary, it was his birthright after all. Returning to the northern coast of Kent had been an odd feeling; well, as odd as his feelings would allow now that he was well and truly undead. It was not home, but a welcome stand-in.

On first arriving back Jakob was careful, believing that some of the residents might still recognise him, the hired hand from the wharf all those years ago. *Pointless paranoia again.* It was not long before it dawned on him that something like eighty years had passed since he was last seen strolling the streets here, an innocent man, a lost boy.

He knew he was being incredibly silly; most of the people who were alive then would certainly have had the common grace to have forgotten all about a foolish foreigner like himself, or would most likely have passed away, after living a sin free life — taken from this world as their faith saw fit.

Free. Jakob knew he would never be free. But at least he was at peace now with who, or what he was — a killer. But what this killer wanted, more than anything else in the world — apart from his regular dose of fresh flowing unfermented blood — was a view of the sea. His home country of Hungary was land-locked and he had never seen the ocean until, well, his parents . . .

He found a small house that overlooked the sea with a small kitchen and a single bedroom. The house was tastefully decorated but Jakob did not really notice. There were few cupboards but the kitchen alone had more space than he would ever need. The vampire was now settled.

Jakob had ended up leaving London with a little money after 'retiring' from the force a year after Abberline had decided to get himself off to Bournemouth in 1913. The two had never been close, but they continued their acquaintance, sharing a kinship in blood. The inspector had been dead for thirty years now. Lusk's legacy living on, some of his mob had finally caught up with him and sent the ex-Inspector First-Class to where he belonged. To where Jakob belonged too. Still, even today, Jakob waits for them every night to cross his threshold and send him straight back to Hell.

Abberline had obviously used Ludwig as a scapegoat, vainly trying to pin the murders of Whitechapel on him, and yet, somehow Ludwig had slipped the net. Perhaps Abberline was more interested in fulfilling his own blood-lust — after all, Jakob himself had investigated another mutilated female torso that had turned up the following year, in 1889.

Sir Melville Macnaughten, the Assistant Commissioner of the CID, wrote in his memoranda:

On 10th Sept. "89 the naked body, with arms, of a woman was found wrapped in some sacking under a railway arch in Pinchin Street: the head & legs were never found nor was the woman ever identified . . . The stomach was split up by a cut, and the head and legs had been severed in a manner identical with that of the woman whose remains were discovered in the Thames, in Battersea Park, and on the Chelsea Embankment on 4th June of the same year; and these murders had no connection whatever with the Whitechapel horrors.

Jakob laughed. In a strange way, Abberline had been right all along about Ludwig, when he had arrested him all those years ago. Time had eventually caught up with Ludwig and he was long dead by now. It turned out that Ludwig had not been his real name at all and he had gone on to perfect his toxins, eventually poisoning and killing at least three women. He had been caught and hanged at Wandsworth Prison on April 7th, 1903. Jakob wondered if he himself had played a part in Ludwig's obsession too?

Jakob had been involved in one of the most infamous killing sprees that England had ever seen and, in one way or another, Jakob had gone down in history forever. The only trouble was, nobody would ever know. Perhaps that was for the best; the 1950s were coming to a close and the Whitechapel murderer was all but a footnote these days. *Why open closed wounds?*

Soon though, the quiet life began to tell on him. He was a doer and could not sit down for long. So one day he just got up and went out to get another job. He found one immediately, his work ethic still the same. Having joined a small but local Estate Agency, Jakob decided he would try his undead hands at selling houses, and hopefully make himself a tidy profit.

It was good work, he did not have to get his hands dirty and, working around the prospective clients, he found he could come and go as he pleased. The houses themselves were quaint — not the cramped and dodgy doss-houses that surrounded the Christ Church in Spitalfields — and easy to sell.

Jakob is still there today and earning nearly £190 a year. Maybe he would get one of those new Mini cars that were due to be released. *Maybe not, it's designed by an Ottoman.*

1959 was turning out to be a good year. Jakob had his little house and he had a good job. A football team from the Midlands, Nottingham Forest, had recently won the FA Cup final — Nicholas Hawksmoor, the famed Baroque architect, would surely be happily celebrating in his grave. To top it all, Jakob had countless miles of sand, sea and countryside to carefully pick off his victims, and indulge in his next meal.

Being of the walking dead also came with its advantages and disadvantages. His appearance never changed and so, in time, he might have to move on again. Unless he left it until someone became suspicious and began questioning him . . . And if they did, it would probably be the last thing they would ever do. After all, it was not the smartest thing to do; to confront a blood thirsty vampire. Jakob did not mind really; he could just do without the hassle.

However, he could only ignore the strange looks from the locals for so long. Moving on was part and parcel of his life, so he would have to get used to it. Besides, if he stayed too long in one place, the death toll could get ridiculous. For now though it was where he wanted to be. As for good old human blood, he had become accustomed to it now; rats and leeches, even prostitutes, were not likely to be on the menu any time soon.

Vampires. Jakob knew good from bad but he also knew that vampires were inherently bad, but the legends, the myths, were something to be taken with a pinch of salt. In the scheme of things few people ever realised that they even existed, until it was too late. Man was the real evil in this brutal world. As soon as evolution had sprouted forth his thumb, it was all he could do to wrap that little dextrous digit around the heaviest piece of wood, shape it into a weapon, wield it high, and go about clubbing his neighbour to death. It was *his* time now, and as a vampire he would wreak vengeance on this world.

Jakob had lived for longer than he ever thought possible. In the time he had been conscious, in Europe alone, he had seen man inflict terrible deeds upon his own kind during the horrors of at least two world wars, but any tales he had relating to those could wait for another time. *Who'd want to listen anyway?*

A mild morning, he had gone to work as normal and sat down at his desk. Readying himself for the coming day, he was straightening some paperwork on his desk when the telephone rang. The cumbersome brown telephone always amazed him. *How on earth does a voice travel down wire?* Lifting the handset from its cradle, he picked it up.

"Good morning, you're speaking to Jake. How may I help you today?" he said, in the manner to which he had been instructed. He liked the trendy shortened version of his name now — these were modern times — and he now used it all the time.

"Hello, my dear Jake, this is Peter," a sincere voice said into his ear.

"Hello, sir, how are you?" Jake inquired politely. *This job really is going to be incredibly easy.*

"I'm extremely well thank you, better if you can give me good news," the voice said.

"And what news would that be, sir?"

"Well, Jake my man, I'm looking to purchase a holiday home in your beautiful town and I had my eye on a particular one," the voice said from the tinny earpiece. It sounded excited.

After discussing the details and the asking price, the polite man on the other end of the telephone continued. "Good Lord," he expressed. "As much as that? But, oh my heavens, it sounds, erm . . . lovely. Helen will just love it, you see. We need to get away from the city air, it stinks to high heaven, but . . . am I talking too much?"

"It's understandable to get excited sir, it's a big move," Jake said.

"Peter, please."

"Peter, yes. Now, if I can arrange a proper viewing, it will only boil down to price."

"Well," the man named Peter admitted, "it seems Humphrey Bogart could do no wrong and I appear to be sharing in his similar fortunes."

The caller explained that he was an actor and had just seen an increase in his popularity and, of course, in his wages. He went on to tell Jake of the success of the horror films he had done with the guidance of a new art-house director named Terence Fisher, under the guise of a studio named after a tool made for bludging someone with — or at least, a nail.

"Hammer," he said.

With a 'bless you my dear boy' and 'I'll see you in a few days', the man named Peter was gone, unknowing that the man with whom he had been talking to was the same thing that his celluloid character had sworn to kill.

Life of the undead always surprised Jake. He had seen and done some awful things, was still doing them in fact — at least weekly. But then he found that behind all the selfish horror and detestable acts that the human race endured, and in turn handed out, there always shone out a ray of hope. Now and then, in-between the pandemonium and horror of daily life, a heroic or happy soul would cross his path.

If Jake still had any of his humanity left it would have lifted him into the air — he was going to sell a house to a famous film star, one Peter Cushing.

Back at his home that evening, Jake spotted the newspaper that lay unread on the table. It fluttered and flapped in the breeze as he stepped through the back door, into the kitchen. Picking it up, Jake smiled to himself in silent amusement as he read an article about the popularity of the horror film genre and of one fictional character in particular.

The character in question was a vampire by the name of Dracula, a fiend who survives only by drinking the blood of humans, the story set partly in the small fishing town of Whitby.

Deciding to sit himself down at the round table and chair, Jake spread the newspaper out and brushed some old letters to one side. Outside, the sun was setting and shone brilliant orange and purple into his eyes. Squinting, he lifted the newspaper to block the evening sun and read some more.

Later that night, Jake went to the house of an older man. He had watched the repugnant man on several occasions, had watched him taking young boys into his house. The man was sick — it was time for Jake to pay him a little visit.

As he broke into the cold house which sat innocently next to the dilapidated old church walls, Jake reached into his pocket to draw out his knife but did not notice a piece of paper fall from his coat and flitter to the floor as he did so. Some minutes later, a muffled cry was heard and Jake reappeared in the dark hallway of the house which was now in urgent need of a new owner and a good cleaner with an even better stain remover.

As he stood there wiping the flat piece of steel in his hands, the sun peaked its head up onto a slightly better town, the bad man was no more. Sunlight edged a solitary beam through the mildewed net curtains that stained the windows. A tiny trickle of scarlet on his chin belied the mischievous deed — he had never got the hang of getting it all into his mouth in one gulp, it was awkward stuff.

About to head off from his latest kill, he noticed something in the corner of his eye. The small piece of white paper that he had dropped from his pocket earlier now caught the light and shone up at him. He glanced down, grinning cheekily to himself. *Well now, will you look at that?* Jake reflected, fresh blood still staining his blue lips.

There, on the hall floor next to his black boots, a small opened envelope lay innocently face up, emptied of its flat contents. He had read the letter the previous day and thought he had discarded the envelope in his kitchen dustbin. Conscious that he better not leave any evidence lying around, he hunkered down in the hallway like a squatting gargoyle and went to pick it up.

As he looked down at the used envelope, in large black bold print, it spelled out his name:

Jake Oláh, Whitstable.

EPILOGUE

Of course he had told the gullible wench of a vampire that he was never going to live on that 'slimy red shit', but Jack had gulped down some of her blood back in the confines of the tiny room at number thirteen that night just the same. He was glad he had, otherwise he would not be here now. He had no choice in it really though, Antonas was not the sort of person — or being — you could easily ignore. Antonas had stood by vigilantly and made him do it, and watched intently.

Becoming a vampire himself was only the start of what he was now to do. After he had dragged himself out of the Thames, his body dumped for dead when Jakob had slit his throat and hauled him out of the warehouse first floor window, Jack had finally realised his ambition.

A destiny of death.

Jack's killing now had clarity, a sense of real purpose. Instead of taking virtuous, impeccant souls, he would turn the nasty, the cruel and the treacherous. An army was needed for the coming apocalypse — Antonas had been quite succinct — when the destruction of Heaven and earth would be recast, remoulded, and ruled by Satan. It was to be an army that walked the earth by day and killed the wicked and sinful by night, continually filling the infernal legions of the underworld with maligned souls.

Jack had not seen Jakob since that night either. Under the guidance of Pura, he was told that he would meet him again someday — they were kindred spirits after all. The dead vampire in Miller's Court had once been Jakob's love and, well, Jakob had not taken it too well once he had found out that he had turned her into a living, or rather dead, art form. *No, it's better to stay out of Jakob's way.*

He laughed. *Anyway, they all think I'm dead.*

Jack may have been laughing but Pura had not been too happy with him and had castigated him. It was Pura who had called forth Emma from the dead many years before and she had actually liked her. As Jack stood in the great hall in front of Antonas — no, Satan — and Pura, the Princess of Sorrow and Conjurer of the Dead, he had felt like a scalded little school boy.

Whatever. Jack dismissed his new bosses — Emma and Mary were one and the same, she had been his masterpiece. Red art.

Having no friends did not bother Jack anymore either. He had reached a higher, or depending on your personal view, a lower plane of existence. With humans he seemed to exude a certain power over their easily-led minds now — he found he could seduce them easily before despatching them with the help of his trusty knife.

He hoped that his other friend, the eager journalist Ernie, had finally got his big scoop, too. No doubt he would read Ernie's reports in the newspapers. Jack had really liked Ernie.

The big question now on his own dead lips was: What should he do now? Where would he go next? He knew what he had to do; of that Antonas had been precise. But that could wait for a while at least. He decided fate would guide him; it would come in time of its own accord. Tonight, he had other things on his mind.

He was hungry.

Throwing his black coat on over his shoulders, he tugged at the front to fasten it. With the hands of a skilful technician, he placed his black hat upon his head gently, reached across his stark new room and picked up his old bag.

Two glass jars inside clinked together softly, offering a salutary 'cheers' as he lifted the bag over the bed and brought it down to his side.

Shutting the door behind him with a sure click, Jack lifted up his collar around his pallid neck and stepped out, once more, into the cold night.

THE END

THE TRUTH . . . Mostly

The 1880s saw London in a transitional stage, shedding its traditional Victorian values for a more modern age. Industrialisation saw large factories take up home there; dye-houses, warehouses, foundries, tanning-houses and mills cluttered the area, all spewing their variant noxious wastes into the surrounding air. The immediate area, suitable only for industry and business, became home to the lowest of workers, the poorest of people — all taking up residence in the most abysmal and wretched lodging houses.

Thoughtless decisions by the Government, such as the 1860 free-trade policy (allowing the duty-free import of French materials), the area saw approximately 50,000 people employed in the silk industry shrink to less than 3,500 by around 1880. You can imagine the knock-on effect this had to the economy in the area. Add to that the London match-girls' strike in July, 1888 due to long hours, poor pay and severe health complications, and you begin to build a picture of the employment problems and feelings of despair felt in the East End.

Tight-fisted, unscrupulous landlords would only deepen their woes by charging ridiculous amounts of money for a night's stay in what was little more than a hovel. In 1883, Queen

Victoria wrote to Prime Minister Gladstone demanding that he 'obtain more precise information as to the true state of affairs in these overcrowded, unhealthy, and squalid abodes'. Gladstone's response was to avoid the issue as much as possible.

Thus the overcrowded, underpaid, unemployed and hungry residents turned to petty crime, racketeering, violence and prostitution — just so they could get 'digs' for the night or a few scraps of barely-edible food as nutritious as week-old mouldy bread.

Soon, conditions of poverty, promiscuity and villainy would set the scene for one of the most notorious of murderers to step forward and put the East End on the historical maps forever.

So, during the real Autumn of Terror, 1888, what really happened? Who was Jack the Ripper – this fiend with a twisted mind? Why was he never caught? Was he a royal? A doctor? A Mason? A butcher? Were there two men involved? Just how many did he really kill? And why did he stop? Or did he? The questions just keep on coming.

This author is afraid we'll never know. Of course, many authors have a preferred suspect who fits the bill, and many make a detailed and even believable argument of who they think he (or she) is — or was.

All we really know about the real Jack the Ripper case is that he has left behind a true conundrum — an enigma.

The story *Partnership from Hell* is a fictional account of what may have happened in the Jack the Ripper case, had vampires been real (who am I to say they are not?). The fictional story could be regarded as being as credible as some of the (absurdly ridiculous) arguments out there and yet it really is totally infeasible. Isn't it?

The facts: Late March 1888, Ada Wilson answered a knock at the door to a man who demanded money from her before being stabbed twice in her throat. The man escaped and Ada Wilson survived to give her side of the story to the authorities. Was she the lucky victim of an early Ripper attack? The fact that the assailer demanded money suggests this was not an attack by a crazed killer.

In April 1888, Emma Smith was viciously attacked by a gang as she made her way home. She initially survived the violent assault only to die four days later from complications arising from a ripped perineum. A Ripper victim? Again, almost certainly not as there is no reason to doubt her given statement of several assailants.

Things appeared to go quiet for the summer (Could it be he was incarcerated against his will by an unknown female vampire somewhere in the London docks?).

Then came the autumn.

Bank Holiday Monday, August 6th 1888 Martha Tabram was out with her friend 'Pearly Poll'. They were seen drinking in several pubs accompanied by two soldiers. Upon leaving the final drinking establishment Martha and the Private ventured into George Yard, and Pearly Poll and the Corporal headed off elsewhere, both probably with the intent of sex. At 2.00 AM, PC Thomas Barrett saw a young Guardsman in Wentworth Street. Barrett questioned the Guardsman who stated that he was waiting for a 'chum who went off with a girl'. Then, around 4.45

AM, laying face upward on the blood-drenched steps of a first-floor landing, Martha Tabram was found dead, brutally stabbed thirty-nine times. It is difficult to say whether she was a Ripper victim or not. Most Ripperologists stand divided on this one. Whether she was or not, the poor woman died in a most terrible and extremely wicked way.

The last day in August 1888 saw havoc in Shadwell Dry Dock when a fire erupted, burning until late the next morning. The fire in the docks later helped to establish John Pizer's (Leather Apron's) innocence as witnesses were able to place him there. But there was also saw another murder — that of Mary Ann Nichols. Found in Buck's Row, her throat was cut, the incision severing the tissues down to the vertebrae. The lower part of her abdomen had been cut, with several deep wounds running down her body. She is generally accepted as the first (or canonical) victim.

September was to see three more murders. On the 8th September 1888 Annie Chapman was found in the rear yard of 29 Hanbury Street, her throat also sliced open, as was her lower abdomen, the contents of which had been lifted out and placed on her shoulder. A passer-by at the time, Elizabeth Long, saw Chapman talking with a man on Hanbury Street. Long heard the man say 'Will you?' to which Annie replied "Yes." Another poor girl had wandered into the unknown with Jack the Ripper.

Late September saw the unprecedented 'double event' when Elizabeth Stride and Catherine Eddowes were killed on the same night. Earlier that evening a man named Israel Schwartz stated to the police that he had seen a man on Berner Street throw a woman to the ground. In fear, Mr

Schwartz crossed the road only to see another man. Before running away he heard the man (who had thrown the woman down) call out: 'Lipski' (not 'Risky?' as in the story). Mr Schwartz couldn't say if the two men were together or even if they knew each other. When he was taken to the mortuary, Mr Schwartz identified the body as that of the woman he had seen. The woman, Elizabeth Stride, was found in Dutfield's Yard. She had a deep gash across her neck, but no other apparent injuries. Was it the Ripper? Had he been interrupted? Forced to leave the scene before he could leave his horrific trademark? If so, he wasn't yet satisfied.

Later that same night, Mitre Square saw the only murder in the City jurisdiction. At 12.55 PM, Catherine Eddowes had just been released from Bishopsgate Police Station after being found drunk on the Aldgate High Street. Less than an hour later she was found dead, this time severely mutilated. Her body opened right up, intestines strewn about, an ear lobe cut away, the nose sliced off. There were more injuries and stab wounds, including the complete removal of her left kidney.

After the victim was found in Mitre Square, the search escalated. PC Alfred Long found a blood-stained piece of apron in an archway at Wentworth Model Dwellings, on Goulston Street. At the same spot was a chalked message on the brick fascia of the open doorway: The Juwes are the men That Will not be Blamed for nothing. Was it evidence? Is it even relevant? Who knows? And in the grime of the East End why would a discarded old piece of cloth interest a policeman? Particularly when it is revealed that PC Long was only on his beat and did not yet know of the murder in Mitre Square? And what did the words on the wall mean? Again, this author believes we will never know — it could go down as the greatest wild goose chase in criminal history.

October 2nd 1888. Known as the Whitehall Mystery the decomposed headless and limbless torso of a woman was found dumped in a cellar vault — a vault on the site of New Scotland Yard. The unidentified woman's arms were found later, dumped in the Thames. Although it was undoubtedly a barbaric crime there is no other evidence that the woman was ever a Ripper victim (or the victim of two hungry vampires).

On the evening of October 16th 1888 George Lusk, head of the Whitechapel Vigilance Committee received a small package wrapped in brown paper. Inside was half a kidney and a letter:

From hell
Mr Lusk
Sor
I send you half the
Kidne I took from one woman
prasarved it for you tother piece
I fried and ate it was very nise. I
may send you the bloody knif that
took it out if you only wate a whil
longer.
Signed   Catch me when
you can
Mishter Lusk

Morning of 9th November 1888. The final victim, Mary Kelly, was butchered beyond comprehension. She was the only victim to be found indoors — the Ripper clearly having more time to do his macabre damage. It is an injustice to her to reveal the extent of her terrible wounds, suffice to say that she was completely unrecognisable, not only as a person, but as a human being. We can only hope the pretty, twenty-five-year-old suffered little and that the first blow she encountered sent her off into eternal slumber.

And at that a truly awful series of crimes suddenly ended, the perpetrator never caught.

Names: It was only too common for people in the 1880s to have more than one name. Why this should be is not quite known. It was common for women to take the surname of their boyfriends, as marriage was clearly far too expensive for most of them. Perhaps they were simply nicknames. Perhaps it was to avoid the police officials.

Martha Tabram was known as Emma Turner. (Jack's victim on the night they pretend to be soldiers. Found in George Yard.)

Mary Ann Nichols was known as Polly. (Jack's victim on the night of the fire. Found in Buck's Row.)

Annie Chapman was also known as Dark Annie or Annie Sivvey. (Abberline's victim. Found in Hanbury Street.)

Elizabeth Stride was known as Long Liz. (First victim on the night of the double event. Jakob was too late in stopping Jack.)

Catherine Eddowes was known as Kate Kelly. (Second victim on the night of the double event. Found in Mitre Square.)

Mary Jane Kelly was known by many names - Marie Jeanette Kelly, Mary Ann Kelly, Ginger and Fair Emma (Jake's girl).

George Chapman was an alias of *Severin Klosowski* who was also known to locals as Ludwig Schloski.

Police officials: Following the murder of Mary Ann Nichols on 31 August 1888 Inspector First-Class Frederick Abberline was seconded back to Whitechapel to head up H. Division. Another detective in H. Division, DC Walter Dew, described Abberline as: 'Sounding and looking like a bank manager'. It was Abberline's extensive knowledge of the Whitechapel and surrounding areas that made him an important member of the murder investigation team. He died in 1929 aged 86 at his home in Bournemouth. Incidentally, his second wife was called Emma. He was never a vampire.

Sergeant William Thick joined the police force in 1868 and was appointed to H. Division in Whitechapel. It was here he earned the nickname 'Johnny Upright' due to both his walk and his moral standing. F. P Wensley, ex- chief Constable CID, described Thick as: 'One of the finest policemen he had ever known'. Thick was involved in the arrest of John Pizer.

Interestingly, Sergeant William Thick was accused of being Jack the Ripper himself by a Mr H.T. Haslewood, who wrote to the police saying he had very good grounds to believe that: 'The person who committed the Whitechapel murders was a member of the police force'. Mr Haslewood's suspicion was based on very tenuous evidence and when he wrote to the police again a few days later, he named his suspect as Sergeant Thicke, misspelling Thick's name. He claimed that: 'Thicke should be watched, and his whereabouts ascertained upon other dates where certain woman have met their end'. Written in the margin of the letter was the official police response: 'I think it is plainly rubbish, perhaps prompted by spite'.

Mr Grand and Mr Batchelor really were two private detectives (Grand was an ex-con) who worked on the case but to what extent, for whom and why are still unclear. Their reputations are sketchy at best and details about them are somewhat scant.

Suspects: There are far too many suspects to mention in this context — and the list is forever growing. It is suffice for this piece to mention the few that appear in *Partnership from Hell.*

On September 10th 1888, John Pizer was arrested as the suspect 'Leather Apron.' Pizer was a Polish Jewish boot finisher who lived at 22 Mulberry Street. Apart from wearing a leather apron as part of his job some locals said he was a sinister-looking man who always carried a knife. This did not mean he was Jack. Later, Pizer received some compensation from newspapers after slanderous stories were printed about him. The wrongly-accused Pizer died in 1897 of gastro-enteritis after being poorly for some time.

George Chapman, a.k.a. Severin Klosowski (known locally as Ludwig Schloski), was a barber at 126 Cable Street.

He'd had tuition as a surgeon in Warsaw, Poland before coming to London. Chapman was hanged at Wandsworth prison on April 7th 1903 after poisoning three women. Was he Jack? Inspector Abberline seemed to think he was for some reason, but there really isn't any evidence that might link Chapman to the Ripper murders. Does a mad serial-killer, known for cutting their throats and disembowelling his victims resort to slow and calculated poisoning?

The East End News reported on the 23rd November 1888: A determined case of suicide occurred in Poplar on Monday morning. A marine store dealer named Edward Buchan, aged 29 years, cut his own throat with a knife. It appears that shortly after ten o'clock a sister of the man heard a strange noise and, on entering the back shop, saw Buchan in the act of cutting his throat. She raised the alarm and the father came to her assistance and attempted to take the knife from the man's hand, but failed. A doctor was at once summoned, but Buchan died shortly after; he had nearly severed his head from his body, he had been strange in his manner for some time.

The fact that this man committed suicide is extremely sad but apart from the above occurring on the very same day of Mary Kelly's funeral there appears to be nothing to link him to the Ripper murders. There is also no evidence to suggest that he killed his own mother as portrayed in *Partnership from Hell* and it is purely used as fiction.

Sir Melville Macnaughten, Chief Constable at the time, wrote a confidential report in which he names the three top suspects, his chief suspect being Montague J. Druitt, a barrister-turned-teacher who ended up committing suicide in December 1888, (he gets a brief mention as the man in *Partnership from*

Hell hanging around the wrong train platform as Jack flees to the docks near the end of the story).

Jake Oláh. Quiet Hungarian farmer's boy. Witnessed his parents murdered, escaped to England, fell in love, became a vampire, paraded as a policeman, aided Jack the Ripper, sold a house to Peter Cushing. Now living in Whitstable. Kills known felons and malefactors for food. Oh, and Jake Oláh sounds remarkably like Dracula when said quickly!

ABOUT THE AUTHOR

Simon Whitmore has been a fan — if that is what one is called — of Jack the Ripper for many years, having read plenty of books on the subject. He also enjoys a good Hammer horror flick on a dark and lonely night. He lives in Leicestershire and writes in his spare time, often burning the candle at both ends.

ACKNOWLEDGEMENTS

I would like to thank my early draft readers who suggested several edits (some that appear, others ignored due to the author's vanity!). Thanks go out to Casebook.org — a huge and well presented website devoted to the many riddles of Jack the Ripper — and their many and devout JTR members; it was an invaluable resource for me as a cross reference.

Sources:

Jack the Ripper — The Definitive History, by Paul Begg.
The Complete History of Jack the Ripper by Philip Sugden.
The Mammoth book of Jack the Ripper by Maxim Jakubowski & Nathan Braund.
Casebook.org - The world's largest public repository of Ripper-related information.

Printed in Great Britain
by Amazon